JACKSON

Tracie Podger

ACKNOWLEDGEMENTS

My heartfelt thanks to the best beta readers a girl could want, Karen Atkinson-Lingham, Marie Mason, and Alison Parkins - your input is invaluable.

Thank you to Sofie Hartley, Hart & Bailey Design, for yet another wonderful cover, and thank you, Leigh Stone of Irish Ink – Formatting & Graphics for making the interior look amazing!

I'd also like to give a huge thank you to my editor, Karen Hrdlicka, and proofreader, Joanne Thompson.

A big hug goes to the ladies in my team. These ladies give up their time to support and promote my books. Alison 'Awesome' Parkins, Karen Atkinson-Lingham, Marina Marinova, Ann Batty, Fran Brisland, Elaine Turner, Kerry-Ann Bell, Jodie Scott, Lou Hands, and Louise White – otherwise known as the Twisted Angels.

My amazing PA, Alison Parkins, keeps me on the straight and narrow, she's the boss! So amazing, I call her Awesome Alison. You can contact her on AlisonParkinsPA@gmail.com

To all the wonderful bloggers that have been involved in promoting my books and joining tours, thank you and I appreciate your support. There are too many to name individually – you know who you are.

CHAPTER ONE

Jackson

Her sobs had quietened as the room darkened. We were lying on her bed, and although it had been six months, her grief and anger still overwhelmed her. With every sob I'd listened to, my heart had broken just a little more. I had her wrapped in my arms; her head was resting on my shoulder and my t-shirt was sodden with her tears. Her breathing had deepened and I knew she had finally dropped off to sleep. Each night I'd lain with her, each day I'd sat with her. She was my best friend, but one I was in love with.

I breathed in deep the scent of her hair, the saltiness of her tears, and the pain she was going through. I wanted to turn back the clock; I wanted to absorb all her hurt but I couldn't. Each day, it was getting harder and harder to conceal my feelings from her. As she turned in my arms to place her back against my chest, I curled into her. I wouldn't sleep, I couldn't. The feelings coursing through my body, hatred for her situation, love for her, and an overwhelming desire to fuck her, had my nerves on edge and my skin itch. For months, I'd been able to control my needs, but it was becoming more difficult. I had to make a choice, a very difficult one. I had to leave her, and that decision would destroy me.

I'd never loved a woman before; I thought I was incapable of that. The emotion needed to love had been taken away from me at a very early age. But the feelings she produced, feelings she was completely unaware of, were fucking with my brain, and I was getting dangerously close to revealing who I really was: one fucked up individual. One fucked up individual, who was about to get worse after receiving a text from someone I'd been hiding from.

I gently slid my arm from under her neck and rolled to the edge of the bed. Her alarm clock showed it to be early morning already. As I stood and looked down at her, I heard her murmur my name and a tear rolled down my cheek.

"I'm sorry," I whispered.

No matter that my brain was telling my legs to move, for a moment my heart was keeping them still. Was I doing the right thing? I crept to the bedroom door and hesitated, taking one last look at her before I left. In my mind it wasn't forever, I just needed to get my shit together. I needed to be honest with her and tell her how I felt, but I was scared it was too soon. I was terrified of her rejection and of tarnishing our friendship. If I couldn't have her, the way I wanted, I'd take whatever she offered, but right at that moment, I was about to combust.

Birds had started to chirp as I let myself out of her apartment door. The sun was slowly rising on the horizon and already the streets of London were busy. Partygoers made their way home, builders made their way to the many construction sites to get an early start, and even the early riser businessmen, making their way to offices, bustled along the pavement. It had rained earlier and the pavement was wet, the air damp, and the clouds above as grey as my mood. I turned up the collar of my jacket and walked.

I sat at a window table in the all-night café I often frequented. The window had steamed up and I used my jacket sleeve to wipe clean a small area. I watched London wake up fully as I sipped on my coffee. I knew what I needed to do as I took my phone from my pocket. I scrolled to the number I wanted and dialled.

"Shit, Jackson, it's five in the morning," I heard, as my sister, Perri, answered.

"I thought you'd be at your desk by now," I replied.

"No, not even for the love of protecting you and your money would I be at my desk this early. What's up?"

"I need to go, I can't stay anymore."

"Okay, has he been in contact?"

"No, but I did get a..." I couldn't finish my sentence as thoughts of him flooded my mind.

"It's okay, you know I have bought a house, do you want to go there for a while?"

"Yeah, I need a change of scenery."

"Where are you now? I can give you all the details."

"Email them over, I don't want you traipsing across London for me."

"Do you have money, Jack? I can transfer some for you."

"I'm good, I have enough, just need someplace to stay until I decide what to do."

"I'll email the address now and details of where to collect the keys. Please let me send you some money, I worry about you."

"I don't want it, Perri. I'll get by, I always do. I have enough to get me there with a little left over, and then I'll find a job. I'll call when I get there."

I wanted to finish the call. As much as I loved my sister, she was a reminder of all that was wrong with me, and one of the reasons I needed to get out of the country. I screwed my eyelids tight, partly to block out his voice and partly to stop the tears from falling.

"Be safe, Jackson. Call me when you get there, promise me?"

"I will, love you."

As I walked back to my apartment, I was filled with dread. I checked my watch, Summer wouldn't wake yet, and as cowardly as it was, I wanted to at least be at the airport with my phone off before she did. I felt like a complete shit for bailing on her when she needed me the most, but I had no choice. For her sake, and mine, it was time to leave.

My apartment was rented and sterile. I'd never felt at home within its stark white walls, devoid of colour. Had it been mine, it would have been decorated with my art. I packed what few belongings I had into a backpack and a small holdall, locked up the door and deposited the keys back through the letterbox. Perri would deal with it; she dealt with everything.

I headed for the train station and purchased a ticket to Gatwick. I had no idea if I would get a flight, how much the ticket would be, or how long the journey would take. I didn't care at that point. I'd blocked my life in the UK from my mind as I walked through to the ticket desks. American Airlines was the first I came to, and after a brief discussion, I purchased a seat on the next available flight to California.

CHAPTER TWO

Summer

Something felt off as I opened my eyes. I was lying, fully clothed, on top of the duvet but there was no warmth. There was no body curled in behind me, no warm breath on my neck, and no strong arms wrapped around me. His absence was immediately felt.

"Jackson," I called out as I sat up.

There was no reply and I stared towards the bathroom, listening for sounds of the shower running. Perhaps he hadn't heard me. I climbed from the bed and made my way to the living room. The apartment felt empty, and without needing to look any further, I knew he had left.

I made my way to the kitchen and set the kettle to boil, placed two teaspoons of tea in a pot, and waited for the water. I hated the silence of my empty apartment. I hated more that Jack was gone. It wouldn't be the first time he'd left before I'd woken, he would return with pastries and coffee, but that morning my gut was telling me something was wrong. I reached for my phone, still charging on the countertop, and brought up his number. I dialled. The call went straight to voicemail and I left a message.

"Jack, I'm making tea, can you call me?"

When my tea was brewed, I poured a cupful and sat on the sofa. I hated the apartment; I hated the circumstances that had me sitting on my own. I hated more that I was left to deal with its sale alone.

I tried not to think, I wouldn't look at the mantel above the gas fire that housed photographs and memories. I stared at my phone, waiting for a call or a text message. An hour passed and I began to get anxious.

Jack, can you call me, please? I'm worried about you.

I looked at the text I'd sent waiting for a reply; nothing came. I pulled a comforter from the back of the sofa and wrapped myself up in it. I missed his arms around me; I missed the warmth of his body and the sigh he gave every time he wrapped me in his arms.

Jackson had been my constant, the friend I was in love with, not that I had ever told him that. For the past six months, he'd comforted me, listened to my anguish and the anger that spewed from me. He'd been here day and night, sleeping next to me.

It had been a shock to realise I loved Jackson, that perhaps I'd always been in love with him. He was the one I confided in, the one I turned toward to solve a dilemma or mediate an argument. He was the one who held my hand when I'd found out about Dane, who had held me to his chest when all I wanted to do was to tear down the apartment, wall by wall.

I'd tried to deny my feelings for him for a long time. I'd reasoned that he was my best friend, it was okay to be a little in love with him. But it was the times when he was gone that I missed him the most, that I wished for him to be with me. I'd spent a while deciding if I had a need for him, or if I was in love with him, and I could come to no other conclusion. He consumed my thoughts, day and night, my body sparked whenever he touched me, and my stomach flipped at the thought of him. But it was too soon after Dane for either of us.

At some point, I must have dozed off; I woke to the sound of traffic outside my window and the sun high in the sky. I checked my phone, and disappointment flooded me when I saw there was no reply. I called him again, left another message on his voicemail, and sent another text.

I was confused. Maybe he'd had enough of my misery. I'd suspected Jackson had his own troubles for as long as I'd know him. Perhaps he couldn't cope with mine anymore. I remembered the erotic dream I'd had of him the previous evening, and prayed to God I hadn't called out his name, or spoken in my sleep. I had no idea whether Jackson thought of us as anything more than friends. He was as closed with his emotions as a brick wall, totally unreadable.

⸺

I spent that day, and the following, attempting to contact Jack. As the hours went by, my messages and voicemails became more frantic. I cried until eventually, I became angry.

"You fucking shit, Jackson. You bailed on me, didn't you? Why? Just tell me why?"

That was the last voicemail message I left for him. No matter how angry, I could not dampen down those feelings of want and desire for him.

It wasn't the first time he had done a disappearing act. He was known for it, but I thought he'd stick around for just a little longer. I remembered back to a couple of years previous. One minute we'd been at a party, the next he called a month later from Australia. He spent most of his time travelling; I knew that. He never stayed in one place for too long, especially London, but I hoped I would have had longer with him. Six months of seeing him every single day, of sleeping beside him, always fully clothed, made his disappearance all the more hurtful.

The days turned into weeks and I survived, obviously. I placed the apartment up for sale and smiled as I showed prospective buyers around. I smiled as I spent time with friends and family, but it was fake. Inside I was dying, just a little each day. I would stare at a photograph of Jackson each night as I struggled to sleep. I would hear his voice in my head or imagined his heartbeat as I lay my head on the pillow. Finally, he called.

It was the middle of the night when my phone lit up on the bedside cabinet. I hadn't been sleeping, just dozing. I reached over, not expecting any calls, and my heart stilled when I saw his name. I hesitated before answering his call.

"Hey," he said.

"What do you want, Jack? It's late," I replied, trying to keep the harshness from my voice.

"I'm sorry, I forgot the time difference."

"Time difference? Where the fuck are you?"

"California."

"You left without a word, I've been trying to contact you, and now you ring me in the middle of the night from California!"

"I had to, Summer. If there could have been any other way, believe me, I would have stayed. I'm sorry. I wanted to get in touch so many times, but I had some things to do, for me, before I could."

"I don't understand. What things?"

"I can't tell you over the phone, I want you to come out here. Come for a visit, Summer."

I should have been fuming; I should have been calling him out on his behaviour, but the minute he asked me to visit, my heart fluttered in my chest. Maybe it was also because he'd done this before. Despite my anger, somewhere deep inside, I always knew he would return. I could never stay angry with him for any length of time, despite wanting to at times.

"I can't, I have the apartment up for sale, and I don't have the money."

"I'll pay for your ticket and you can stay with me. I have a house on the beach. You'd love it, say you'll come?"

"How can you pay for my ticket? And if I did, then what? Are you actually going to tell me why you bailed on me?"

"I'm working, I have some pieces of art to finish and I work behind a bar."

"When?" I asked.

"Soon as you can."

I sighed. "I can't for a couple of weeks, I have appointments. How about I text you over a date, and we can sort it out for then?"

"Cool. And I am sorry, Summer, really I am."

"Will you promise me one thing? Tell me what I did wrong?"

I hated that my breath hitched, causing my voice to crack. I hated that the tears started to flow.

"Summer, you could never do wrong. I had to leave because of me, because of my shit. It had nothing to do with you, and I was fucking wrong to just walk. I was a coward, okay? I have stuff going on that I find difficult to talk about. Just come out here. Spend some time with me, let me make it up to you."

I found myself nodding because I didn't trust my voice.

"Summer?"

"Okay, I'll text you, Jack. And if you don't answer me, don't ever call me again."

"I'll answer, trust me."

I stifled a snort at the 'trust me,' but we said our goodbyes, and I placed the phone back on the cabinet. He was in California. I wasn't aware of anyone he knew out there, but then, I wasn't aware of anyone Jackson knew.

CHAPTER THREE

Jackson

It had been months since I'd seen her last: months of thinking of her, dreaming about her, wanting her. I'd known her for a few years; I'd been in love with her for as long. But she was never mine to have. She was Dane's. I was there when he died. I was the prick that took her grief as an excuse to lay next to her, in an effort to comfort her. I was the arsehole that held her in my arms as she cried because I wanted to feel her body next to mine.

I thought back to the day I'd left. Summer had recently found out that Dane had a child; he hadn't been faithful to her through their marriage. She believed it to be only the once; I knew differently. I hated him for what he did to her. I hated that she loved him. I hated that I was a coward and never told her the truth. I'd watched her go from inconsolable to angry, and then sadness. I'd been with her nearly every day of that process. I'd held her hand at Dane's funeral, at the solicitor's when she'd discovered his child, and all the time I wanted to tell her.

Instead, I'd run away. I ran away because the feelings that coursed through my body whenever I was near her, were becoming harder to hide. How could she love me the way I loved her? If she knew me, really knew me, she'd hate me.

———

"What time is Summer getting in?" I heard.

I was sitting on my deck, watching the sun set over the Pacific. Dexter was walking up the stairs from the beach.

"Hey, want a beer? She gets in tomorrow morning."

I'd met Dexter when I'd first arrived in California. He was Australian by birth but left some years prior. Although I didn't know his history, I was aware that he'd left under terrible circumstances; he'd fled, hoping to leave his demons behind. It was a surfer I'd met, D-J, who introduced us. D-J had stumbled across me one night while I was too drunk to get off the beach and up to the house. It had been the first or second night after I'd arrived. I was lonely; I was missing Summer and feeling pretty shit about bailing out on her. And I had just received a second text message from my demon.

"Are you collecting her?" Dexter asked, as he took the beer I was holding out and sat beside me.

"No, thought I'd let her walk. Of course I'm picking her up."

He gave me the look. Dexter had been a licenced therapist back in Australia; in Cali, he became the unlicenced therapist, the man everyone went to with their troubles and one of my best friends. But, boy, could he freeze with his stare.

"You missed your session today," he said.

"Is that why you're here?"

"Yes, you don't think I choose to chase you around the coast, do you?"

After D-J had tripped over my drunken body that night, he'd introduced me to Dexter. The first thing Dex noticed was the way I kept one of my sleeves down, the way I gripped the edge with my fingers to stop it rising. He'd grabbed my arm and slid my sleeve up. He never said a word as he reached for his medical box and took out an antiseptic wipe. He didn't look at me as he cleaned the cuts to my arm. From that day on he'd counselled me. He'd got further in helping me than any of the expensive waste of space therapists I'd had back home.

It had been Dexter that had encouraged me to contact Summer, to return one of her many calls. She was angry with me, but it took the knowledge that someone had my back for once in my life, for me to contact her. I was so glad that I had. She cried, and that killed me because I couldn't put my arms around her, because I couldn't wipe those tears from her cheeks. She asked me why I'd left but that wasn't a question I wanted to answer over the phone. Despite what I'd told her, I wasn't even sure I'd be able to tell her face-to-face. How do you confess to the one you love that you've been living a lie?

"So, I repeat, you missed your session today," Dexter said, bringing me back out of my thoughts.

"I'm scared, Dex. I don't know that I can be normal around her. That I can act that well anymore."

"Then don't do either. Just be you. Maybe it's time to be honest with her."

"There's too much I can't tell her, she'd fucking hate me."

"Then tell her what you can, for now. Tell her how you feel about her. You've told me many times that you think she feels the same, so why not open up and find out, once and for all, where you stand?"

"Because I don't want her rejection."

"Her rejection isn't the same as you've had all your life, Jack. You walked away from her and that must have hurt both of you. But here she is, on a plane, about to spend three weeks with you. She certainly hasn't rejected you as a friend—that's your starting point."

After finishing his beer, Dexter left. I replayed his words through my mind. Summer hadn't rejected me as a friend, he was correct on that, but having her as a friend wasn't what I wanted. But to have a relationship with her, should that be on the cards, was also impossible. I'd have to return to the UK and that was something I couldn't do, not while he was alive.

Just the thought of him had my skin itch, had the wounds on my body start to burn with a desire and need I swallowed down. Most days I controlled that desire—that need. Some days I couldn't, I didn't want to. It was those days that Dexter had helped me find outlets, as he called them. Like he did with D-J, like he did with all the misfits that found their way as if by instinct to Passion, the bar he owned.

I stood and stretched my arms over my head. The sound of the sea soothed me, the gentle lapping of the waves as they broke on the sand was a comforting sound. From the minute I'd stepped back on U.S. soil, I'd felt at home. I intended to stay; I just had to figure out a way to do that.

I took the two bottles and dumped them in the trash before making my way to my bedroom. I kept the sliding glass doors open, so I could hear the sea as I stripped off my jeans and t-shirt. I lay on the bed, not bothering to cover myself with the top sheet, it was too warm for anything else and I didn't like air-conditioning. I stared at a stark white wall just crying out for some of my art.

I drew, all the time. I designed and those designs either adorned my body in the form of tattoos, or walls, and I earned from it. I didn't earn a fortune, but enough to survive. D-J thought that I didn't charge enough for what I did, I was just happy to have my art appreciated. It hadn't been for so many years.

Anxiety started to settle in my stomach. Whether I wanted to admit it or not, I was nervous about meeting Summer again. I was nervous of not being able to control myself around her. She didn't mean to, but she affected me in ways that I struggled to keep on top of. I'd lied to her; I'd kept the truth from her for so long with good intent. I didn't want to see her hurt; I didn't want to be the one to hurt her with the truth.

It was her face I saw in my mind as I fell asleep.

—————

I hated airports, I hated anywhere busy, but I parked the car and made my way inside. I'd deliberately arrived after her plane had landed. She'd be held up in immigration and baggage collection, and I hoped that I wouldn't have to wait long. My palms began to sweat a little as my nerves increased.

A throng of people weaved their way through the foyer. I scanned the crowd until I caught a glimpse of auburn hair. I watched her shoulder barge her way through a family that had stopped, without warning, in front of her—causing a mini pile-up of tourists. I laughed, and she looked my way. Her smile floored me, it always did. Her eyes shined as they focused on me. She ran, dragging her oversized suitcase behind her until she let go and flung herself into my arms. She wrapped her arms around my neck as I lifted her from her feet.

"Jack. Oh, Jack, it's so good to see you," she said.

I nuzzled into the side of her neck and inhaled. She smelled the same; her scent was as comforting to me as the sound of the sea.

"It's good to see you, too," I said, as I lowered her to her feet.

She stood and looked at me for a few seconds, tears formed in her eyes. She took a slight step back and raised her arm. Her slap across my chest had the couple standing next to us look over sharply.

"You shit, you're a fucking shit for running away, Jackson," Summer said.

I tried not to laugh; I bit down hard on my lower lip as she struck me again. She had clenched her fist and tried her hardest to pound on my chest. She was a little over five feet tall, I was more than a foot taller, and I stifled my laughter as she bounced on her toes to reach. I wrapped my arms around her and pulled her close.

"I know, baby. I know," I said.

"Repeat after me, I am a fucking shit," she said, looking up at me.

"You are a..."

She fucking pinched me! Pinched me on the side, and it hurt.

"I am a fucking shit," I said between laughs.

"I have missed you so much. One day you were there and the next, gone. Not a word, Jack. Not a word. You made me fucking cry, and I vowed I'd never cry over a man again."

I slung my arm over her shoulder and grabbed her case. Her words had me internally wincing, for sure.

"Summer, I'm sorry. I'm so sorry, okay? Let's get home and you can beat the shit out of me there. Doesn't do my street cred any good being attacked by a five foot girl in a crowded airport."

She laughed as she tucked her arm around my waist and we walked to the car park.

"Is it always this hot?" she asked.

"Yep. Wait until you see my place. It's right on the beach."

I loaded her case into the beat-up car I'd borrowed from Dexter and opened the passenger door for her. She smiled up at me, and for a moment, we stood and looked at each other. Despite her smile, her eyes were full of sadness and my chest constricted at the thought that I'd done that.

"I've missed you so much," I whispered.

She reached up and placed her palm on the side of my face, I closed my eyes.

"You're not going to slap me again, are you?" I asked.

She laughed. "No. I want to know why, though."

"Let's get home first." I wanted the delay to gather my thoughts.

I watched her rub her palms over her eyes as we drove. She'd flown through the night and I doubted she'd gotten much sleep.

We pulled up into the driveway and I ran around the car to open her door. I dragged her suitcase from the trunk and led her to the front door. She paused just after she walked in, taking in the expanse of space.

"Wow!" she said, as she stood on the landing and looked down to the open plan living space on the lower floor.

"It's pretty amazing, right?"

"It is."

She made her way down the stairs and I followed, bumping her suitcase behind me. She walked straight over to the sliding glass doors that led to the balcony.

"Let me show you," I said, as I reached past her and unlocked the door.

"Oh, Jack, it's..." she said as she stepped out.

"I know. I've never felt so comfortable anyplace else."

She placed her hands on the balcony wall and looked out to sea.

"Why did you run, Jack?" she asked, without turning to face me.

I took a step closer to her. The slight breeze ruffled her hair, and the closer I got, I could see her knuckles whiten as if she was holding on tight.

"Because...Because I was finding it hard to be around you."

I swallowed hard, waiting for her to speak; she didn't. Instead, she turned to face me and simply nodded. She gave me a sad smile as she lifted my arm and placed it over her shoulder. She nestled against my chest and I heard her sigh.

"But not now?"

"Not now."

I wrapped my arms around her again and closed my eyes. I felt like I had finally come home.

⸺

Summer tried to stay awake, but as the day wore on I could see her struggling. We had taken a stroll along the beach; we'd sat on the daybed and drank beer. We talked, we didn't stop talking and laughing. It was like old times, we fell instantly back into that easy friendship we'd always had.

I watched her yawn and insist that she needed to stay awake to adjust to the time difference. Eventually, she gave in. I led her to one of the downstairs bedrooms, the one next to mine. I hesitated by the door after she'd walked in, towing her case behind her. I wanted to lay on the bed with her, to have her wrapped in my arms as she fell asleep. I wanted to kiss her goodnight, to make the sadness in her eyes disappear. I wanted to do so many things.

"Good night, Jack," she said as she turned away, leaving me outside.

I could hear her moving around, the unzip of her case, and the opening and closing of closet doors as she put her things away. I heard the shower run, and at that point, I had to walk away. My cock hardened at the thought of her in the shower. I pulled off my t-shirt as the heat had it sticking to my back.

I grabbed another beer and sat on the daybed. The sun had set and subtle floor lights lit the balcony. I strained my ears, listening for any sounds from the bedroom. One of the many reasons I'd left her was because of the effect she had on me. No matter how hard I tried to conceal it, my cock was permanently hard when she was around.

However, it was the turmoil in my mind that had been my main reason for leaving. Summer didn't know me, not the real me. She didn't know what I did to myself and the closer I got to her, the more afraid of discovery I became. It was only having that time apart that I could think about that. Dexter had convinced me I could deal with it; I only hoped he was right.

CHAPTER FOUR

Summer

I woke feeling disorientated. Perhaps it was the time difference or the warm breeze that flowed through the room because I'd left the bedroom door open to the balcony outside. I climbed from the bed and pulled on a vest top before making my way outside.

The sky was clear and a thousand stars shimmered above me. I leaned on the balcony and listened to the sea as it gently lapped the shore.

"Can't sleep?" I heard; his voice had startled me.

I turned to see him, dressed just in jeans, sitting astride the daybed.

"It's too warm. I guess the time difference has caught up with me. And I need to take my pill, it doesn't appreciate I'm not in the UK right now."

I was conscious of the fact I wore just a pair of panties and the vest top, but my stomach flipped at the intense stare he gave me. To distract myself, I looked up at the sky.

"That's Orion's Belt," I said.

He stood and walked towards me. "Where?"

I pointed. "There, look."

"I don't see it."

I tried to describe what I was looking at. He stood to my side, close enough for me to smell his musky scent and the slight sweat from his body. His stomach was muscular, and I willed my eyes to keep looking at the sky and not give away that I wanted to take in every plane of his body.

I took a step forward. "Stand behind me, look along my arm, and you'll see what I'm pointing at," I said.

Once he had, I wondered if I'd made a mistake. His body pressed against mine and I felt goose bumps travel over my skin. I felt his breath on my neck as he looked over my shoulder and a spark of static on my skin as he rested his hand on my hip.

"Nope, still don't see it," he whispered. His breath caressed my ear.

I struggled to keep my finger pointing; my hand had a very slight shake to it.

"Three stars in a straight line, how can you not see that?" I asked, inwardly cursing that there was huskiness to my voice.

His fingers tightened on my hip as he pulled me tighter to his chest. I prayed I hadn't imagined the hardness of his cock as I leaned further against him. His breath was a steady rhythm against my neck, and I realised he wasn't looking along my arm. I slowly lowered it.

I felt his lips very gently brush against the skin just below my ear, and my heart rate increased. I tilted my head slightly away, giving him access. His hand moved from my hip and splayed across my lower stomach, his fingers brushed under the material of my vest top and left a tingle on my skin in their wake.

His tongue licked a path from my neck to my shoulder, and I failed to stop the moan from leaving my mouth. I bit down on my lower lip to quieten myself. He used his free hand to slide the strap of my top over my shoulder and his lips followed. His cool breath set my skin alight.

I placed my hands on his thighs, gripping his jeans as his mouth moved back up the side of my neck. He nipped, he licked, and he kissed his way back to my ear.

I had closed my eyes, absorbing the delicious sensations flowing through my body. My stomach quivered and a heat travelled over my skin. My clitoris throbbed, desperate for his touch. I wanted his hand to move from my stomach, to lower and relieve me of the frustration that was starting to build.

I felt a gentle moan against my skin and my heart fluttered in my chest. His hand slowly slid up my stomach, moving my vest up with it. My exposed, flaming skin was cooled by the night breeze. His fingers slid under the material until he found what he was searching for. His hand cupped a breast and his palm ran over my erect nipple.

I gasped as his hand closed around my breast. His kisses to my neck became feverish, and with that my heart rate increased further. My legs started to gently shake at the building orgasm. I'd never been brought to an orgasm that way before. I gripped his thighs tighter as my lips parted and I drew in a deep breath. I ground my backside against his cock and felt his breath quicken, his hand roughly kneaded my breast.

As his lips moved to the back of my neck, I let my head fall forwards. His hand released my breast from its grip and slid back down my stomach; with his other, he gently pushed my shoulders forward, bending me slightly at the waist as his mouth assaulted my back, my neck, and my shoulders. He wrapped his hand in my hair, pulling it to one side.

Not one word had been spoken for however long those kisses had taken. It felt like hours. My skin was a mass of static and the throbbing between my legs escalated. I released my grip from one of his thighs and ran it over my hip to the top of my panties. I wasn't sure I had the courage to pleasure myself but I needed touch, whether it was his or mine.

My wrist brushed gently over his hand and his mouth stilled on my neck.

"Do it," he whispered. "Fuck yourself."

I raised my head and leaned back against his chest, as my fingers slid under the band of my panties. His head was on my shoulder, watching. As my fingers met my clitoris, a shockwave rolled over me. He rolled his hips against me as I gasped.

I felt him move, my support was gone and I pulled my hand away. He had circled me, pushing me back against the cool glass of the balcony. His body pressed against me once again, and he placed his hands either side of my face. His fingers tangled in my hair as he lowered his mouth to mine. I felt them dig into my skin and his pelvis push into me as his lips found mine, as his tongue swiped across mine.

I wrapped my arms around him, my fingers dug into his back as our kiss became deeper, more urgent. I clawed at his back as his moan filled my mouth. Never in my life had I experienced a kiss like that. It was a kiss that literally took my breath away. It sucked all the oxygen from my lungs, my brain scrambled, and my blood pumped faster. My heart raced as I tried to draw in air through my nose. His kiss was intense, demanding; he devoured me.

Just as I moaned, as my body was about to give in to the heat, he pulled his head away. I struggled to catch my breath as he rested his forehead on mine. His chest rose and fell in time with mine.

"I'm sorry," he said and then took a step back.

My brow furrowed in confusion. I looked at him, his blue eyes, darkened with the desire I knew he felt, stared back at me.

He took a step away and ran one hand through his hair. He closed his eyes and took a deep breath.

"I'm not," I said. "I'm not sorry you kissed me and I kissed you back. I'm not sorry that was about the most passionate kiss I've ever experienced. I'm not sorry that you were aroused, that I still am."

He didn't speak. His hand fell to his side and he sighed as he let his head fall back. He looked up at the stars.

The frustration I felt threatened to overwhelm. We'd danced around a need for each other for nearly a year. Tears welled in my eyes and I balled my fists by my side. I walked past him and back to my room without a backward glance. I was embarrassed; I was aroused. My heart still pumped hard in my chest that had constricted at his rejection.

I threw myself onto the bed and covered my eyes with my arm.

What the fuck was that? I thought.

JACKSON

I squeezed my thighs together, trying to gain some relief from the pulsing I felt. I measured my breaths as a way to slow my racing heart. My fist pounded the bed as a tear rolled down my cheek.

"You're my best friend's wife," I heard, whispered from the door.

I stilled but kept my arm over my eyes as a shield.

"And your best friend is dead," I replied.

I choked on the words as they left my lips. I didn't need reminding, and I didn't need his rejection. As hard as I tried, I couldn't stop the sob leaving my body. I curled on my side, silently cursing him.

I knew he was still there, I could hear the soft shuffle of his bare feet against the wooden floor. I felt the dip of the bed as he sat on the edge.

"I'm not the person you think I am, Summer."

I turned to face him. He sat facing the doors, staring out to sea as he spoke.

"So who are you? Who is Jackson, the man I've known for over three years?"

He didn't answer immediately. "I feel like I'm betraying Dane."

"That didn't answer my question."

"I'm not ready to answer your question. I'm sorry, okay?"

"No, it's not okay. Your best friend, my husband has been dead a year now. We're not betraying anyone. I don't know what happened out there, but I do know we both wanted it—we both enjoyed it."

My voice had trailed off to a whisper. I wasn't about to beg him. I'd known Jackson for so long, we had been great friends, we'd flirted innocently, and I was terrified that friendship had been soured. I needed him; I'd be devastated if I lost him.

I sighed and placed my hand on his back.

"If that kiss damages our friendship, I'd be devastated, Jack. I need you in my life. If you want to just forget it ever happened, then that's what we'll do."

"That's the problem, I don't want to forget. I can still taste your skin on my lips; I can smell your perfume, the scent of your hair. I can feel your tongue against mine. Out there? I wanted to fuck you so hard."

My stomach knotted at his words. "Then why didn't you?" I whispered.

"Because my head is a little fucked up right now."

I watched his body tense. He slowly turned to look at me and I was surprised at the intensity of his stare. His face had changed, hardened. He reached forwards and smoothed a piece of hair from my face, pushing it behind my ear. It was a tender gesture from a body held so stiff and wound so tight.

"I want to sleep next to you, just sleep. I need the company tonight," he said.

I shuffled over the bed and he climbed on beside me. He lay facing me but without touching. For a while, we lay quiet just staring at each other. I wished I could have read his mind; I wanted to know what was troubling him so much. I watched as his eyelids gently closed and listened as his breathing deepened.

Sleep eluded me for a long time. I tried not to move so as not to disturb him. I studied his face. I wanted to run my hand through the slight stubble around his jaw and his short blond hair. I wanted to trail my hand over his shoulders and down his muscular arms. Instead, I just watched him. His body was covered in tattoos. I loved them; most hated them. He looked like a thug but I knew different.

Jackson was a troubled man. His tattoos, his street art, were his way of expressing himself. He was a nomad, he never settled anywhere or with anyone. For years, I had been desperate for him to find a nice woman and settle down. But he never did. His circle of friends, of which my husband was one, had teased him constantly. I was sure most were jealous of his freedom, of his choice to turn his back on his wealth and travel the world. I was jealous of all that.

I had loved him for a long time, but initially, in a way that wouldn't have threatened my marriage. Jackson and I had a connection that went beyond friends. I understood him when no one else did. My last thoughts as I fell asleep were that I hoped that connection, that friendship, had not been jeopardised by what had happened. We were both needy, and to me, it was natural we would gravitate towards each other. Obviously, he hadn't felt the same.

I felt the weight of an arm across my chest when I woke. I was lying on my side and Jackson was tucked in behind me. He had one arm under my neck and across my chest, the other rested on my hip. I didn't want to move, I didn't want to disturb him or have him move away. It felt comfortable to be in his arms, whether that was intentional or not.

I must have drifted off into sleep again. When I opened my eyes for a second time, he was gone. I turned to face the doors. They were left open and the sun was high in the sky. I checked my watch to see it was mid-morning. I swung my legs from the bed and walked to the bathroom. I needed to shower and wash the stickiness I felt from the humidity off my skin.

California in August was playing havoc with my hair. I pulled it back into a bun as I stepped under the shower. Jackson had invited me to spend some time with him, and I was happy to leave London. Although it had been a year since I had buried my husband, it was still hard to be in the apartment, to be surrounded by his things, possessions I'd struggled to put away. Three weeks with my friend had sounded like an ideal way to get my mind straight and start the process of moving on.

I'd grieved, I would always grieve, but I was only twenty-nine. I needed to get on with my life. I needed a job for starters. What little life insurance Dane had was long since used to pay off his debts and funeral expenses. As much as Jackson had told me I didn't know who he was, it had come as a greater shock to know I didn't know my husband either. I'd discovered an adulterer, someone with a child, and a debtor. I had been crushed beyond belief and Jackson had been my saviour.

Not only had my husband been taken from me in an accident, I'd discovered everything I knew about him had been a lie. Our life, our happiness, it had all been fake. What stung the most was the circle of friends, that I believed to be so close, knew. It was a conversation I had intended to have with Jackson during that holiday.

I turned off the shower and wrapped a towel around myself. I walked back into the bedroom and dressed quickly in shorts and a t-shirt. I headed out to the balcony, which ran the length of the house and into the door that led to the kitchen.

It was an amazing house, nestled in the cliff overlooking a white sand beach. From the front, the house looked one storey and

I'd been surprised when we had arrived. Jackson had opened the front door and I stepped on a glass landing. There was a corridor to one side with two bedrooms and a glass and wooden staircase to the other. It was down those stairs that the main living areas were, with a further two bedrooms. Each room opened to the balcony.

There was no sign of Jackson as I filled a glass with cold water from the fridge. I stepped out onto the balcony to see him jogging along the water's edge. He'd obviously been for his usual morning run. I watched as he slowed, jogging on the spot for a moment, before resting his hands on his knees as he caught his breath. I'd never looked at Jackson the way I did then. He was fit, always had been, but his body was sculptured almost. His shoulders were broad and his biceps bulged. The muscles on his stomach were taut and defined as he stood and raised his arms above his head in a stretch.

His chest, arms, sides, and his back were covered in tattoos. They extended down beyond the waistband of his shorts, and it left me feeling a little uncomfortable that I wanted to know just how far down that ink went.

The man I had known before Dane's death had been a good friend. Someone who always made me laugh, who always made a point to single me out and talk to me. He was Dane's friend but always seemed to be slightly on the outside of the circle, as was I. It was as if we were two misfits that found something in each other. But as I looked at him when he strode back to the house, I saw someone different. I saw the man women couldn't take their eyes from. The man other men were wary of, without understanding why. I saw the free spirit, the artist, and it disturbed me.

"Hey, did you sleep okay?" he asked, as he climbed the steps to the balcony.

"I did, best night's sleep I've had in ages," I answered with a smile.

His body was covered in a sheen of sweat, and I swallowed down the thought that I wanted to lick that from his body.

"How far did you run?" I asked.

"Not far, a couple of miles, I imagine. It got too hot. I need to shower," he said as he walked past.

"Do you want coffee?" I called out.

"Sure, be back in a minute."

I stood from the daybed I had been sitting on and made my way back to the kitchen. I switched on the coffee machine and searched the cupboard for tea. I didn't want my nerves jangling any more than they already were by adding caffeine. Although we had spoken normally, there was an undercurrent of tension. I prayed that would quickly dissipate. I wouldn't mention the kiss, I'd pretend it hadn't happened and I'd need to get my emotions under control.

Jackson arrived back in the kitchen just a few minutes later. His hair was wet from his shower and spiked on top. It was as if he'd just run a towel over his head and nothing more. He wore jeans and a white t-shirt that melded to his body. He took the cup of coffee from me and gave me a smile.

"What do you want to do today?" he asked as he took a sip.

"Are you going to show me the bar?"

"Can do. Then I want to take you to lunch at an amazing beachfront shack I found."

"A shack? You take me to all the best places but it sounds interesting."

"It is, fantastic food. One of the guys from the bar owns it."

We moved to the balcony and sat at a small metal table

overlooking the beach.

"Are you staying here?" I asked.

He sighed. "For now, but I don't know what Perri's plans are. She wants this as a holiday home, I think. There's an apartment over the bar, but it's pretty shit at the moment. I might fix that up."

Jackson had told me he'd met an older guy, another nomad, who owned the bar. He'd seen some of Jack's art and wanted him to decorate the inside of the bar. He also wanted Jack to buy in. The trouble was, by walking away from his family, Jackson had also walked away from considerable wealth. His father owned a private bank and was about the biggest arsehole I'd ever had the pleasure of meeting.

"Can you afford that?"

"Doubt it. I'm earning well, but maybe it's time to put down roots," he said with a laugh.

"You? Never!"

"I know, but I guess I have to grow up at some point."

He chuckled some more as he drained his coffee.

"Any news on the apartment?" he asked.

"There's a buyer and I've accepted their offer, so I guess it's just all the paperwork now."

"Where are you going after?"

"I have no idea. I'm still processing, shall we say."

"Any news from her."

I took a deep breath. I had wanted to talk to Jackson about her but when I was ready to.

"She wants money of course. For the child."

As much as Dane's son was an innocent, I couldn't speak his name.

"Did you know about her? It appears everyone else did," I asked.

He placed his cup on the table and leaned back in his chair. He looked at me and sighed.

"Yes. Although, not for a long time. I guess Dane didn't trust me as much as I thought he had."

"Why didn't you tell me?"

"How could I? I threatened him that I would. I gave him an ultimatum; tell you himself or I would. I guess I couldn't bring myself to destroy your world."

"But it got destroyed anyway," I said quietly.

Jackson leaned forwards and took one of my hands in his. His thumb ran across my knuckles and I kept my gaze out to sea. I didn't want to see any pity in his eyes, and I didn't want him to the see the tears in mine.

I'd found out about her, and my husband's child, just a month after his death. I believed us to have had the perfect marriage. We worked hard and we holidayed twice a year. We had a nice apartment and great friends, we dined out—all the things a happily married couple did. It was a solicitor that told me. Dane had left a will and the child was mentioned, he was entitled to Dane's share of our apartment—that cut through me like a knife. Although they weren't together, the child had been conceived during our marriage. The news had totally shattered me.

"Will you tell me what you know?" I asked, turning my gaze back to him.

"Will it help?"

"I don't know, to be honest. I just know my life was a lie for so many years, and I can't get my head around that. How could someone so close to me do that?"

"He loved you."

"Not enough to keep his cock in his pants though, did he?" There was a bitter edge to my voice.

"He was a prick at times. He didn't know what he had with you."

We fell silent for a while. I remembered back to when I'd first met Dane. It had been at a bar and Jackson was with him. They'd known each other from school but were miles apart where their personalities was concerned. Where Dane was everyone's best friend, Jackson was reserved. One never truly got to know Jack. There was always layer upon layer that was never revealed, and no one was able to peel those back. He'd fascinated me for a long time. But he was the one who was always on my side, the one that backed me up in an argument; the one that collected me from whatever night out I'd been on and Dane had forgotten. In fact, the more I thought about it, the more I realised; Jackson had been more of a husband than Dane, at times. He'd become my best friend and not Dane's.

He leaned back in his chair and I missed his touch. I stared down at my hand on the table.

"Let's not talk about it anymore. I want to enjoy being here with my best friend." I gave him a smile, which was returned, although I noticed the smile didn't quite meet his eyes.

CHAPTER FIVE

Jackson

I stared at her as she looked out to sea. I could see the tears that she tried desperately to hold back and my stomach knotted with hatred. If her husband was still alive, I'd fucking bury the prick myself for what he'd done.

Dane had been my best friend through school. In fact, he'd been the only kid to want to know me. I had a difficult childhood and most thought I was aloof, the other kids were wary of me and kept their distance. I'd been with Dane when he met Summer, we were mid-twenties by then and at a bar in the city. I'd spotted her across the room and gave him a nudge. I remembered telling him that I was going to talk to her, buy her a drink. It was her long auburn hair and dark brown eyes that had caught my attention. She looked like a deer caught in headlights, at first. She was scanning the bar, looking for someone, and her face lit up with a broad smile when she caught sight of her friend. Before I had the chance to approach her, Dane was off. I watched her laugh at something he'd said, subtly tossing her hair over her shoulder, and I knew that was it. She was lost to me.

Over the years we grew close, very close. But at times I couldn't stand to be near her. I wanted her, I'd never stopped, and I knew what a fucking shit Dane was in real life, in the life she knew nothing about. He gambled, he fucked women like they were going out of fashion: hookers, skanks, anyone. I started to distance myself from him, but I couldn't do that to her, so I stayed on the outskirts of our circle of friends. I would have walked away, but I wanted to be just close enough to be sure I was there when she needed me. And I knew, one day, she'd need me.

I closed my eyes and raised my face to the sun as I recalled the previous evening. For years I had wanted to kiss her, to taste her, and feel her arms around me in a gesture other than friendship. I'd always managed to hold back those feelings. Something snapped in me though. My usual strength and resolve had failed me. It was when she had leaned back against my chest and pointed to stars I could quite clearly see, that I felt it. My heart broke a little, because I'd always known I couldn't give her the life she deserved. I couldn't be the man she would want to grow old with because I was too fucked up. I swallowed down the anger I felt towards my father, the man that tried to break me until I had the strength to walk away. The man that, in my mind, screwed me over so much I was unable to love that woman the way she needed to be.

"Come on, let me show you my empire," I said as I stood. I wanted her to see the bar and the artwork I'd already started.

Summer had been the only one, other than my sister, who understood my need for my art. Whether that art translated as tattoos covering my body or graffiti on a wall, it was my way of expressing myself in pictures instead of words. Some of it was dark, clearly displaying the damage I felt. Some of it was uplifting; giving me hope for a future I desperately wanted.

We walked into the house and I watched as she bent down to retrieve her shoes. She was perfect to me, petite and curvy. Not slim, not overweight, just right. Not that her size would have mattered in the slightest. It was her mind, her nature, not her body that I loved.

I opened the car door for her after I'd locked the front door.

"Ever the gentleman," she said with a laugh.

Yeah, and that's not what I want to be, I thought.

"Tell me about the bar?" she asked as we drove along the highway.

"It's called Passion. It's a great place; imagine the bar in the movie, *Coyote Ugly*. It's about the same, but with three hot guys behind the bar. We've closed it down for a few days but it's really buzzing at night."

"Three hot guys? You'll have to introduce me," she teased, but a knot formed in my stomach at her words.

I didn't answer. The guys would love her; it was going to be a difficult morning. I had half a wall done and wanted it finished before the official reopening. We pulled into the car park and I leapt from the car to open her door for her. I held out my hand to help her but pulled away at the feel of the static that jumped between our fingers. She frowned at me but said nothing.

"Come on, and watch out for those hot guys, of whom I'm one, by the way," I said, then laughed to let her think I was joking.

"And here's my favourite man, but that sweetie sure can't be your girlfriend," I heard as we walked through the door.

I laughed and shook my head. Dexter stood behind the bar polishing some glasses.

"You're way too old, my friend, to stand a chance with her. Summer, meet Dexter, the *old* bloke who owns the place," I said.

"Enough of the fucking old, Jack. Summer, it's a pleasure to finally meet you. I've heard a lot."

Summer laughed as he not only took her hand in his, but also raised it to his lips.

"All good, I hope," she said.

"Sure, all good. Now, what can I get you drink?" he asked her.

Dexter led her to a stool, while I pulled off my t-shirt and picked up a bucket of spray paint that I'd left the previous day at the side of the bar. I watched as Summer sat and chatted with him. He handed her a cold bottle of beer, and I swallowed hard as I saw her tongue gently lick around the rim before she placed the bottle to her lips. My cock twitched in my jeans. I turned on my heels and headed for the half-finished wall. The only way I could get her mouth around that bottle out of my mind was to immerse myself in my other passion, my art.

I soon lost myself in the smell of paint and in the design on the wall. It was hell, or my interpretation of it. If anyone studied it, they'd see a small figure that resembled my father. It wasn't macabre; in the centre I'd replicated *The Last Judgment* but placed it in hell. To me, heaven and hell were one and the same. I'd lived in both. I'd lived in hell that masqueraded as heaven. As much as

Summer believed she'd lived a lie in her marriage, I'd lived a lie my whole life.

James Bay's, *Scars* a song that resonated with me, blasted through the speakers as I worked. I quietly sang along until I felt a hand on my shoulder. I straightened and turned towards her.

"Jack, it's amazing. This has to be your best work yet," she said, as she studied the wall.

I watched her face, so animated and full of pride at what I was doing.

"Talk me through it?" she asked, as she stepped closer to the wall.

"It's heaven and hell, it's a contradiction, it's my life," I said.

"And that's your father?"

She had been the first to question the suited guy that stood to one side and was completely out of place amongst the naked men and women, amongst the monsters and debauchery.

"Yes."

We fell silent while she took in my art. What she didn't see, or maybe she did but never mentioned it, was the woman that featured in every piece I did. A woman with auburn hair and brown eyes, a woman that stood out pure and clean against the bloodshed and slaughter.

"I think it's stunning, I love it. Wherever I end up, I want you to do something on my bedroom wall. I saw the pictures of that piece you did a couple of years ago."

I wondered how she'd seen that particular piece. I'd taken the picture. I took pictures of them all: partly to remember and partly to showcase my work.

"I know exactly what I'd like to do against your bedroom wall,"

I said before picking up a spray can and continuing.

She looked sharply at me but said nothing. I cursed myself; I didn't want to play with her. If I could take back those words, I would have. I heard her walk to the bar and fall back into a conversation with Dexter. I smiled as I heard him regale her with stories from Australia. How he'd fought off an imaginary shark one day when he'd surfed. I chuckled and shook my head at his tales.

I wasn't sure of how much time had passed; I knew my back ached. I stood and stretched and my stomach grumbled, reminding me that I hadn't eaten that morning. I capped the cans and placed them back in the bucket. I took a deep breath, inhaling the scent of paint then picked up a rag to wipe my hands with. I turned and walked towards her as I wiped the rag over my chest. I saw her tongue very slightly wet her lips.

I knew she wanted me; her kiss and her body the previous night, had left me with no doubt. She knew I wanted her, too. But to have her the way I wanted, the way she deserved, would mean opening up to her, and I wasn't ready for that. I wasn't ready to tell her my past, to be honest with her, and have her discover the fucked up individual I really was. I also wasn't ready for her rejection.

"Lunchtime," I said, as I got close.

"Aw, you're not taking her away? She's about the prettiest thing in this shithole."

D-J walked through the bar and towards us. I made introductions and laughed as Dexter threw a bar towel at him. D-J was the third cog in the wheel. He was a true Californian, with his long blond hair, perfect teeth, and a tanned, toned body. He carried his surfboard under his arm and leaned it against the bar.

"Dude, that is fucking awesome," he said, as he looked at the wall.

"Oh, I forgot to add, D-J is about as clichéd as you can get. You ever want an advert for Cali, that's it," I said pointing at him.

"What can I say? I'm a perfect specimen of man. I mean, come on, Summer. Look at us: a half Brit that looks like a fucking criminal, an old Australian that should have retired centuries ago, and me. Who do you think attracts the chicks here night after night?"

I watched Summer throw back her head and laugh. I hadn't seen her laugh like that for a long time and I smiled at the sight.

"Yes, I totally get it, D-J," she said with a wink. "Clichéd!"

To the sound of laughter, although I doubted D-J actually understood what had been said, we left the bar and walked to the car.

"I like your friends, and I can really see you behind that bar," she said as she climbed in.

"They're good guys, especially Dex. He took me under his wing. He became the father I would have loved," I said, quickly closing my mouth before I said too much.

"Your father's not very nice, is he?"

"That's the understatement of the year. Now, buckle up."

"Do you want to talk about it?"

"No," I said, perhaps a little too abruptly.

I saw her glance at me as she clipped in her seat belt. I kept my gaze firmly on the road ahead, but I felt my jaw working side to side with the immediate tension I felt whenever I thought about him.

I placed a CD into the stereo and cranked up the music. I wound down the windows and let the breeze flow through the car. It was a beat-up old Mustang that Dex had given me, a far cry from the sleek Mercedes I'd left behind in London. But it got me around and I had no interest in material things. The only reason I'd kept the Merc was because it pissed off my father. He'd cut off my trust, a trust my grandfather had set up, but he couldn't take my car away. I shook all thoughts of my family from my mind. I was in California, doing something I loved, with a woman by my side that I loved. I would not allow that fucker to bring me down that day.

We pulled into a small car park alongside the beach and I watched her smile. Surfers were out on their boards, waiting for that one wave that would have their adrenalin flowing. People walked or sat on the sand and the sun beat down.

"So I promised you a fantastic lunch and there it is," I said as I helped her from the car, absorbing the spark that time.

I pointed to a beach shack. A wooden hut with a shutter that was propped open at the front. Two sides were covered in my art, it was the first thing I'd done when I'd arrived. On the sand were tables and chairs and large cushions to sit on.

"Jackson, my man. Introduce me," Alfie said as we approached.

"Alfie, meet Summer. Summer, Alfie tells me he was the best at, and I quote, 'No one can make a jambalaya like a native from New Orleans.' And, boy, is he right," I said.

There was no menu, Alfie served one dish a day, and it was usually whatever he had to hand, or what he fancied himself, but it was always amazing. He used a ladle to scoop the food into bowls, gave us a couple of plastic spoons, and retrieved two cold beers from the fridge. I fished in my jeans for some dollars but he waved his hand.

"On the house, I've had more customers than ever since this boy drew all over my shack."

46

"I'd hope you see it as more than just a drawing, but thanks," I replied.

I liked Alfie; he was Dexter's partner in crime, as we called him. I think there was a little more to their friendship but it was something never spoken about. They were both the same age, mid-sixties I guessed, and I loved his company. We would sit on the beach at night and he'd tell me all about his life prior to Cali. Visiting his family in New Orleans was on my 'to-do list.'

Balancing my bowl and bottle in one hand, I held Summer's as she kicked off her shoes, then lowered to one of the oversized cushions. She sat cross-legged and smiled up at me. I dropped down on the sand beside her and then pulled my t-shirt over my head to catch some sun.

"You still have paint all over you," she said.

"Checking me out?"

"I, erm..."

"I'm kidding. I know, it's a bitch to get off."

For years we'd flirted in fun and she'd always been able to come back with something to put me in my place. That time, she concentrated on getting the spoon of food into her mouth, as if she needed the distraction. It saddened me a little. I recalled her words, if our friendship was damaged by that fucking kiss, I'd be as devastated as her.

I took a sip from my bottle of beer. I saw her glance from the corner of her eye once or twice. I pulled my t-shirt back on.

"Jackson!" I heard and winced at the screech of Honey's—although I doubted that was her real name—voice.

I sighed as she walked over; she was all tits and arse in the skimpiest bikini. I'd fucked her a few times; she frequented the bar, but I had no desire to have a friendship, let alone a relationship with her. Did that make me a jerk? Probably.

'Honey," I said without a smile.

She stood with her perfect model pose, twiddling her hair in the fingers of one hand. She was a society girl, originally from New York, and totally fucked up.

"When is the bar opening? I've missed you," she said with a purr, which made her sound more like a child than the seductive temptress I believed she thought she was.

"Couple of days."

I kept my answer deliberately short and curt. I didn't want to get into a conversation with her. I looked at Summer, who stared back at me with a smirk on her face. An awkward silence ensued. Honey looked between Summer and me.

"Okay, you let me know when that bar's open, won't you?" she said before turning and walking away.

"Honey?" Summer said.

"Don't go there. A mistake, okay?"

Summer chuckled as she finished her lunch. She placed her bowl on the sand beside her and lay back, stretching out her legs beside me. As her feet brushed against mine, I felt that spark jump between us.

"That was delicious," she said, as she turned her head towards me.

I stretched out beside her. "Simple food suits my simple mind," I said.

"There's nothing simple about you, Jack. You're about the most complicated man I've ever known."

"What makes you say that?"

"There's no body language with you. You have a closed-off look sometimes, and it's hard to read you. That's some suit of armour you wear," she said, as she rolled to her back and closed her eyes.

I propped myself on my elbow and looked at her. She stretched her arms above her head, and her t-shirt rose showing her stomach. My heart lurched in my chest at her pose. I reached over and gently touched just below her navel.

"You need a tattoo here," I said quietly.

She opened her eyes to look at me. "I might just do that, what should I get? And does it hurt?"

As much as I didn't want to, I removed my fingers. "Would you let me design something?"

"I'd love that. How amazing to have a piece of your art on my body. Let's do it," she replied, there was excitement in her voice, again something I hadn't heard in a while.

"It can be step one on my 'getting my shit together' list," she added.

"You'll end up with piercings next."

"I might get my belly button pierced, or my nipples."

"Your..."

"I'm kidding, that must fucking hurt!"

"Maybe, you get yours done and I'll get mine," I said, not for once believing she would.

"Is this our mid-life crisis, do you think?"

"If it is, I hit mine fucking years ago," I said with a laugh, pointing at my arm.

"When did you get your first tattoo and why?" She had turned on her side to face me.

"I think I was about fourteen. I lied about my age, I imagine. It was this one," I pointed to a small skull just below my shoulder. "As for why, that's a long story."

"One you don't want to talk about?"

I smiled at her. "Shall we get back? I need to shower off this paint."

No, I didn't want to talk about it. She'd never understand the compulsion to cover my skin. To cover the scars from the razor blade or the imaginary scars from the psychological abuse. People expressed their pain in many ways; mine was to transform myself, to cover every inch of the skin he, or I, had fucked with. When I was younger it became a choice; I could cut myself or I could draw art. I combined the two. The sting of the needle as it etched over my scars was pleasurable, as pleasurable as the slice of the rusty razor blade.

I still had the blade; it was wrapped in some tissue paper and stored in a small cardboard box. I often took it out and looked at it. It was a reminder of who I had been and a reminder of how far I'd come from those days. From a life no one knew about. And it was for that reason that I couldn't tell her. Like her husband, I'd lived a lie for many years. But it wasn't that which kept me from wanting a relationship with her. That was something far worse. A familiar feeling began to wash over me, a feeling of needing to control. It sickened me in one way, and I swallowed down the bile that rose to my throat.

I stood and reached down for her. I needed to shower, not just to remove the paint but the nastiness that had started to creep over my body.

CHAPTER SIX

Summer

The journey back to the house was made in silence. Well, I say silence; there was no opportunity to speak. Jackson had his music on, Eminem's, *The Monster* blasted from the stereo. I watched as he nodded his head in time with the music, and for a moment, I wondered how much the lyrics meant to him. He seemed engrossed in them. His lips moved as he silently sang along in his head.

As the song came to an end, he turned down the volume.

"I'm going to cook you dinner tonight. I need to run to the shop after I've showered though," he said.

"Can you cook?"

"The best beans on toast you'll ever eat."

I laughed, the earlier tension seemed to have been forgotten.

"Why don't we just stop now? Seems silly to shower then go back out."

I noticed his jaw clench.

"Unless you want to, of course. It's fine, I can shower while you're out," I added.

Maybe he needed some time away from me. Whatever it was, it confused me. I let it go, though. Jack was a solitary person; perhaps he just needed a half hour to himself. I smiled at him as he looked over.

I'd never known Jack to have a long-term partner. I'd seen him with many women over the years, none of which seemed to have lasted any length of time. I worried for him; our male friends slapped him on the back. I guessed I was the only female, other than his sister, that he had any kind of friendship or relationship with.

I liked Perri; she was the total opposite to Jack, in looks and in personality. It often took people by surprise to discover they were siblings. Whereas Jack was blond, she was dark. He had blue eyes; she had brown. He was the spit of his father but with a far nicer manner. She was two years older than him. I'd never met his mother, but from what he'd said, she took after her in looks. He was as vague about her as he was his father at times. Talking about anyone other than Perri was a no go where Jackson was concerned.

"You want a beer?" he asked as we walked through the front door to the house.

"Sure. I can get it if you want to shower."

He gave me a smile and wink before he headed off to his bedroom, the room next to the one he had given to me. Each bedroom had an en suite and I had to temper down the feelings of knowing he was naked in the shower. I could hear the water run as he hadn't closed his bedroom door. To distract myself, I took my beer and opened the patio door to the balcony. It was late afternoon and the beach below was still full of people. Laughter drifted up to where I sat. I took a long draw on the bottle and let the alcohol fizz around my system. I wasn't a drinker, and although the beer was nowhere near as strong as back home, it didn't take much for my head to feel a little fuzzy. I heard Jackson stride into the kitchen and grab his car keys from the counter.

"I won't be long. Is there anything you fancy?" he called out.

It was on the tip of my tongue to say, "You," but I didn't. "Whatever you want to cook, but please, not beans on toast."

He laughed as he left the room and climbed the stairs to the front door. I placed the bottle on the floor beside the daybed and closed my eyes. I needed to get a grip. I'd always flirted with him but we'd both known it was just for fun. Something had changed though; I didn't want it to be 'just for fun' anymore. I tried to understand why I was seeing him in a different way than usual. It occurred to me that I hadn't seen him in six months; he'd left the UK without so much as a goodbye and he'd changed.

It hadn't taken me long to forgive him, I was pleased he'd found somewhere to settle, but I had wished that had been in the UK. When he'd rung and asked me to stay with him, I'd been over the moon and booked the first available flight. It had felt good to be hugged by him as I arrived at the airport. It felt good to hear that sigh, which often left his lips when he wrapped his arms around me as a way of saying hello or goodbye.

I'd always known there was a connection between us but it was one we'd never pursued, for obvious reasons. I sighed; I had a sinking feeling that life was about to get complicated.

———

I woke with a start at the noise of Jackson in the kitchen and the smell of something grilling on the barbecue.

"Shit, how long have you been back?" I asked.

"About a half hour. You were out for the count, I thought I'd leave you to sleep."

I looked at my watch and noticed it had been two hours since he'd left for shopping. I wondered where he had been. I rose from the daybed and walked into the kitchen. Jackson had some steaks on the go and was preparing a salad. I watched him expertly cut vegetables for the salad.

"You can cook!" I said.

"I have to eat, Summer. Of course I can cook," he replied, giving me one of his killer smiles.

It was as he smiled at me that I noticed a thin trail of dried blood on the side of his neck.

"You've cut yourself, let me get a tissue," I said.

I pulled a tissue from a box on the counter and reached up; as I did he backed away. There was a moment of awkwardness before I saw him relax. I dabbed the scratch with the tissue.

"Someone got their claws into you?" I said with a laugh, praying I was way off the truth.

"Must have got too close to a bush or something," he replied, not convincingly.

I did something I really didn't want to do. I inhaled deeply. What the fuck I thought I was doing was beyond me, but I relaxed when I couldn't smell the scent of a woman on him.

Jackson turned away and pressed play on the music centre he had on the counter. Another James Bay song played and I sat opposite as he sang, *Move Together*. He looked at me as he sang certain lyrics and once again, my stomach somersaulted. Was he singing to me?

"You have a beautiful voice," I said.

I wished I could have taken the words back, not that I didn't mean them but it seemed an inappropriate thing to say.

"I like this song," he mumbled as he threw the salad into a bowl. "If you want to grab some plates, I think the steaks will be ready."

I slid from the stool and followed him to the balcony with the plates and cutlery. He took each plate and laid a steak on it. We sat as the song filtered from the kitchen. For a moment I listened to the words, it was a haunting song and I swallowed back the lump that had jumped to my throat. I wished he *had* sung that song to me.

The sun began to set and we chatted about everything and nothing. He told me all about the bar, Dexter, and D-J. I laughed at some of their antics. He became animated when he spoke about Passion.

"You've certainly found your passion in Passion," I said.

"That's so corny, but you're right. For once I feel like I fit in somewhere."

"I'm so glad for you. I miss you, of course, but I'm glad you've found somewhere to settle."

"You miss me? Let me guess, you miss my wonderful array of jokes. The ones you always rolled your eyes at. Or you miss my wit and charm. I think you called me a miserable bastard many times."

"I miss having you close," I said.

He closed his eyes briefly then reached for his beer and took a long sip.

"I miss you, too, but I had to do this."

"Dexter wants you to buy into the bar, will you do that?"

"Doubt I could afford it right now. I'd like to think I might at some point."

"So you'll never come back home?"

"One day. You are always welcome here, Summer. What the fuck have you got to rush home for? Extend your stay. I mean, you've only been here for a few days but stay for the month."

I rested back in my chair, having finished my meal. "That's tempting, for sure. But I don't know. I need to find a job soon. And I need to be back home for the apartment sale."

"Think about it?"

"I will. You cooked, I'll clear up."

I stood, I wasn't rushing to clear up because I wanted to; I wanted to end the conversation. Jack piled the plates and I carried them in, he followed wanting to replenish his beer. As I loaded the dishwasher, he stood to my side at the fridge. I could feel the heat radiate from his body, he was so close. I could smell his aftershave and wondered what brand it was. I liked the smell of him. I'd always liked the smell of him.

As he made to pass me, he placed his hand on my hip. An electrical current ran through my body at his touch. He walked back to the balcony with two beers, and I watched through the window as he lay on one of the daybeds. I followed him. He shuffled to one side and patted it. I climbed on beside him. He handed me a beer and we clinked bottles.

The sun had set and the balcony was lit by subtle uplighters in the decking.

"Can you see the stars this time?" I asked as I rested my head back.

"I could see them last night."

"So you just pretended you couldn't?"

He chuckled. We fell into a comfortable silence as we drank our beers. The beach had emptied and the only sound was the waves breaking on the shore.

"I love that sound," Jackson said.

"So do I. That and the sound of a heartbeat."

He raised his arm and placed it around my neck, pulling me closer. My head rested on his chest. In one ear I could hear his heart, and the other, the sea. I placed my bottle on the floor and rested my hand on his stomach. My fingers bunched in his t-shirt.

"So tell me about this tattoo I'm getting? You'll have to hold my hand," I said.

"I think you deserve a butterfly. You've come out of your cocoon and you're spreading your wings now."

"That's a lovely thought but you have to get one, too," I said, with a laugh.

"Okay. Where do you propose I get mine?"

"You don't have a great deal of space left. How far down do yours go?"

He chuckled, again. "All the way down."

I raised my head to look at him. "Not all the way down, surely?"

"No, not all the way down but pretty close. I've seen some people have their cock tattooed, can't for the life of me imagine why," he said.

As I settled back in his arms, I laughed out loud. "Got mine pierced, though," he added.

"You're kidding me? No way! Why would you do that?"

"I'm told it gives a lot of pleasure."

"Jesus, Jackson. I don't want to know anymore." I did, fuck, I did! "What...what have you got there?" I asked.

"A small bar, just on the underside."

"I can't believe we're having a conversation about your cock piercing."

"I guess we'd have to be pretty good friends to," he replied. "I want a nipple piercing next."

"I'll get my belly button done and you get your nipple," I said.

"Deal, but back to the tattoo. Sit up for a minute."

I did as he'd asked and he slid from the bed. He disappeared into his bedroom for a moment and then returned with a handful of pens. He knelt beside the bed and putting his fingers in the loops of my jean shorts, he pulled me down and closer. He pushed my t-shirt up and popped the button of my shorts, and then he slowly lowered them just a little. My heart hammered in my chest as he placed his hand on my stomach; his fingers traced an image he was seeing in his mind.

My skin goose bumped. His touch was so light that it tickled. He flipped off the lid from the pens and I noticed they weren't your average felt-tips. The pens looked more like very fine paintbrushes. He didn't look at me as he drew. The brush tickled more, and once or twice, he tutted at me as my body involuntary drew away from the pen. I stifled a giggle.

"Keep still," he mumbled.

"I'm trying but it tickles."

I watched the concentration on his face and felt the heat from under the hand that was still splayed on my stomach, just below my navel, and so very close to where I really wanted him to be. I rested my head back and waited. Once or twice he scrubbed at my skin to erase before continuing. After what seemed like an age, he sat back on his heels and smiled at me. He stood and held out his hand. He led me to my bedroom and stood behind me as I studied his artwork on my stomach in the mirror.

In line with my hip, and just under my navel, was the most beautiful butterfly I'd ever seen. The colours were vibrant and it was if it had been done in three dimensions. It looked like it was real and about to fly from my body.

"Oh, wow, Jackson, I love it. I don't know what to say. It's beautiful."

I looked at his reflection in the mirror. He was close and his smile was broad. There was a change to his face.

"This is going to seriously hurt," he whispered.

"Pain is good sometimes, if something so beautiful comes out of it."

I wasn't sure exactly what it was I'd said but he took a sharp intake of breath, and I saw him swallow hard. He held my gaze; there was something in his eyes. He looked at me as if I'd recognised something in him, but I had no idea the significance of what I'd said. I wasn't even sure if it was my words that had his eyes darken, his eyelids partly close.

I watched him blink a couple of times before his features relaxed and he smiled again.

"I'm glad you like it," he said. He took a step back. "I need to crash, I'll see you in the morning."

He placed a kiss to the top of my head and walked away. I stared at the butterfly, the wings were spread, shades of blues and greens adorned its body, and I noticed what made it look three-dimensional was the shading of black underneath. I gently touched it to see if it was dry. I didn't want to smudge it.

CHAPTER SEVEN

Jackson

"Fuck!" I said as I entered my bedroom.

I paced and my fists balled at my sides. My body started to shake with a need I hadn't felt for a while. My breath quickened.

Not now, not the fuck now, I thought.

I walked to the mirror and looked at the scratch on my neck. The bitch will pay for that. She'd broken my rule; no one marks my body but me. I took several deep breaths to calm my racing heart. That was why I needed to distance myself from Summer sometimes. She had a way of getting under my armour, as she'd called it. She got to me in a way no one, other than him, had ever done. It frustrated the hell out of me and I'd taken that frustration out on

Honey. I scrubbed my hands over my face. I could do it; I could quell the compulsion, I just had to breathe. I had to remember all the coping techniques Dex had taught me. I picked up my phone and scrolled through my contacts, his number was highlighted but I wouldn't press the call button. I'd wait and see.

I took the phone and lay on my bed. I closed my eyes; the only image in my mind was of Summer laying on the daybed. Her shorts were pulled down to the top of her white panties. Her skin was screaming at me to touch, to taste, and to decorate.

Maybe it was a mistake to invite her. I thought I had my impulses under control. I had an outlet. I kept telling myself, I didn't need to cut. I needed to fuck. But who? Who needed to be my outlet?

I heard her moving around the room, readying herself for bed I imagined. I'd give her a half hour or so then leave. Hopefully she would be asleep and not hear me. I could be out and back within an hour.

I studied the clock on my bedside table, the minutes ticked by and I could still hear her. I heard the slide of the door as she left her room and stepped out onto the balcony. I silently cursed her. The knot in my stomach tightened, my hands shook, and the white noise in my head increased. If I didn't get my release soon—I felt I was going to explode.

The warning signs normally started off gently, I always had plenty of time, but it was all crashing over me way too quickly. I had no choice. I slid from the bed and pulled open the dresser drawer. I took out the small cardboard box and opened it. With shaking hands, I unwrapped the blade. Sweat had beaded on my upper lip and I licked at it.

My heart pounded as I made the first cut. As the skin parted on my stomach and the blood seeped out, I felt an immediate rush of pleasure. My cock hardened. As the warm blood trickled, I undid my jeans and grabbed my cock in my hand. I watched in the mirror as my fist pumped and the fingers of my other hand smeared the blood across my skin.

It wasn't enough though. I sliced again. The rush of adrenalin I felt had my heart racing further, but the noise in my head quietened. I needed to come; I needed release. My legs quivered slightly as my orgasm built. I wasn't quite there so I cut again, and again. I closed my eyes and quickly drew the blade across my stomach. I was normally very measured in what I did; I cut precisely within my tattoos so they weren't noticeable, but that night I didn't care. I didn't want precise; I wanted pain and pleasure. I wanted to see, to smell the metallic tang of my blood. I wanted to feel my cock pulse in one hand while my hot blood coated the fingers of my other.

As my cum spurted over my hand, peace washed over me. I fell to my knees and let my chin fall to my chest. Eventually I opened my eyes. I wished I hadn't. I counted them; eight slash marks crisscrossed my body. I'd done worse in the past, but those cuts were deep. I dropped the blade on the floor beside me.

I rose and on shaking legs made my way to the bathroom. I stripped and turned on the shower. As I climbed under the jets of water, I watched the water turn red as it washed away my shame and guilt. I wanted to cry. I wanted to scream out. I wanted to punch the fuck out of the tiled wall in front of me.

I stepped from the shower and wrapped a towel around my waist. My wounds still bled and the blood diluted with the water on my body. It looked a lot worse that it actually was. I grabbed a fistful of tissues and held them to my stomach.

I sat on the edge of the bed and picked up the phone. I closed my eyes and pressed the call button.

"I cut," I said as Dexter answered.

"Okay, do you need me? Or someone?"

"No."

"Are you safe, Jack?"

"I am."

"Can you deal with it?"

"Yes."

"What caused it?"

"I don't know. I was fine and then the compulsion hit me like a fucking train. I couldn't get out. Summer was still awake, I couldn't leave without her knowing."

"Have you got something over your cuts?"

"Yes."

"Okay, son. Lie down; keep the phone to your ear. I want you here first thing in the morning, okay?"

I did as he said. He talked me down, his voice was calming and soothing. He had done this for me so many times. Either that or gave me an alternative, the alternative that I was getting addicted to.

———————

I woke sore. My stomach stung as I stretched. My phone was still on the pillow beside my head. Dex had obviously cut off the call when I'd failed to answer after I'd fallen asleep. I sat up and winced. It was always the same the morning after. I felt a wave of shame wash over me. I stood and walked to the mirror. What I saw wasn't as bad as I was expecting. I'd need to keep a t-shirt on for a few days, though.

I bent down to pick up the blade. I traced my thumb along the edge, stained with my blood. I wrapped it up, without cleaning it, and placed it back in the box. I heard the swish of Summer's bedroom door open and pulled on a pair of board shorts and a t-shirt.

By the time I'd made it outside, she was standing at the water's edge, holding a cup in her hands. She wore the same jean shorts but with a red bikini top and I watched her for a while. My phone beeped in my pocket, alerting me to a text message.

Am I expecting you soon? Dexter had written.

Give me a little time. I'm okay, I replied.

I placed the phone on the table and descended the steps to join her. She startled as I placed my hand on her shoulder.

"Good morning, I thought you'd gone for a run," she said as she smiled up at me.

"Not today."

"I can't imagine what it must feel like to wake up to this view every morning, you're so lucky," she said.

I wouldn't class myself as lucky but I nodded my head. The view was one of the reasons I had fallen in love with the house. As we walked back, I remembered the day I'd arrived.

Perri had arranged for me to collect the keys from the agent and a taxi had spent way longer than was probably necessary driving me from the airport. When we'd first pulled up outside, I thought we had the wrong address. It didn't look like the type of property Perri had described. But I was blown away once I'd stepped through the front door.

I loved that every room on the ground floor opened to the

balcony. I rarely shut the bedroom door at night, opting to fall asleep to the sound of the sea instead.

We walked back to the house and Summer placed her hand on my stomach as we stopped at the steps. She raised one foot to brush off the sand. As hard as I tried, I couldn't stop the wince when her hand connected with my cuts.

"Are you okay?" she asked.

"Sure, I think I pulled a muscle or something. Probably in my sleep."

"Pulled a muscle? Are you sure?"

"Yeah. What do you want to do today?" I asked, diverting her attention.

"How about a day on the beach? Unless you have to go to the bar."

"I'll shoot over there now for an hour then be back, how does that sound?"

"Okay, want me to come with you?" she asked.

"It's fine, you relax and while I'm out, I'm booking that tattoo for this afternoon, before you change your mind."

She laughed and looked down at her stomach. The butterfly was still perfect; it would take some scrubbing to get the ink from her skin. I had a stack of alcohol wipes that I normally used for my cuts; they would remove the ink.

"Do you need to copy this on paper, so the tattoo person can copy it?"

"No, because I'll tattoo it on you."

"You?"

"I am a man of many talents, Summer."

"That you are. In just a few days I've learned more about you

66

than in the past couple of years. I'm beginning to wonder why."

I placed my arm around her shoulders and side by side we walked up the steps and into the kitchen.

"Breakfast?" I asked.

"No, I'll have a cup of tea, though."

I refreshed her cup and she sat outside, waiting for me to join her. I grabbed a coffee and sat at the end of the daybed.

"You might need to get someone to look at your stomach," she said.

I guessed she'd noticed the way I'd gingerly sat down. "Dex will fix me up."

"Dex?"

"He's the fixer-upper," I said, and then stood. "Will you be okay for an hour?"

"Of course, I'll sunbathe for a while. There are no sharks out there, are there?"

"No. Well, I don't know, actually. Stay on the beach."

She laughed as I walked away.

———

Dexter was in the safe room when I walked behind the bar and through the stockroom. I paused, as was the rule, at the door. I listened for a moment, wondering who was inside. I'd only known Dex was in there because the door was closed. It was always left open to those who knew what and where it was.

I tapped on the brown wooden door and waited. A shadow fell across the peephole before it was opened. Dex held the door open wide for me to enter.

"He okay?" I asked, indicating with my head to D-J, who was

asleep on the bed.

"He will be. Come and sit, talk to me."

The room was large and had been all Dexter's idea. Against one wall was a double bed and a dark wooden unit stood flush against another, in a corner were two leather armchairs with a small table in between. The walls were painted indigo; Dex gave me some bullshit about its calming effects when I'd first had reason to use the room.

I slumped into one of the leather chairs, Dex sat opposite.

"What did he do?" I asked as I looked at D-J. He hadn't stirred at all.

"Overdosed, although not to the point of danger. Somehow he got hold of some pills and took them on top of his regulated dose."

"So you had me and him to deal with last night."

Dex chuckled quietly. "Will you get him clean?" I asked.

"I believe so. I've done it plenty of times before. He's fighting against it right now. Addicts are all the same, Jack. It takes a lot to kick it and it's normal to relapse every now and again."

I guessed he was referring to me. No matter what we did, whether it was snorting shit up our noses, cutting our skin, or doing what else I did, we were all addicts.

"I feel like shit."

"I imagine you do. Can you tell me about it?"

I rested back in the chair and closed my eyes. I recounted the previous evening and how frustrated I was that I didn't understand what set it off. Dex made me analyse everything I said until I came to understand that, as much as I didn't want it to be, it was the presence of Summer. She reminded me of home, she reminded me of all that was wrong with home.

"I don't want to send her away. I need another outlet."

He nodded at me; he understood exactly what I needed. And he would be there to pick me up after when he found me, sobbing on the floor, clawing at the dirt and depravity I would believe crawled over my skin. It was the same every time.

"I don't know how long this can go on for, Jack."

"I know. One last time, I need it, Dex."

"I'll get in touch. But I'm going to have to stop this soon, son. You know the drill. It's time to face the demons and conquer them, not give in anymore."

D-J stirred, saving me from answering. I wasn't sure I wanted to face the demons, and I wasn't sure I wanted to conquer them. There was a sick part of me that enjoyed what I did. But like Dex said, we were all addicts and I guessed, any addiction was bad if not under control. I was getting out of control; I knew that. My episodes were becoming too frequent for his, or my, liking.

"Man, my fucking head," D-J whispered. He turned on his side and immediately vomited.

Dex jumped to his feet and helped D-J into the recovery position. I pulled the sheet from under his body and rolled it into a ball, which I deposited by the door. D-J immediately settled again. I watched Dex fill a syringe and give D-J a dose of something.

"Sit back down, we haven't finished," he said, indicating with his hand towards the chair. "Show me."

I lifted my t-shirt as he walked towards me with a medical box in his hand. He closed his eyes and sighed at the red angry marks.

"I thought you said you cleaned those up," he said.

"I did."

"Not well enough, that looks a little infected already. Stand up."

Dexter took some wipes from his box and gently cleaned the wounds. One cut had swollen slightly; I guessed it had been the deepest. He popped a couple of pills from a blister pack and handed them to me. I eyed his hand before accepting.

"Antibiotic, nothing more," he said.

I swallowed them dry and then sat back down.

"I didn't get much warning, it just fucking hit me," I told him.

"You said. Tell me, what would you have done if Summer hadn't been awake?"

"Trawled the streets, I guess."

"You know how dangerous that is?"

I closed my eyes and nodded my head.

"You never do that, okay? We have it under control, Jack. You need to remember that but from tomorrow on we need to work some more on this. Did you run today?"

People thought I ran to keep fit, I didn't. I ran to pump the blood around my system, to have my heart and body pushed to its limit, and to quell the compulsion. I lifted weights for the same reason. I didn't desire the physique, the muscles; it was just a by-product of my need to punish myself.

"Cunt," I whispered.

My hands had gripped the sides of the leather chair and I closed my eyes again.

"You, or him?"

"Both."

"You need to stop hating on yourself, Jack. What happened to you wasn't your fault. He's not in your life anymore, he'll never be in your life, but he will always be on the periphery. We need to deal with this."

"I know. I thought I had it under control, I really did. I haven't done this for months."

"You haven't cut but you've done other stuff. Is there going to be a problem with Honey?"

"No, she fucking loves it. But I'll cut her loose. I don't want to go there anymore."

I'd told Summer I was heading for the shops, I had, but with a detour to Honey's apartment. As soon as she opened the door, she knew what I wanted—what I always wanted. And it was what she needed too. Rough sex, very rough sex between two fucked up people. She was a narcissist, she wanted only what she wanted and thankfully, she served my purpose.

I'd fucked her mouth and her arse. It left her sated beyond belief, but I walked out of her apartment feeling hollow.

"I need the rough, Dex," I quietly said.

"Then we need another outlet for that, Jack. One day, you'll fuck up, bad."

I knew exactly what was wrong with me. I needed to fight, to punish. In my mind I was fighting off my father. Not that he ever laid a finger on me; it was his words that had destroyed me.

From as young as I could remember, it was always the words. He'd lock us in a small room at the back of the house and just stand in front of me in the dark. His vileness spewed from his mouth. He hated me, I was a mistake that should have been aborted, I was a disgusting human being, and I'd ruined my mother. I was the child that should have died at birth; I was weak.

His words flowed through my mind and I became that small boy again, scared of the dark, scared of his voice, and even more scared to tell anyone. I wished he'd beaten me; I could have handled that. Wounds heal, but his words had cut so deep they were embedded within me. I wanted to carve them out.

I'd started cutting when I was eleven years old. I recalled what triggered the need, and I could remember, distinctly, the pleasure and relief I gained from it. I'd been cutting myself for years. I could go a couple of months without it, if I had another means to gain that relief. But just lately, the time frame between each episode was getting shorter.

We sat in silence for a while. "What happens when she finds out?" I whispered.

"When who finds out?"

"Summer. What happens when she finds out I killed her husband?"

CHAPTER EIGHT

Summer

I'd grown bored of lying on the sun bed, as much as the thought was wonderful, sunbathing actually wasn't for me. Perhaps it was the paranoia that my fairly pale skin would end up red and peeling, or perhaps it was that I found it difficult to sit still for any length of time on my own. Sitting still meant thinking and that wasn't something I wanted to do.

Jackson had been gone longer than the hour he'd initially said, but I wasn't worried. He had the wall to finish and the bar to prepare for opening night. I was looking forward to opening night. I wanted to see Jack in action, he could make a mean cocktail and having him at a party had always been fun. In fact, I think I danced with him more at my wedding than Dane.

Sadness swept over me at the thought of Dane. I sighed as I poured a glass of cold water. We had been married for just under three years, yet to start a family. He was the life and soul wherever he went. He worked hard; in fact he worked for Jackson's father. I knew that had caused some tension between them. Dane liked Brett Walker, I'd met him once and it was an instant dislike. Brett didn't like women, yet doted on his daughter. And no one could fail to notice the obvious distaste Brett showed towards his son. It had baffled me that Dane could be so disloyal to his friend by taking up the offer of a job. However, Dane always did what Dane wanted to do. If I sat and really analysed my marriage, it wasn't all hearts and roses; it was very much one-sided.

I picked up the CD case that sat on top of the music centre while I pressed play. It was the James Bay CD that Jack seemed to be constantly playing. He had an eclectic taste in music. I'd heard him listen to rap, rock, and classical. He was the kind of man that loved whatever his mood wanted at the time. Some days he was mild, chilled out, yet on others, he was erratic, hyped. For three years I'd wanted to know more about him. He was an enigma. I remembered having a conversation with Dane about him to be told Jack wasn't someone anyone knew, he never allowed people to get close.

Perhaps it was a man thing, I'd have wanted to unravel the man had I known him from childhood. I would have wanted to peel back the layers but maybe that was just too hard with Jack.

When Dane and I had fought he would always finish with, "Go on, run to the pussy." Jackson was my go-to when life got tough. Somehow, he always knew without my calling that I needed him. He would appear or call. I believed Dane to be jealous of Jack. Jealous of the easy friendship we had; yet they remained friends, sort of, until the end. Jackson had been with Dane on a night out when he had been killed. He'd fallen from a bridge into the path of a train, drunk, so the pathologist report said. It was a tragic accident that affected not just Jack and me, but the train driver as well.

Jackson and I had never really talked about that night. It seemed too hard for both of us. I'd lost my husband, but he had lost his lifelong friend.

———

I heard the front door open and looked up towards the landing. He smiled when he saw me, although there seemed to be sadness about him that day. As he descended the stairs, his music started to play. He strode towards me and picked up one of my hands, he placed the other around my waist, and without a word he danced with me. I laughed as we made our way around the kitchen. He pulled me close to his chest, I rested my cheek on his shoulder, and he rested his chin on the top of my head. I heard the familiar sigh. He let go of my hand and I wound my arms around his neck. He looked down at me as he gently sang along to *Incomplete*. He tightened his arms around me and I could feel his heart beat in his chest. We'd danced that way many times in the past, but something felt different. There was neediness about him.

When the song changed to something a little more upbeat, he stepped back, held one hand, and twirled me under his arm. He laughed as I did.

"Did you finish your wall?" I asked as we came to a stop.

"Not yet. What did you do this morning?"

"Sunbathed for a little while but I got bored. I guess I don't like my own company anymore."

"I'm sorry, I shouldn't have left you."

"It's fine, please don't worry. You have work to do. Life doesn't stop just because you have a visitor."

He still held onto my hand and his thumb ran across my knuckles. I watched him look down at them. His thumb brushed over my wedding band, he twisted it, just the once, before letting go.

"I need to eat," he said abruptly.

"Let me make you something, you cooked last night."

"Okay, I'll be outside."

I watched him walk away and I was a little confused. Maybe we needed to sit and talk about what was happening to us, something clearly was. We'd spent days and nights together when Dane had first died. He'd even slept beside me in my bed; he'd cradled my head to his chest and let me cry myself to sleep. But then we had a few months apart. Something had changed in him, in me, in that time.

I leaned on the countertop and looked at him through the window. He had his back to me and his hands rested on the balcony rail. A slight breeze came in off the sea; it ruffled his t-shirt, exposing his back. His body fascinated me, and many a time I would just sit and study his art. It was seeing him that reminded me.

"Are we getting that tattoo today?" I called out as I made him a sandwich.

I carried the plate out and handed it to him with a bottle of beer.

"We are. Are you ready to be permanently inked by me?"

"I'd rather you did it than a stranger."

"Good, I wouldn't let anyone else touch your skin anyway."

He had taken a bite of his sandwich and stared at me. That statement could have so many different meanings.

I took a seat next to him on the daybed, nudging him with my shoulder to shuffle over.

"Will it hurt really bad? You know how much of a coward I am."

"Yes. It will burn, but I'll take care of you."

"If it's that painful, why did you have so many?" I asked.

"Because I like the pain."

I looked sharply at him. He was staring out to sea as he finished his sandwich.

"What was it you said last night? Pain is good if something beautiful comes out of it," he said.

"I think you're beautiful," I whispered.

He slowly looked at me. "Not on the inside, Summer."

Before I had a chance to reply, he stood and held out his hand for me. I took it and silently, he led me back into the kitchen. He locked the doors and picked up his keys before leading me to the front door. Once again there was no opportunity for conversation as his songs blasted in the car. I began to wonder if music was his shield. The louder it was, the less chance of talk.

We drove for a while, following the coastal road. Eventually we arrived outside a small parade of shops. Nestled in the middle was a tattoo shop. Jack parked the car and we climbed out. He took hold of my hand as we entered the shop. The smell of antiseptic, the sound of rock music, and the buzz of a tattoo gun assaulted my senses.

"Jack, buddy. How the fuck are you?"

Sitting in a chair, tattooing himself, was a man. He had a shaved head, holes where his earlobes should have been, and not one piece of bare skin.

"Summer, this is the famous Bridge," Jackson said.

"Bridge?"

"Dumb name, I know."

Bridge rose from his chair and walked towards us. He gripped Jackson's hand and they bumped shoulders. He gave me a broad smile and I tried to hide the shock at the sight of the piercings on his face. He had a ring through his nose, two in his lower lip, numerous barbells in each eyebrow, and I had no idea if the row of small silver studs that crossed his brow were piercings or stuck on.

"Hey, Summer. It's good to meet you. What are you here for, bro?" Bridge said, turning back to Jack.

"She needs marking, my friend," Jackson replied.

"You know where it all is. I have a client in about twenty minutes. You guys want a beer? I'm not supposed to offer alcohol but..."

"Sure. I think I might need a little Dutch courage," I replied.

He chuckled as he walked away. Jackson led me to a black chair in front of a mirrored wall. A shelf held all the ink and a metal tray with the gun was placed to one side of it.

"Sit," he said, after he wiped the seat down with a paper towel soaked in something.

He used his foot to control a pedal underneath and the chair turned into a bed. I giggled as I fell backwards. My giggles stopped when I felt his fingers on the buttons on my shorts. Like he had the previous night, he raised my top until it was just under my breasts and pulled my shorts down to the top of my panties. I watched him tear off a piece of absorbent paper from a roll. I tried hard not to convulse off the bed when he tucked that paper under the waistband of my panties. His fingers very gently brushed against my skin.

Bridge came back and placed two bottles on the shelf beside us.

"Shit, man, that is fucked," he said, as he examined the drawing Jack had done on my stomach.

"Does that mean fucked as in good or bad?" I asked.

"It's fucking awesome, we need that in the catalogue," he replied.

"No, this is exclusive, just for her," Jackson replied.

Bridge placed his hand on Jackson's shoulder and laughed.

"How's D-J?" he asked.

"Good. Now, go sort out your client," Jack replied.

The tinkle of the doorbell had alerted us that the client had arrived a little early.

"What's up with D-J?" I asked.

"He had a little too much to drink last night, nothing more."

For the first time, I wasn't sure I believed him. There was something in the way his eyes shifted to Bridge as he spoke. And the loudness of his voice led me to believe that statement wasn't just for my ears.

"Are you ready for this?" he said.

"No, but go ahead."

He laughed as he wiped the drawing from my stomach.

"Don't you need that, to copy from?"

"No, it's imprinted in my mind. I can see it perfectly, even when it's not there."

He picked up a gun that was wrapped in plastic, opened some small pots of coloured ink and then ran his fingers over my hip.

"Don't you need gloves on?" I asked.

"You don't have some nasty disease I should know about, do

you?" he teased.

"No, of course not. But won't it bleed?"

"A little, but I'm not worried about your blood on my hands."

He took a swig from his bottle, although I wasn't sure he should be drinking just before he tattooed me. I looked at him; he stared back at me. He gave me a gentle nod of his head.

I let out a hiss as the needle of the gun connected with my skin.

"Breathe through it, baby," he whispered.

I stilled at the sentiment. He'd never called me anything other than my name before I'd arrived. His arm rested on my hipbone and I watched the concentration on his face. He bit down on his lower lip and I was grateful. Watching him, wanting to bite that lip myself, distracted me from the painful sting I was feeling.

He was right on one thing; it was a burn that spread across my body. I closed my eyes, trying to absorb the pain. I winced, I hissed, I even cried out at one point. But it was a strange pain. At times it hurt; at times it tickled. After he'd completed the outline, he rested back and studied his work. He wiped my skin and then applied a lotion.

"That will numb it a little," he said, as he dipped the gun in another pot of ink.

Maybe he had lied, maybe the lotion hadn't worked, but the longer he continued—the more it hurt. I tensed, my hands fisted by my sides, and I screwed my eyes shut. I took deep breaths and clenched my jaw shut.

"How are you doing?" he asked, without looking up at me.

"I don't know. How much longer?"

"We're about a third done."

"Oh, fuck."

He chuckled. "I'm not stopping, no matter how much you beg me, okay?"

"That's not nice."

"A half done tattoo looks shit. This is my art on your body; it has to get finished. Talk to me, about anything, take your mind off it."

It was only during the times he took the needle from my skin, to dip into yet another pot of ink that I was able to speak. At one point, I'd tried to arch my body off the bed; he had placed his hand way too close to my pussy for comfort and held me down. Part of me wanted to arch up again, if only to keep his hand in that exact spot.

I lost track of time. People came and went, the music changed many times, and Bridge came over to inspect Jack's handiwork.

"That's your best one yet. You need to work for me," he said.

"I should have asked, how many tattoos have you actually done?" I said.

"Five or six, not sure," Jackson answered.

"Five or six! Is that all?"

He chuckled, "Baby, if you hate it, Bridge can do a cover up."

"This is bad enough, Jack. If you've fucked it up, it stays fucked up. I'm never doing this again."

He looked over to me and gave me a wink. "It's perfect, now quit whining."

"Bridge, get your piercing gun out. She needs something to take her mind off this," he called.

"Whoa, wait up," I replied.

"My nipple, your belly button, that was the..."

He didn't finish his sentence immediately. After a pause, he added, "Maybe another time for that."

"No, it's fine, let's do it."

"Another time, Summer, okay?"

His abruptness startled me a little. I watched him take a breath in and let it out slowly. "I'll tell you what, your belly button, my brow, for now," he said.

"Okay."

As Bridge walked over, Jackson pointed to his brow without taking his eyes from my stomach.

"Shouldn't have let the previous one close up, bro," Bridge said.

I watched in utter fascination as he clamped Jackson's skin, and then without any tenderness, pierced a fucking large needle through it. Jackson didn't make a sound, but I did notice his pupils dilate and a smile played on his lips. It was a wicked smile though. Bridge threaded a silver bar through and screwed a small ball to one end, before removing the needle. I'd never seen a piercing performed before so had no idea if that was normal. I had my ears pierced but they had been done when I was child.

"Done," Bridge said.

"Didn't that hurt?" I asked.

"No."

Jackson hadn't broken his stride the whole time his piercing had taken place. A small trickle of blood ran just past his eye. Before Bridge could wipe it away, I raised my hand and caught it with my fingers. Jackson looked at me before placing the gun on the metal table and grabbing hold of my wrist. He raised my fingers to his lips and licked his blood from them. I was frozen, but the sight and feeling of his tongue on my fingertips had my stomach in a knot and my clitoris throb. He released my wrist and picked up the gun to continue. I turned my head away slightly and closed my eyes.

There shouldn't have been anything erotic in what he had done, but it affected me to the core. Jackson continued in silence.

"Belly bar?" Bridge said, rousing me from the dark thoughts whirling through my mind.

I looked between him and Jackson. "We are well over half done here, if you want to take a break," Jack said.

I nodded. I ran my hands over my face. I'd shed a couple of silent tears with the pain, or frustration, I wasn't sure. Bridge was holding a tray, and I tried to raise my head without shifting my stomach for fear of yet more pain.

"That one," I heard Jackson say. He'd chosen the belly bar for me.

"Are you consenting or is he making you do this?" Bridge asked, as he snapped on a fresh pair of latex gloves.

"I'm consenting. Jack, hold my hand, please."

He reached down and took my hand in his. "Look at me, baby," he whispered as Bridge got to work.

I screamed out but thankfully it was a quick process. Before my brain had time to register, it was done. I looked down to see a silver dragon's head above my belly button and its tail trailing underneath. A blue stone for an eye looked up at me. It was the same colour of blue as Jackson's eyes. I smiled.

"I love it," I said, as I wiped my eyes with my free hand.

"Sit up for a bit, have a look," Jackson said.

I shuffled up the bed. Although bloody and red, the butterfly had an outline, the shading underneath had been done and one wing was coloured in. It was absolutely stunning. It was situated exactly where the drawing had been, in line with my hip and just off to one side. Jackson handed me my beer, although not cold, I welcomed it. My lips were dry.

"I hurt," I said with a chuckle.

"I'll make it better when we get home," he said.

"I hope so."

"You need to keep moving the bar, it will sting a little but we can't let it scab up."

I smiled at him and then lay back down. He continued with the butterfly without speaking. Finally, he sprayed something on my stomach and wiped a tissue over it. He rested back on his stool and stretched out his back by raising his arms above his head. It was as he did that I noticed a large cut, just above the waistline of his jeans. Having seen me look, he quickly pulled his t-shirt down and stood.

I stared at his back as he turned to clean up the metal trolley. I was glad he had. I had half an idea what that cut was. His quickness to cover it, his lack of explanation, gave him away. I wanted to reach out to him, I wanted to speak but I didn't. I had no words.

"Can I look now?" I asked. I wanted to break the silence.

He slowly turned to me. "Sure, here."

He reached out with his hand to help me from the bed. We walked to a full-length mirror and what I saw took my breath away, again.

"Oh, Jack. It's stunning. I don't know what to say."

He gently pulled the paper towel away from the top of my panties. I watched his reflection in the mirror as he studied the tattoo. I also looked at the belly bar.

"Dane would have freaked," I said.

"Good."

"I love it, thank you."

I raised my hand to his cheek and he leaned into my touch

before reaching up and sliding my hand to his lips. He gently kissed my palm.

"You're welcome."

He turned to finish cleaning his workstation and I stood at the mirror. I gently ran my fingers over the tattoo, it was sore, very sore, and although Jack had told me when it healed I'd be able to see the colours better, the vibrancy of the blues and green popped out against my pale skin.

"Jack, can you do something for me?"

I turned to walk back to the bed and climbed on. "Put your name underneath, sign it for me."

"You want my name on your body? Forever?" he said.

"Yes, forever."

He must have known that I'd seen the word, 'Summer' on his side. Although a dragon snaked around the letters, it was clear to see. It was another thing that we'd never spoken about.

He dipped the gun in black ink and swiftly drew his signature under the tattoo. It took no more than a minute, and I loved that it was his signature and not just his name; it felt a little more personal.

CHAPTER NINE

Jackson

We drove home slowly, Summer shifted in her seat, trying to get comfortable. The seat belt had rubbed against her tattoo and she'd winced once or twice. I thought of her request, she had wanted my name under the butterfly, and a surge of something I found hard to name went through me. It was a mixture of pride, of love, of longing for the body to really belong to me, and I was in awe of her strength. She'd endured over two hours of pain, I'd seen the tears but she'd soldiered on. Her butterfly was exceptionally detailed for a first tattoo; it was a big deal. Most people opted for something simple and in one colour; she'd let me mark her, permanently, with what I believed to be my best tattoo.

However, I was also troubled. I knew she'd seen the largest cut, whether she understood what she'd seen, I had no idea. She hadn't said a word and I wondered if she would. But I'd seen the pain flash through her eyes, and I guessed I should have been grateful it wasn't pity.

"Don't sit in the sun for a bit, okay?" I said, as we walked into the house.

"I have no intention of burning my skin any more than it already is. I want to look at it again. Come with me?"

I followed her to her bedroom. She undid her shorts and peeled off the film I'd placed over the tattoo to protect it. I stood behind her as she studied herself in the mirror.

"I can't believe that didn't hurt," she said quietly.

"What?"

"The bar through your eyebrow."

"I guess I have a high pain threshold and I'd had it done there before."

"Your pupils dilated, Jack. The pain pleased you," she said, her voice had dropped to a whisper.

I didn't answer immediately. "Didn't we have a conversation about this yesterday?"

"No, we didn't have a conversation about pain *pleasing* you."

I sighed. "Summer, people get their kicks all sorts of ways."

"You get a kick out of pain? Receiving or inflicting?"

I didn't answer. I clenched my jaw shut, but I could feel my anxiety levels rising and I was getting agitated.

"I saw, Jack."

"I know."

"That wasn't a scratch from a bush."

I didn't answer her, not that it was a question.

"Why?"

She turned to look at me. Her hands slowly moved to the hem of my t-shirt. I could have stopped her but I didn't. I wanted the shame to wash over me. She slowly lifted, and I watched as her eyes widened before tears pooled in them. Her hands shook as she held my t-shirt to my chest. I watched a solitary tear roll down her cheek and I closed my eyes.

It was the touch of her lips on my skin that had my eyelids fly open. She'd placed a gentle kiss on one of the cuts. I grabbed the hair at the back of her head and pulled her head away, roughly.

"Don't. Don't feel for me."

I took a step away from her but she held on to my t-shirt. I grabbed her wrists and wrenched them away. I turned and walked away from her.

"Jack, please don't walk away. Talk to me," she said.

I stopped by the door.

"You want a conversation, about that?" I pointed to my stomach.

"Yes. I want to understand why."

"There's nothing to understand. I like it."

"I don't believe that. No one could enjoy doing that to themselves."

"I don't care what you believe, baby. Conversation over, okay? You don't and can't ever understand." I was aware of the aggressive tone to my voice.

"You're not exactly giving me a chance to, either. Carry on walking away, Jack, run, go on, do what you do, be a coward."

"You're a coward, Jackson. You'll never be anything more,"

88

my father's voice resounded in my head.

"Fuck you," I whispered, not entirely sure who the statement was directed at.

I left the room then.

I grabbed a bottle of Jack from the kitchen, laughing at the irony. I was going to drown my sorrows in alcohol with the same name. I headed down the steps and kept walking along the beach. I found a spot some distance from the house and sat. I unscrewed the cap and took a large gulp. I screamed out expletives. Thankfully, that end of the beach was empty, save for a few guys out on boards. I needed to drown out his voice.

I took another gulp, then another. I watched the sun set through a hazy vision. It was with disgust that I realised I'd finished the bottle. I threw it towards the water and then laughed when it landed no more than a few feet from me. I tried to stand, the beach swayed.

"Fuck, keep fucking still," I said, and then laughed again.

I took a few steps before falling to my knees. I rolled over to my back and watch the night sky swirl.

"That's Orion's Belt," I said to no one in particular.

A wave of nausea washed over me and I rolled to my side. I heaved my guts up into the sand. The alcohol burned my throat as it was expelled from my body. I wiped my mouth with my t-shirt and tried to stand again. Somehow I made it back to the steps, but not before trying to climb the neighbour's.

All the lights were on, including the one in my bedroom. I staggered up the steps and crashed, head first onto the decking.

"Oh, Jack," I heard. I rolled to my back to see her looming over me.

I laughed. "Think I'm fucked," I said.

She reached down to grab my shoulders. There was no way she was strong enough to lift me. I rolled to my stomach and winced as the rough wood scraped against my cuts. Somehow I managed to get to my knees. She wrapped her hands under my arms to steady me. I stood and wrapped my arm around her shoulder to anchor myself. With her arm around my waist, she walked me to my bedroom.

"I fucking hate you for this, Jack," she said between gritted teeth,

"No more than I fucking hate myself, darling."

"Why? What did getting pissed ever solve?" She had managed to get me to my bed and I tried to sit. I ended up lying across the bed.

She lifted my legs and swung them on the bed. I laughed as I was scrunched at an angle. She pulled on my arm to straighten me. I felt her remove my trainers and socks. I laughed as her nail slid down the underside of my foot.

"That tickles," I mumbled with eyes closed.

She grabbed the hem of my t-shirt and tried to lift. I was not in a position to help her. Somehow she got the t-shirt off over my head. I smelled my own vomit as it passed my nose.

Somewhere in my consciousness, I felt her hand move to the top of my jeans. She unbuckled my belt, popped open the button, and before she lowered the zipper, I placed my hand over hers.

"No shorts," I said with a slur.

I held her hand at my groin though. I wanted her to feel how hard my cock was. I felt her flatten her palm against me. She gently squeezed and I moaned. I released her hand and threw my arms above my head. That action must have caused my wounds to open slightly. I felt the trickle of hot blood run down my side.

Summer pulled her hand away and I opened my eyes to look at her. I tried but failed to get her focus.

"What did you do to yourself?" she said.

I ran one hand over my stomach; I dragged my nails across and opened my wounds. I coated my fingers in my blood and brought them to my face, to my lips. I heard her sob.

"It's not what I did, baby. It's what he did."

Those were the last words I remembered before I passed out.

CHAPTER TEN

Summer

I couldn't stop the tears; they rolled freely down my cheeks as I looked at him. His mouth was smeared with his blood, it ran down his side and soaked into the white sheet he lay on. He mumbled incoherently, and for a few minutes, I was stunned into paralysis.

Four words swam through my mind and I reached for Jackson's phone.

Dex is the fixer-upper, I remembered Jack saying.

I scrolled through his contacts and pressed call when I came to his name.

"Jack," I heard.

"It's Summer, Jack is…" My voice caught in my throat.

"I'm on my way." Dexter cut off the call without waiting for an explanation.

I rushed to the bathroom and wet a washcloth. I sat on the edge of the bed and wiped it over his stomach. It was as I studied his cuts, I noticed so many scars. Most were covered over by his ink, and I wondered why I'd never noticed them before. Raised skin in straight lines covered his stomach, up his chest and down the undersides of both arms.

"Oh, Jack," I cried as I wiped away his blood.

I watched my tears drip onto his skin, mingle with the blood that continued to seep from one wound, the one I'd seen that extended down to the waistband of his jeans. I gently lowered the zip and parted the top of them. Old scars followed the ink down to a patch of dark blond hair.

I closed my eyes and slid from the bed. I rested my back against it and cried for my friend. I folded my arms across my knees and lowered my head. Some time after, I heard heavy footsteps on the decking. I scrambled to my feet as Dexter walked through the bedroom doors. He carried a plastic box in one hand.

"What happened?" he asked, as he made his way to the side of the bed.

"He got drunk, I tried to help him but he fell up the steps. I guess he opened those..." I struggled to finish the sentence.

"Why did he get drunk?" he asked, as he placed his box on the bedside table and opened it.

"I saw...he freaked. He...he cuts..."

"I know, Summer. I know."

I watched as Dexter filled a syringe with something and injected a liquid into Jackson's arm.

"What is that?"

"Something to help with the massive headache he's going to wake up with," he said, and it surprised me to hear him chuckle.

I hadn't found the situation remotely funny. Dexter opened a couple of packets of small wipes, which he ran over the open cut.

"Thank fuck he's out of it, this stuff stings like a bitch," he said.

The wipes left an orange smear over Jack's skin. He closely inspected the largest one. I watched as he placed some small strips of a sticky fabric over the wound to hold it closed. He then taped gauze over it and rolled Jack onto his side.

"That's about all I can do for him tonight. He came to me this morning."

Dexter straightened and closed his box. He took my arm and led me from the room. I slumped into the daybed and he sat on a chair facing me.

"Why did he come to you?" I asked.

"He's struggling, Summer, emotionally, and when that happens, this is what he does."

"How long have you known?"

"D-J found him on the beach one day, pretty much in the same condition, he brought him to me. I patched him up. I counsel him, I counsel them all."

"Why does he do it?"

"That's for him to tell you, if he ever will."

"He said something like, 'it's what he did.' Who is he?"

"Again, that's not something I can tell you. He talks; they all talk to me in confidence, Summer. I hold all their secrets and all I can do is help them through it."

"What do I do?"

"Be his friend, don't question him until he's ready. I warn you, he's going to feel pretty shitty in the morning, and I don't mean from the drink. He's going to be full of shame and guilt, he might disappear for a couple of hours and that's okay. Let him go. He has to purge himself."

"Purge himself?"

"Purge the guilt, the shame, and the anger that will follow."

"How?"

"That's not something you want to know. Call me if anything else happens tonight, but I'll expect him at some point tomorrow."

Dexter stood and with a pat to my shoulder, he left the way he'd come, down the steps and along the beach to the car park.

I walked back to Jackson, he hadn't moved from the position we'd left him in. I lay behind him, curled my body around his, and placed my arm across his chest, careful not to touch his wounds.

It was at some point during the night, I felt his hand close over mine. I hadn't slept but dozed on and off. He gave my hand a squeeze, and I flexed my fingers on his chest to let him know I'd felt him.

He brought his knees closer to his chest; I tucked mine in behind him. My face was close to the back of his neck and I kissed it. I breathed in his scent, his aftershave, his sweat, and Jack Daniels. He murmured something under his breath, I didn't catch what he'd said but I kissed him again. He straightened his legs slightly, and slid my hand down his stomach, to where I'd left his jeans open. I wasn't sure if he was completely awake or if he was conscious of what he was doing. My fingers slid through the downy hair until I reached his hard cock. I closed my hand around it and heard him sigh. He straightened his legs further and rolled slightly onto his back.

I slid my hand up and down, and ran my thumb over the tip, catching a drop of fluid. A small moan left his lips but his eyes stayed closed. I released his cock and pulled on his jeans to lower them a little. I closed my fist around him again, feeling the metal bar he had pierced on the underside. I watched as his chest rose and fell, his breathing quickened as I pleasured him. His lips parted and his tongue ran across his lower one.

His cock felt so silky and smooth in my palm. I let my nails gently scratch against him and I heard the sharp intake of breath. I felt him shift and slightly raise his hips; I upped the pace and squeezed harder.

His hand gripped the bedding at his side as I brought him close to his release. Tears rolled down my cheeks as he came. His milky cum spurted over my hand and coated my fingers as I pumped him dry. He moaned out loud, he arched his back off the bed, and I saw one tear leak from his closed eyes. I gently kissed the tear away as he slumped back onto the bed.

He didn't speak, nor did he move. I climbed from the bed and headed to the bathroom. After washing my hands, I grabbed a handful of tissues and cleaned him up. I pulled his jeans back up to his hips and sat on the edge of the bed for a while, just looking at him.

I quietly closed his bedroom door and headed to my own. I peeled off my shorts, my top and underwear, and lay on the sheet. It was too warm to climb underneath. I was frustrated, aroused, scared. I was all emotions mixed up. Despite his drink-fuelled brain, had he wanted to fuck me, I think I would have let him.

I ran my hand down my stomach; I needed to get some relief.

Pleasuring myself wasn't something I had done much of. My fingers trailed over my opening, spreading the wetness to my clitoris, which throbbed. A heat travelled over my skin from my stomach to my neck. I was desperate for my release but unable to achieve it. I kicked my heels against the bed and growled out in frustration.

I heard his footsteps across the floor and quickly pulled my hand away. I opened my eyes to see him beside the bed and my cheeks flamed. He didn't speak as he climbed on at the bottom and positioned himself between my thighs. He propped himself up on his elbows, his hands rested on my hips, and while he kept his eyes fixed on mine; he lowered his head.

I heard him inhale before his tongue swiped over me. I wanted to raise my hips from the bed. A spark of electrical current surged over my body and I gasped. I placed my hands on his head and gripped his hair. He licked, he sucked gently on my clitoris, and he pushed his tongue inside me. I was a mass of static, of heat, my legs quivered and my stomach knotted with pleasure. I tilted my pelvis; I wanted his tongue deeper inside me. I cried out his name and felt his fingers dig into my skin as I did. Tears rolled down the side of my face as wave after wave of pleasure, of desire, washed over me. I brought my heels closer to my backside and let my knees fall to the sides. I wanted to give him as much access as he needed. He forced his face closer to me and his mouth covered my opening. I could feel his breath on my burning skin and when he moaned, that was my undoing. My body convulsed and I screamed out as I came.

I'd never had an orgasm from oral before. I'd never felt the emotions coursing through me; I'd never felt the heat that continued to travel over my skin, followed by goose bumps. I'd never felt anything like Jackson before.

He raised his head, his chin glistened, and I watched as he swiped his tongue over his lips. He placed his lips on my pubis and his tongue gently swirled around in my hair. He kissed up to my navel and very gently sucked the dragon into his mouth. It stung as the bar pulled against the newly made hole and I think that was his intention.

While his mouth explored my body, he removed the film from my tattoo. As I came down from my orgasm, his tongue swiped over his artwork. I was struggling to catch my breath and had closed my eyes when I felt him move above me. He placed his hands either side of my head, and I opened my eyes to see piercing dark blue staring back at me. He lowered his head to the side of my neck.

"Thank you," he whispered.

Then he rolled to one side and stood. Before he left, he leaned down and his fingers trailed down my cheek, catching the tear before it dripped onto the sheet.

"I want you so badly, but right now, I want to sort out my head more."

I watched him walk away. Once he'd left the room, I pulled the sheet around my body, not for warmth but protection. I curled into a ball and cried into my pillow.

CHAPTER ELEVEN

Jackson

I could taste her on my lips and tongue as I walked, still a little unsteady, back to my bedroom. I heard her cry. It tore at my heart but I kept on walking. I angrily brushed the tears from my cheeks before falling onto the bed.

I lay on my back for ages, listening to her. Every nerve willed me to move. My legs jerked in protest at not climbing from that bed and holding her in my arms. I was finished. I was exhausted and I cried along with her. She quietened; I guessed it was her turn to listen to me.

My hand twitched with the urge to reach for that box, but my resolve was stronger. I opened the drawer and pulled out a pad and a pencil. I flipped it open and I drew. I drew her naked form. I knew every inch of her and I sketched from memory. Her hair was fanned out around her head, tears rolled down her cheeks, and her body arched from the bed. She was in the throes of her orgasm. Her hands gripped the bedding, exactly as I had seen her. When I was done, I flipped the page over and started again. I drew her again and again in different positions on that bed. In one she was on all fours, in another she was spread-eagled with her hands above her head. Each time she was crying. I threw the pad to the floor just as the sun started to rise.

I rolled to my stomach and buried my face in my arms to block out the light. I slept.

———

I glanced at the clock when I woke; it was mid-afternoon. I rolled to my side and faced the doors. Something was off though. I scanned the floor and noticed the sketchpad missing. I sat up and saw it closed on the bedside table. I swung my legs to the side and was surprised to not feel even the slightest thump in my head. The shake to my hands was the only evidence of the alcohol poisoning I had narrowly missed. Alongside the sketchpad were some used wipes, although it would take me a few moments to piece the early part of the evening together, I knew Dexter had been there.

I took in a deep breath and wet my dry lips with my tongue. I could taste her still.

"Fuck," I whispered.

Images flooded my brain. She'd brought me to an orgasm; I'd done the same to her. Those memories were very clear in my mind; it was what came before that I couldn't remember. The sound of the sea and laughter drifting up from the beach reminded me of sitting out there and drinking a bottle of Jack. But it was the bit in the middle that I struggled with. I inspected the crook of my arms. I saw the very small red hole and chuckled. Whatever the fuck it was that Dexter swore by, worked. There was not one wave of nausea as I stood, no pounding in my head as I made my way to the bathroom.

I switched on the shower and slid out of the jeans I'd slept in. I climbed under the water while peeling away the gauze. I stood and raised my face. I let the water wash the shame that had started to creep over me from my body.

I wasn't sure I'd hit rock bottom; in fact I doubted it. But I'd done the one thing I'd never done before. I'd exposed my cuts to someone other than Dex. Fear replaced the shame. I wondered if she would still be there or would she have run. In one way, I was thankful we were in the U.S.; it wasn't so easy to pack up in the night and leave.

I stepped from the shower and pulled a towel from the rack. I patted my stomach dry and wrapped it around my waist. As I walked from the bathroom, I came to an abrupt halt. Summer stood in the middle of my bedroom with a cup in her hand.

At first we didn't speak. She kept her eyes cast down for a while. Eventually she looked up at me.

"Coffee, I thought you might need it," she said.

I walked towards her and it killed me to see her take a slight step back. I stopped and sighed. I reached out for the coffee.

"Thanks, yes, it's needed."

"I…"

"It's okay, no need for words," I said. I turned away and placed the coffee on the table next to the pad.

"I'll, err, I'll make something to eat. I'm sure you're hungry."

"Starving," I replied. I gave her a smile, a fake one, and I wasn't sure if she knew it was.

She smiled, a small one, before leaving the room. I dressed and picked up the coffee before making my way out on the balcony. Summer was in the kitchen and when I arrived I saw her stiffen her back.

"How's the tattoo, I need to see it's healing okay," I said.

"It's fine, itchy, but fine."

She had kept her back to me. I stood and an awkward silence developed.

"Want me to help?"

"No, I got this. You go and sit, I'll be out in a minute."

I left her and grabbed a bottle of water from the side as I passed. I was thirsty. Dexter's magic potion stopped a headache and the nausea, but not the dehydration itself. I unscrewed the cap and brought the bottle to my lips, I drank it down in one go.

"I made turkey sandwiches," she said as she joined me.

She hadn't exactly joined me, she kept her distance and whereas I sat on the daybed, she opted for the chair.

"Thank you, this looks really good."

"It's just a sandwich," she snapped back at me.

I sighed and scrubbed my hand over my face, feeling the stubble around my chin. She started to nibble on her sandwich but I could tell she wasn't enjoying it.

I placed my plate on the decking beside the bed and swung my legs over the side so I was sitting and facing her.

"You have every right to be totally pissed off with me..."

"No shit, Sherlock," she said cutting off my sentence.

I wanted to chuckle. I hadn't heard that phrase in a long time.

"You scared me, Jack. And then you gave me the most amazing orgasm. I'm confused. I don't know whether to hate or love you, right now. Dexter is expecting you and I really think you need to go and see him. I don't know what's going on, I want to. I want to help but I don't know if you'll let me."

"You don't want to help me."

"Don't tell me what the fuck I want to do, okay?"

"I'm sorry, that wasn't what I meant."

"What did you mean then?"

"I meant, don't waste your time on me."

She stood and walked towards me, she knelt in between my legs. She cupped my face in her hands.

"Do I mean anything to you? You tell me the truth. We've been skirting around this for days, for weeks, fucking years, Jackson. Do I mean anything to you? And don't you dare lie to me."

I swallowed hard as I looked straight back into her piercing stare. She didn't blink and her eyes demanded an honest answer.

"I've loved you from the first moment I saw you. You're all I think about, all day. You're all I dream about. Your name is etched on my body, in my heart. You're in every painting I do. But you don't know me, Summer. You don't know what I've done, what I do. When you do, you'll hate me with way more passion that you're showing now."

"Give me the chance to make that decision," she said in a whisper.

"I can't do that. I can't live knowing you hate me. I need help, Summer; I know I do. And I was fine for a while. I can't promise you last night was a one off, because it won't be. I fall, I get up, and then

103

I fall again. But I promise you this; I'm working on it. I can't tell you everything, maybe I never will. Call me a coward, you won't be the first, but I can't let you make that decision because I know what you'll choose if you knew it all."

She placed her hands on my thighs and her head fell forwards onto my chest. I wrapped my arms around her and held her. I breathed in the smell of her hair, of her body, and committed it to memory. I knew her body; I wanted to memorize her smell because she would leave me. I had no doubt about that.

"Go see Dexter, please?" she whispered.

"I will. And then we'll talk some more. Please be here when I get back, don't leave, not yet."

"I'm not going anywhere, for the moment."

She stood and held out her hands. I took them and stood myself.

"I love you, Jackson. I love you more than I ever loved Dane, and that's the honest truth."

I smiled at her. "Opposed to the dishonest truth?"

"You know what I mean. I love you. You know I do. But I can't help you if you don't help yourself. I don't know how."

I kissed her forehead and gently pushed her away. "I'll be an hour, maybe two. He'll kick my arse, scream at me a little, and then counsel. It's probably best you don't see that."

"Just come back sober and..." Her eyes flicked to my stomach.

"I will."

I walked into the kitchen and grabbed my car keys. While she took the seat I'd vacated on the daybed, I grabbed her handbag and rifled through. I pulled out her passport and placed it in my pocket. I wasn't going to take any chances.

"Jack," D-J said as he walked towards me.

I'd climbed from my car at the same time as D-J had flicked his cigarette butt to the ground and pushed himself off the wall.

"Is he in a good mood?" I asked as D-J gave me a fist bump.

"No, I think we're both in for it." He laughed as he spoke.

D-J was the only other person who knew it all. He knew every seedy detail about me and I knew the same of him. His drug taking was a result of being abused as a child. Not only abused by his father but pimped out for years. When his demons took over, he fought them with coke, pills, pretty much anything he could get his hands on. He was one of the many that Dexter fixed.

"Bad one, was it?" he asked.

"Been worse. But Summer saw me on a downer, it wasn't pretty."

"Dude, that sucks."

"Yeah."

We walked through the doors and into the bar. Dexter was standing in his usual spot behind the bar. He looked up and without a word pointed to the door behind him. The three of us made our way to the safe room.

He closed the door and slid the bolt across behind us. "Sit," he commanded.

D-J sat on the edge of the bed and I took one of the chairs. Dexter sat facing me.

"Show me," he said and I raised my t-shirt.

He leaned closer and inspected. "Okay, you'll live."

He turned slowly to D-J. "You know the drill, piss in a bottle."

D-J rose and headed to the cabinet. He knew which drawer was his, it contained all that Dexter needed but was normally kept locked. I guessed it had been opened for our arrival. D-J took a small sample bottle and in front of us, pissed in it. He grabbed a testing kit and took both to Dex. I noticed the shake of his hand as he placed them both on the table. He wasn't expecting a good result, I suspected. Dex pulled off the cap from the testing kit, poured a small amount of urine in it and then replaced the testing strips. He let it sit for a moment.

"Do you need to tell me anything?" he asked.

He always gave us the opportunity to confess before he produced the evidence.

"A little Ketamine," D-J said.

Dexter closed his eyes and sighed. "You ain't no horse, son. That stuff will finish you off and there is nothing I can do with that shit."

Dexter inspected the kit and nodded. D-J had confessed all. There had been a time, not too along ago, where that kit would register every drug known to man. Dexter's mission was to wean him off slowly. He bought the drugs, he administered them, but there was no stopping D-J from obtaining his own if he wanted to.

There was nothing legal about what Dexter did. He had been a registered psychotherapist at one time, but he'd hit the bottle when he'd misdiagnosed a young boy who had then gone on to take his own life. He'd left Australia and settled in New Orleans with Alfie, as an alcoholic, but turned his life around. When the storms wiped out his neighbourhood, they'd moved again, bought the bar, and he'd made it his life's mission to help the misfits that couldn't afford regular therapy. And whatever it was he did, it worked. Most of the patrons had been in his care at one time. Most were able, stable young people.

"Now you. How was it this morning?" He turned back to me.

"Okay, I didn't wake until mid-afternoon, I think. Summer was still there; I half expected to have found her gone. She was scared, she wants to help me but I can't let her do that. I stole her passport," I confessed.

"You replace that the minute you return, you hear me? Why do you think you can't let her in?"

"Because if she finds out what I need, it's not something she can give me, and she'd be disgusted with me. If she finds out what I did, she'll hate me."

"There is no reason for her to find out. But we need to wind it down, Jack."

"I know. I'm trying. Give me some other outlet, tell me what to do?"

"If you had a regular relationship with her, how would that work?" D-J chimed in.

"I've never had a normal relationship, I have no fucking idea."

The circle of friends we'd had thought I was the eternal playboy. They had no idea. Most of the women I had were prostitutes, women I paid because no sane woman would put up with what I needed. I needed the rough sex I could exert when I paid for it. Those women knew exactly what they were getting involved with and they charged heavily for it.

I hated myself every time I fucked one of those women. I had no idea why I did it even. It sickened me to my very core. And that produced a circle that I was struggling to break. The more sickened I'd feel, the more I'd want to hurt. The more I wanted to hurt, the more I needed to...

I didn't want to think about it.

"I think she may be the one to break you down, Jack. And that will be hard for you both, but it's the only way to break the cycle you're in. If we can get one thing under control, the rest will fall into place," Dex said.

"She's here on holiday and I sure as fuck am not going back there."

"That's where your demon is, dude. Might be worth hitting it head on."

"Says he who won't go to the police," I snapped.

"It's too long ago for me, and my old man happens to be the ex-governor. Who the fuck is going to believe me?"

The safe room was the only place we argued. It was policy to be honest and to speak freely. D-J and I had come to blows before, but the minute we stepped out that door it was all left behind.

We argued back and forth for another half hour. Dex would often sit back and let us battle it out. He believed in everyone being able to chime in with advice until we came to a collective decision. It exhausted me though.

"I'll tell her some of it. I'll give an explanation as to the cutting, is that fair enough?" I asked.

Both nodded. "It's a start."

We stood and although we would never embrace, Dex was way too manly for that, he gave us both a squeeze to the shoulder. Session over, we made our way out.

"Beer?" D-J asked as he helped himself.

"Probably not wise right now," Dex said.

"You'll have to tell us what the fuck is in that jab you give us," I said.

All I knew about it was it was not wise to touch a drop of alcohol for twenty-four hours after. I'd made that mistake once, never again. I don't think I'd ever been as sick in my life.

"It works, doesn't it? That's all you need to know."

"I'm heading home. I'll be here in the morning to finish the wall then we can get ready for opening," I said, as I made my way to the door.

I began to get nervous on the journey home. Although Summer had told me she loved me, and I'd confessed my feelings, I was unsure of the future. We lived in two different countries for a start, and there was no way I was about to return the UK. I just had no idea how, if, a relationship would work.

I parked on the drive and sat for a moment in the car. I removed her passport from my pocket, and although I felt like a complete shit, I hid it in the pocket in the car door.

I walked through the house and out onto the balcony. Summer was sitting on the beach. She was hugging her knees and her head rested on her forearms. I stood for a while, just watching her. My emotions were all over the place and my heart started to flutter in my chest. I needed to explain, to tell her something, but I was unsure as to what.

I strode across the beach and sat beside her.

"Hey," she said without looking up.

"How are you doing?"

"I'm not sure, to be honest." She raised her head and looked out to sea. "I'm confused."

"I can imagine. I don't know what to say to you."

"I want to know why, but I guess that's about the hardest question I can ask, isn't it?"

"It is. Not because I don't want to tell you, I just don't know how or where to start. My head is totally fucked up and has been for years. The man you know...knew, it's me, but it isn't me."

"So you're a lie as well."

"No. There's the real me, the one you know, and then there's the me that has demons that take over and I can't control them."

"I think I understand. Jack, I don't know what to do. You being drunk doesn't bother me, you hurting yourself does. I don't get why you would do that to yourself."

"I like the pain, Summer. I like to hurt sometimes, I get a rush from it," I said quietly.

"So skydive or something," she replied.

I sighed. I reached over and took her hand in mine. She hadn't looked at me the whole time we had sat.

"What happened today?" she asked.

"I talked, Dex talked."

"Who is he?"

"He's a psychotherapist but not licenced here. He battled his demons for a long time and then bought the bar. He fixes us all up, it seems to be his mission in life to help others."

"And how is that going?" she asked, I detected a slight hint of sarcasm in her voice. "Is it me? Did I cause this?"

She turned her head on its side and looked at me.

"No, maybe. But I need you here, Summer."

"You said, last night, 'it's what he did.' What did you mean by that?"

My heart missed a beat. "Did I say anything else?"

"No, just that. Who did this to you, Jack?"

I took a deep breath and looked out to sea. The sun shimmered off the water; it was a beautiful day, way too beautiful to be talking about something so ugly. But then I thought of D-J, and it pained me that I was so fucked up for something nowhere near as serious as his childhood.

"My father, the great Brett Walker. The cunt with a capital C."

"What did he do to you?"

"That's a conversation for another day. I'm exhausted, I need sleep right now."

I stood and brushed the sand from my jeans. "Sleep with me?"

She looked up at me. I held out my hand and waited, praying that she would take it and stand. It took a moment or two before she reached up and I helped her to stand.

We walked hand in hand back to the house and into my bedroom. I pulled my t-shirt over my head but left my jeans on. As I climbed on the bed, Summer lay beside me. At first we lay side by side without touching, until I placed my arm under her neck and pulled her into my side. She turned on her side and nestled her head on my shoulder. She placed her hand on my chest.

"What do I do, Jack, to help?" she whispered.

"I don't know, just be here, I guess."

"What happens when I leave?"

I sighed. "I don't want to think that far ahead yet."

We fell silent and as exhaustion washed over me, I let my eyelids drop.

———

It was dark when I woke; the muslin drapes blew gently as a breeze wafted through the room. I was alone and my stomach knotted in panic. I rolled to the edge of the bed and stood. I quickly walked to the doors and out onto the balcony. I stopped outside Summer's bedroom; the door was open and the bed empty. I carried on walking. My heart rate started to increase as I searched each room without success.

"Summer," I called out. Silence responded.

I ran from room to room and then back outside. I sprinted down the steps onto the beach and scanned first one way, then the other. It was too dark to see far and I prayed she hadn't decided on a walk. I pulled my mobile from my jeans and dialled, I could hear her ringtone back in the house.

"Where the fuck are you?" I said, as I made my way back to the kitchen.

It was as I slammed my mobile down on the countertop that the front door opened. I looked up the stairs. Summer walked through carrying a paper bag in her arms.

"Where have you been? I got worried," I said, as I met her at the bottom of the stairs.

"I went for food, Jack."

"You left your phone here."

"So I did. I've been gone twenty minutes, that's all. We needed to eat and you have nothing in."

"How did you get to the shops?"

"I took your car. Took me ages to remember to stay on the wrong side of the road, but thankfully I didn't meet anyone head on," she said with a chuckle.

"You won't be insured, please don't do that again."

She placed the bag on the countertop and reached in.

"And please don't do this again," she said, as she waved her passport in front of me.

"I…"

"I don't need to know."

I watched as she returned the passport to her handbag and zipped it closed.

"Do I need to hide this?"

I shook my head.

"I've got two weeks of holiday left, Jack, but if I need to leave, I will," she added.

She unpacked the groceries as I took a stool at the breakfast bar. "Need any help?" I asked.

"No, I only got a few things, enough for now. I'm hungry, go and fire up the barbecue." She handed me a plate of meat to grill.

She joined me on the deck with burger buns, salad, plates, and cutlery. When the meat was grilled, we sat and ate. I watched as she took a bite from her burger and then licked her fingers clean of the juice that had dribbled. My cock hardened, and I shifted to get comfortable on the metal chair.

"Do you want a beer?" she asked as she wiped her mouth with a napkin.

"No, too early. I'll have water instead."

"Too early?"

"Too soon after that injection, it will make me sick. Which I guess is the point of it, really."

"What did Dex give you?"

"I have no idea but whatever it is, it works. Whether it's booze or drugs, we wake without too many after-effects."

"Should he be injecting you with something you know nothing about? And care to explain the 'drugs' comment?"

"I don't take drugs, figure of speech. I trust him. D-J trusts him." I cringed at the mistake I'd made.

Summer stood and walked to the kitchen, she snapped the top off a bottle of beer and unscrewed the cap from the water. As she passed, she placed my water on the table next to me. Instead of sitting, she stood against the balcony.

"Did you mean everything you said earlier?"

"I've meant everything I've ever said to you."

"I'm scared, Jack. I don't know what to do." She turned to look out to sea.

I rose from my chair and walked to stand behind her. I rested my hands on the rails beside hers and pressed my body against hers.

"Tell me what scares you, other than the obvious," I said.

"You scare me. I don't know if I can have a relationship with you, but I love you."

Her honesty cut me to the core. I rested my chin on her shoulder, and for a moment, we just looked out into the darkness.

"What can you see?" I asked.

"Nothing, it's too dark."

"Does the darkness scare you?"

"Sometimes."

"Why?"

She shrugged her shoulders. "I know there's nothing out there to frighten me, though."

"Then think of me in the same way. It's the darkness about me that scares you; it does me too. But that darkness has never hurt you, has it?"

"For someone so fucked up, you're very deep."

"The two go hand in hand."

"Will you answer just one question for me?"

"I don't know. I guess it depends on your question."

"Did your father abuse you?"

I didn't answer immediately. "I guess that depends on what type of abuse you mean."

"Did he...you know...sexually..."

"No."

I felt her body sag, relax back into mine a little, and heard the soft exhale of a held breath.

"Then..."

"No more questions, not yet. When you make me think about him, it doesn't help."

"I'm sorry, I just needed to know that one thing," she said quietly.

"And if he had? How high would your level of disgust at me be?"

She turned in my arms.

"That's not why I asked."

"Then why do you need to know?"

"I just need something to understand why you do that. What did your father do to make you want to cut yourself? If you can just give me something to help me understand, I can help." She placed her hand on my stomach and I flinched.

"I'm asking again, Summer. Stop the questions, okay? Now I have his fucking voice in my head." I made a conscious effort to not allow the emotion to show in my voice.

"I only want to understand why, is that so wrong? What was it that he did to you? Did he beat you? Can't you tell me something? No one cuts themselves for fun, Jackson."

"I. Like. The. Pain." I growled out the statement as I pushed my body further into her, pinning her.

I felt her body tremble but she held my gaze.

"Can we find another way?" Her voice cracked.

"I have other ways, Summer. Now quit talking."

Her probing had done its usual. Just the mere mention of him had his words swimming around my head. As my mouth crashed on hers, I heard him. As the darkness of the night engulfed me, I felt him.

'Scared of the dark, aren't you?' he'd say as he locked me in the closet.

'You're nothing but a snivelling shit,' he'd say, as his large, rough hands gripped my chin, forcing my head up.

'You should have died, Jackson. You killed your mother, did you know that?' he'd scream at me.

'I don't think I've disliked anything more than you. I begged the hospital to abort you, wash you down the sewer,' he'd say.

"Jack, stop. Jack!"

I blinked as my vision came into focus. The voices quietened in my head. I took a step back and looked at her. Her face was flushed, her hair was tangled, and her t-shirt ripped. She held her hand to the side of her head.

"Huh?"

I looked at my hand and saw a fistful of her hair. I opened it and watched the hair fall to the floor. When I looked back at her, her lips were swollen and bruised.

"I killed my mum," I blurted out, then turned and walked away.

"Jack?"

I carried on walking until I got to my bedroom. I closed the doors behind me, sliding the bolt across. I heard her footsteps and the rattle as she tried to open them. I then heard her walk away. I paced the room with my fists gripping the sides of my head.

"Fuck!" I screamed. I wanted to punch the fuck out of myself for saying what I had.

In my confusion, I'd forgotten to lock the internal door, the one leading to the hallway. I had my back to it as it opened and I heard her walk across the room. She didn't speak at first but placed her hand gently on my back.

"Talk to me, Jack. What did you mean out there?"

"You need to go back to your room. I can't do this right now."

"I'm not going anywhere until you at least talk to me. You kissed me like I've never been kissed by anyone before. You were like a man hungry, desperate for me. That was beyond passion, that was...well, I don't actually know what it was. Please, Jack, talk to me."

I spun on my heels and continued to pace. "You don't get it, do you? I will hurt you physically, Summer, because that's all I know. You need to get as far away from me as possible. It creeps over me, it takes over, and I can't stop it."

"I don't know what you're talking about. What creeps over you?"

"The anger, the fucking anger. Now go, get out of my sight before I do what I want to do."

"What do you want to do, Jackson?" she said so quietly I nearly missed it.

"I want to fuck you so hard. I want to hear you scream, cry. I want my name to drip off your tongue as you beg me to stop."

"So you want to hurt me?"

CHAPTER TWELVE

Summer

Confusion crossed his face and he stopped his pacing.

"So you want to hurt me? That's what you would be doing, Jackson. You want me tied up so you can *fuck me hard*. You want to hurt me, just so you can release your anger?"

"No! Not that..." he said.

His chest was heaving, sweat beaded on his forehead, and his nostrils flared as he tried to drag in enough air to keep his heart beating. And it was pounding at a rapid pace; I could see a vein bulge and throb at the side of his neck.

I tried very hard to hide the shaking and to keep my voice even. I watched as he blinked rapidly, his pupils were dilated and I wasn't entirely sure he could focus on me. I tried, subtly, to shift my weight onto the balls of my feet so I could push off and run if I needed to.

I also watched him grip the front of his t-shirt and dig his nails into his stomach.

"I need..." he whispered.

"You don't need that, baby."

I flinched as he used the heel of his hand to hit the side of his head. He growled something incoherent about his father. I watched as his eyes shifted to his bedside cabinet.

"Lie down, Jackson," I said, I tried to keep my voice firm and controlled.

I gave him a wide berth as he made his way to the bed and did as I'd instructed.

"Take off your t-shirt," I said. He did. "Now raise your arms and grip the headboard. If you so much as let go and touch me, I leave, okay?"

He closed his eyes and I truly believed he knew exactly what I was about to do. I sat across his thighs and placed my fingertips to the largest wound. He took in a sharp breath.

With the tears rolling down my cheeks that I had no control over, I drew my fingernails across his cut. I opened it up and allowed him to feel.

His arms were rigid, his body arched off the bed and his cock hardened, straining against the confines of his jeans. He moaned as if the experience was pleasurable, and I guessed to him, it was.

"Again," he hissed through clenched teeth.

I watched my tears drip onto his stomach and dilute his blood. It ran down his side as I dug my nails in further. I swallowed down the nausea, the bile that rose to my throat and burned. Each pass I made with my nails caused him to moan and writhe underneath me. He tilted his pelvis, grinding his cock into me. It sickened me to realise I was aroused. My clitoris throbbed with every thrust he gave.

He parted his lips; his tongue ran across his lower one to moisten it. I wanted to kiss him, I wanted to hold him to me and comfort him. I didn't want to do what I was doing.

I didn't believe Jackson wanted to hurt me. I'd used that line to hopefully shock him into understanding. Dexter had talked about outlets and purging his guilt, was that how he did it? Did he rough fuck women to release his aggression? I looked down on the man I loved, the man I thought I knew yet realised I didn't, and my heart broke for him.

I placed my palm on his stomach, my fingers were coated with his blood and I smeared it across his tattoos. It was as I stared that I realised what I was running my hand over—a pregnant woman I'd never noticed before. Most of his cuts were over her stomach and I wondered if that was significant.

His breathing was rapid and shallow but his body had relaxed back on the bed. He had kept his eyes closed the whole time but opened them as I shuffled slightly down his legs. I undid the buckle of his belt, the button and zip on his jeans. I dragged them down slightly and his cock sprang free. I wrapped one hand around him and stroked gently at first, then harder and faster. I squeezed him tight; there was a part of me that wanted to hurt him more, not to pleasure him, but to punish him for what I had done.

I sobbed as he came.

Tears rolled down his cheeks as he called out my name. I leaned down and cupped his cheeks. Cum and blood smeared on them and he opened his eyes again and looked at me. They were full of pain and self-loathing. While I cried, while he cried, I kissed his lips. I'd never felt so hurt, so sad, yet so in love with the broken man whose head I held in my hands.

Our kiss deepened; there was a need to connect, to taste, and to clear our minds of the horror with something pleasurable. His arms snaked around my body and he lifted my t-shirt. I sat up and pulled it over my head, stretching my legs out until I was lying on top of him. I felt the wetness against my stomach as our skin connected.

His arms tightened and he rolled us until I was on my back, without breaking his kiss. He took hold of my hands in his and raised my arms above my head; I stiffened slightly as a wave of apprehension washed over me.

Jackson removed his lips from mine; he kissed along my jawbone and down my neck. As hard as I tried, I couldn't stop the moan leaving my lips. Despite what I had done, despite the situation, I couldn't recall a time I'd felt so aroused. His need, his desperation, and my feelings for him all seemed to pool in my groin. I hooked my legs over his calves and raised my pelvis to grind against his.

Jackson slid his hands down my arms and along my side. I lifted my shoulders from the bed as he reached underneath to unclip my bra. His mouth trailed a path down my chest as he pushed my bra up and his lips found a nipple. He licked, he sucked, and then gently bit down.

With his hands at either side of me; he pushed himself down the bed. As his tongue swirled over my stomach and through his own blood, I removed my bra. He undid my shorts, and as he slid down my body, he lowered them. I raised my hips and he hooked his fingers under my panties, dragging them down with the shorts. I kicked them off my feet. He sat across my thighs and stared at me while lowering his jeans to his knees.

His hands were on my hips, his fingers gently brushed over my tattoo as he lowered his head. I cried out his name as his tongue swiped over my clitoris, sending a shockwave through my stomach. My fists bunched in the sheet as his lips closed and his tongue flicked. I wanted his tongue inside me; I was desperate for his touch so I raised my hips.

Instead of giving me what I wanted, Jackson sat back on his heels. He trailed his fingers over my lower stomach and down as he slid to one side. With his free hand he pushed his jeans lower and then kicked them off before he settled beside me.

He lay on his side, one hand held my wrists above my head and the fingers on the other teased me. I parted my legs as he inserted two fingers inside me. Fire raged at his touch. He hooked his fingers and stroked in a place that had me crying out his name. I wrenched my wrists from his grip and placed one hand on the back of his head. I pulled his face towards me, and his mouth crashed down on mine. He bit and sucked on my lower lip, still tender from our earlier kiss.

I needed to come; my stomach was in knots and heat travelled over my body. As his fingers stroked faster, I fell apart around them. Before I'd come down from the high, he rolled on top of me. I opened my eyes to look at him as his cock brushed against my entrance. He held himself above me on his hands, and he pushed into me then stilled, I wrapped my arms around him.

"Promise you won't hurt me," I whispered.

"I can't promise you anything." He pulled back and then

slammed into me so hard my body jolted up the bed.

I could feel the bar underneath the tip of his cock roll against me and it heightened every sensation. He fucked me fast. Beads of sweat dripped from his brow, and he growled out my name as I clawed down his back.

I wrapped my legs around him; I needed him deeper. He thrust into me harder but it wasn't enough. I was a bundle of static, of nerve endings screaming out, and my body shook with want. I struggled to catch my breath at times and as my orgasm rolled over me, I screamed out.

Jackson pulled out of me, and before I could register, he had flipped me onto my stomach and was pulling at my hips, raising them. I scrambled to my knees. I had just about stabilised myself before be pushed into me. He wrapped one hand in my hair and pulled my head up. His other hand held my hip and his fingers dug into my flesh.

My arms shook as I held myself steady. I sunk to my elbows and Jackson continued to fuck me. Every time he pulled back, I pushed myself towards him; I felt the void he had left.

I lost track of time, I lost count of the orgasms I'd experienced. My body ached and I was coated in both his sweat and mine. I couldn't hold myself up any longer, and with Jackson still inside, I slumped to the bed. He pulled out and while I lay on my stomach, I felt his hand run over my backside. His finger gently slid down and probed at a place that had me tense my body. I could feel his other hand slide up and down his cock and then his hot cum as it spurted over me.

Jackson collapsed beside me. His breathing was as erratic as mine. He lay on his back and closed his eyes until he got himself under control. We stayed that way in silence for a while.

"Is that the hardest?" I whispered.

He turned on his side and opened his eyes. "Huh?"

"Is that the hardest you could have fucked me?"

He didn't answer immediately. "No."

I didn't want to know anymore. He held me to him as I started to cry. Emotion flooded over me, I felt drained, emotionally and physically. I felt shame and guilt at what I'd done and allowed to be done.

CHAPTER THIRTEEN

Jackson

Summer's cries subsided and she drifted into sleep. I felt peace wash over me, until she rolled onto her side. My blood, our sweat, and my cum was smeared over her body. I enjoyed that sight normally. I got a sense of empowerment when the woman beneath me was covered in my fluids, as if it degraded her in some way. But not Summer. It saddened me to see her that way. The sheets were tangled around us, again smeared with blood and cum, my stomach the same.

I gently pulled my arm from under her and slid from the bed. I wet a washcloth in warm water and returned. While she slept I cleaned her. My tears dripped onto her stomach as I washed my nastiness from her body. I gently pulled the sheet from underneath and rolled it into a ball, leaving it by the bedroom door as I headed for the shower.

I knew I wouldn't get any more sleep, so I dressed. I wrote a note and placed it on the bedside table for her, before covering her with a fresh sheet, and then left.

I drove to the bar. I needed to finish that wall, I needed to lose myself and settle my mind in my art. I unlocked the door and turned on a light. I collected my paint, put in my earbuds, jacked up the music, removed my t-shirt, and then got to work.

The sun had risen when I finally stood, stretched my back, and rolled my neck to relieve the tension in my shoulders. I got a little high on the paint fumes, higher still on the sight of something that was most definitely my best work. I took a few paces back and stared. I pulled the earbuds from my ears. In one way it was a shame it was in the bar, an area not well lit. To fully appreciate it, it should be viewed in daylight. It was so detailed and that one wall represented me, and my life. I scanned the wall, it was my biography running from left to right; the darkest depths of my mind to my saving grace, Summer.

"Wanna talk?" I heard and turn to see Dexter.

"How long have you been there?" I asked.

"An hour. I've been watching you."

"An hour? I didn't hear you come in."

"Why are you here? It's six in the morning; you should be getting some sleep. And come closer, I want to see."

His eyes had trailed down to my stomach.

"Oh, Jack. What the fuck did you do?" he said.

"I needed it, Dex. She asked about my father, I told her I killed my mother. I flipped, we fucked; she helped me feel." I was rambling.

I sank to my knees and cradled my head in my hands. I heard the scrape of the barstool Dex had been sitting on. He knelt in front of me.

"How did she help you, son?"

"She cut me, with her nails. She sat astride me and helped me. I needed it."

I heard his sharp intake of breath and I felt the hand he had placed on my shoulder tense.

"She didn't do it willingly, Dex. She did it so I wouldn't hurt her," I said.

"Where is she?"

"She's home, she's fine, sleeping."

"Did you hurt her?"

"I don't think so."

I watched him sigh and nod his head. We sat that way for a while, I watched my tears drip through my fingers and pool on the dusty wooden floor. I don't think I'd cried as much in my whole life than I had those past few days. Perhaps the end was coming; perhaps I was closing on rock bottom, finally. I would welcome it with open arms.

He stood and walked behind the bar. I rose and followed him, taking a seat on one of the stools as he grabbed two bottles of beer. He snapped the caps off and handed me one.

"I think your episodes are getting closer, Jack. I'm worried about you. One day you'll take this too far and seriously hurt yourself. That cut is infected. I think you need a different strategy."

"Don't quit on me, Dex, please."

"I'm not going to, I just need to rethink this."

I swigged on my beer bottle as we fell into silence. "I'm close, Dex. I'm close to rock bottom, that's a good thing, isn't it?"

"And where do you think rock bottom is going to take you? Are you strong enough to come back up from that? Or do I find you hanging as well?"

I'd never learned the full details of what had happened to the kid he had misdiagnosed. All I knew was that Dexter had been brought in to deal with him, he didn't think he was at rock bottom, but he was. The kid had threatened to take his own life, and in Dexter's mind, he'd missed the seriousness of that.

"Did you find him?" I asked.

He closed his eyes and nodded his head.

"He was a good kid, like you and D-J. His mum had brought him to me, I counselled but I missed it, Jack. I saw the cheerfulness, the shine to his eyes, and thought we were on the other side. He didn't turn up for an appointment and I went to call on him. He was hanging from the rafters in a barn."

"I'm sorry, but how could you have..."

"I should have, it was my job to know, to not be fooled by the fake high."

We fell silent and sipped on our beers. "How do I stop myself from hanging?" I said quietly.

There had been plenty of days when my father's voice would not quieten. When the thought that I had killed my mother overwhelmed me. Had she lived, she would have loved me, I was sure of that. I wouldn't have endured years of his constant psychological abuse. I wouldn't have felt so scared of the dark that I pissed the bed, night after night, instead of going to the bathroom.

I wouldn't have endured him rubbing my face in my piss-stained sheets like one would do to a dog. It was those days that I would have gladly hung.

"You don't give him the satisfaction, Jack. You don't give him the space in your head to fester. Until now, until Summer, it's been an empty void filled with him. Now you have her, if even for a short period of time. I want you, every day, to fill your mind with her. Memorize, like I've told you to, her scent, her body, the colour of her eyes, and her smile. Every time he gets in there, bring her to mind, think only of her."

"I drew her, naked and as if I was fucking her."

"Draw her some more. Draw her smiling at you, laughing at something you've said. Draw all the happy times, Jack. You need a permanent reminder of her to focus on."

I stared at him for a moment. "I need to go."

"Jack, wait..."

"I'm fine, I'll be back later." I rushed from the bar and started my car.

The wheels spun as they lost their grip on the gravel of the car park and I headed along the coast. I parked the car and ran to the shop, it was closed of course but I banged on the door, rang the bell continuously.

I saw him, in a pair of shorts and rubbing his eyes, come to the door.

"What the fuck, Jack? What's the time?"

"Bridge, I need to do something. It's important."

He stood to one side and let me in. I grabbed a piece of transfer paper and drew. I pasted the transfer to the last piece of skin without ink on the underside of my forearm, just above my wrist.

It was a smaller version. It took about an hour of pleasurable pain before it was complete. I wiped the ink, the blood, and studied it. I cleaned the station before rushing back out of the shop, without a word to Bridge.

I started the car and sped home.

———

Summer was sitting on the balcony, she had a cup of tea in her hands and her face was raised to the sun. She wore a sundress that exposed her shoulders and I noticed some marks to her neck. I shut them from my mind.

"Hey," I said as I walked through.

She looked up but didn't give me her usual broad smile. Her eyes were red and puffy, she'd been crying again.

I sat beside her and reached up to run my fingers down her cheek.

"Look what I got," I said, as I showed her my wrist.

She smiled at the sight of a butterfly, a replica of the one I'd tattooed on her. I'd even scrawled her name underneath.

"It's lovely, Jack," she whispered.

I took the cup from her hands and climbed on the daybed beside her. I wrapped my arm around her shoulders and pulled her into my chest. I felt her tears through my t-shirt and for a while we sat in silence.

"Do you want to talk about it?" I asked.

"I'm not sure I know what to say. I'm disgusted with myself, with you. I'm confused as hell."

Her word, 'disgusted' was like a bolt of lightning had shot through me. I'd heard that word so many times. I pulled my arm away and stood.

"I disgust a lot of people, I'm sorry you're one of them. I'm going for a run."

I left her crying and walked to my bedroom. She had remade the bed with fresh sheets; the bloodied one was gone. I stripped off and changed into shorts. I didn't care about exposing my stomach as I jogged down the steps and onto the beach. I ran, for miles. The sun beat down, the sweat dripped from my body, stinging the cuts as it rolled over them. My muscles screamed with the exertion, and I kept on running.

After a while I stopped, turned, and jogged back the way I'd come. As I came close to the house, I kicked off my trainers and dived into the sea. The sting of the salt water was welcomed. I swam until my chest hurt then gently made my way back to shore. I crawled onto the beach, my legs had given out, and I lay on my back as the waves gently lapped around my body. The sun continued to beat down and I closed my eyes.

"Jack, you need to get out of the sun," I heard.

I opened my eyes to see Summer standing over me. I rolled to my side and stood. My legs quivered a little and she placed her arm around my waist to steady me. Silently, I walked to the house and straight to my bedroom. I took a shower and with just the towel around my waist, I lay on the bed.

CHAPTER FOURTEEN

Summer

I'd watched Jack for a while as he lay at the water's edge. He looked exhausted. I'd hoped he would have stood and walked back to the house, but after an hour I went to him. I'd thought on his words the whole time he had been running. I needed to explain what I was disgusted with but it was hard; I wasn't entirely sure.

I heard the shower running and waited some more, fully expecting him to join me on the balcony. When he didn't, I walked to his room. He was lying on the bed with just a towel around his waist and his arm slung across his eyes.

"Jack?"

"I need some sleep, Summer."

I was unsure at first what to do. He was dismissing me but I wasn't about to be. I walked to the edge of the bed and climbed on beside him. I curled into his side and placed my arm across his chest. He didn't speak, he didn't move, and we lay still.

I heard his breathing deepen and knew he had fallen asleep. I studied the tattoo on his wrist, it looked sore, he hadn't covered it like he had mine, and I guessed the salt water must have stung like hell.

As I lay, I saw his phone light up, it had been on silent but Dexter was calling, his name was displayed on the screen. I picked it up and stood from the bed.

"Hi, Jack's asleep, Dex. He's had a rough hour or so," I said as I answered.

"Okay, he left here on a mission and I was worried. What happened last night, Summer?"

I went through the previous evening, omitting most, just hinting at the sex. I heard my voice catch numerous times and more so when I got to recalling our earlier conversation.

"I don't know what to do to help him?" I said. Tears had pooled in my eyes again.

"By being with him, you are. I've been thinking about him all afternoon. He needs a normal relationship; he needs to break the cycle he's in. If he can do that, I think we might be halfway there."

"I'm not here long enough for that," I said.

"Then perhaps he might need to go home."

"It's his dad though," I said.

"I know. I need you to help me, Summer. I don't know if you're able to do that, but he's spiralling out of control. You are the catalyst, but we need that."

"What do I do?"

"He needs to be at the bar tonight, we're opening. Come with him. I want him to have a few days of normal. And then we'll talk."

"I will."

We said our goodbyes and I quietly crept back to the bedroom. I replaced the phone on the table and climbed back on the bed. Jack stirred; he turned on his side to face me. I snaked my arm under his head and held him to my chest.

"I love your tattoo," I whispered.

"Thank you, I want something to remember you by," he replied.

"Can I come tonight?"

"Of course, although I don't know how much time I'll have to spend with you, it gets pretty mad."

"I'll just sit at the bar in the corner, it'll be fun."

He sighed and I kissed the top of his head.

"We need to eat, then get ready."

He rolled away from me and I missed him in my arms. In one way he was so vulnerable, in another so brutal. He was a contradiction. His highs and lows had left me exhausted and my head spinning.

I climbed from the bed and joined him in the kitchen. He had made sandwiches and we sat at the breakfast bar and ate.

"What should I wear?" I asked.

"Jeans would be good, it gets messy."

"Messy?"

He chuckled a little. "Messy."

Once we had eaten, Jack left to dress. I made my way to my bedroom and showered. I dried and straightened my hair, applied some makeup, and pulled on jeans and a fitted t-shirt. I grabbed a pair of heels and joined Jack back in the kitchen. He whistled as I walked towards him.

"I'm not sure that's appropriate," he said.

"Not appropriate?"

"I need to work, and now I'm going to be fighting off the guys hitting on you."

I laughed and it felt good to have that banter with him. "I will sit and only have eyes for you."

"Make sure you do, I get very jealous, Summer."

I shook my head and rolled my eyes. He grabbed the keys and we headed out. Jack cranked up the music in the car; we wound down the windows and drove to the bar as if the past day hadn't occurred. I wondered whether he was bipolar, or had a split personality. His highs and lows gave me whiplash; it was something I stored away on my list of things to talk to Dexter about.

There was a doorman standing outside, with a rail and rope snaking alongside the building. He opened the door to let us in. D-J and Dexter were already behind the bar, lining up bottles and glasses. I watched a guy setting up his amplifiers and guitars on a small stage in one corner. I wandered over to the finished wall and stared at it. It was a masterpiece and probably the best work I'd seen of Jack's.

"Take a seat," Jack said as I walked back to the bar.

He had placed a stool in the corner next to the bar, and a jug of iced water with a couple of glasses on a tray.

"It gets hot in here, you might need that."

I sat and watched as the bar started to fill quickly. Music blasted and Jack was right, it heated up pretty quickly. Dex had handed me a bottle of beer that I sipped at.

The man I watched behind the bar was yet another version of Jackson that I'd never seen before. He danced around, he made cocktails; he laughed and joked. He flipped bottles around as if he'd spent his life behind a bar. At one point he and D-J threw bottles between them and didn't spill a drop.

As the evening wore on, the musician started to play. His cover of Linkin Park's, *What I've Done* had everyone dancing, jumping up and down. Water, beer, alcohol spilled everywhere. It was total madness, but an amazing madness.

I slipped from the stool and joined the throng of dancers. After a few seconds, I felt arms around my waist and Jackson joined me. He sang out loud as he bounced on his toes. His t-shirt was soaked through with sweat and beer. As the song came to an end he held my hand and walked me back to my corner. He vaulted over the bar to cheers.

D-J came to life, too. He had climbed on the bar to dance, and practically strip, using a soda syphon to soak the audience. They screamed for more.

I don't think I'd ever been in a bar so electric, so highly charged before. The place throbbed with music; it pounded against my chest. As the musician came to the end of the next song, I heard Jackson's name being shouted. The crowd started calling for him. I looked over to him. He looked a little unsure as he walked towards me.

"What do they want?" I asked.

"It's a moneymaking thing, it's not what you think, okay?"

"Okay, but I have no idea what you're talking about," I said with a laugh.

Five very busty women, in revealing tops, had lined up in front of the bar, each held a fifty-dollar note in their hands. Jackson lined up five shot glasses and reached for a bottle of Jack Daniels, hidden under the counter. As the cat-calling continued, he poured five shots of whiskey. Each girl then picked up the glass and wedged it between their tits, while slapping their fifty dollars on the bar.

Jackson vaulted over again, why he didn't walk around the bar was beyond me. I laughed as I finally got what was about to happen. He smiled when he saw me laughing. With his hands behind his back he lowered his face to their cleavage and gripped the glass in his teeth. He then threw back his head and drank. The crowd counted the seconds it took for him to down five shots from five pairs of tits. As D-J marked the time on a blackboard behind the bar, the crowd erupted. It appeared Jack had beaten his previous time. And then it was the turn of whoever wanted to beat him.

The men who wanted to compete slapped fifty after fifty on the bar. Some made it to the fifth glass, some didn't. No one beat him. I cheered along with the crowd when the last one was done. Jack raised his arms as he jumped on the wooden bar in victory. D-J aimed the syphon at him, he got soaked, the crowd got soaked, again, and I got soaked.

My throat was sore from laughing and shouting so much. Jack jumped back down and walked towards me. I noticed the women's eyes follow him, lips were licked, and breasts pushed out as he passed. He stood in front of me, cupped my face in his hands and kissed me so passionately, the crowd whistled. Some shouted out to 'get a room' and the musician started up again.

"You don't taste of whiskey," I said as he pulled away.

"Coloured water for me," he said with a wink, before vaulting the bloody bar again.

My head thumped, my feet were tired from dancing, and I was soaked with either sweat or soda. Jackson, D-J, and Dex hadn't stopped for hours. I'd watched as they'd wiped the sweat from their brows. As the evening began to wind down, the music changed, and dropped a pace. Jackson walked around the bar, I guess his vaulting and the evening had exhausted him a little, took my hand, and dragged me on the dance floor. He wrapped his arms around me, pulled me to his chest, and as we danced, he sang gently into my ear.

It had been a perfect evening and I thought the Jackson I had witnessed had been the real man. That was until Honey showed up.

"Jackson, baby," I heard in a slurred voice.

I looked over his shoulder to see her slightly swaying behind him.

"Fuck off, Honey," he replied without looking.

"I need you, baby," she purred, well, tried to anyway.

"Go find someone else, I'm a little busy here," he said as we parted slightly.

"Only you can play, Jack. Want a little daddy payback?"

He stiffened in my arms and my heart stopped a beat.

"What did she say?" I asked.

The crowd had thinned as patrons made their way out into the early morning sunlight.

"Oh, sweetie, you don't know? Jack and me, we like to play. I doubt she does rough, does she? Can she give you what I can, Jackson?" Honey said, over pronouncing his name.

He turned to face her. I stood to his side, looking up at him and into a face I'd already seen. His features had hardened.

"I'll tell you one more time, Honey. Fuck off, now, before I drag

138

you out." His voice was so low it was almost a growl.

She licked her lips and I saw her chest heave as her breath hitched in her throat.

"Make me, Jack," she challenged.

I placed my hand on his arm. "Don't," I said.

"Daddy needs his punishment, Jack. Daddy hates you. Mommy doesn't love you, Jack," she said.

I was about to step forward and shut her up myself when I saw him reach out. As quick as a flash, he grabbed her by the arm. I screamed, D-J jumped across the bar, and the crowd parted as he walked her backwards towards the bar.

He moved so fast, she lost her footing and stumbled. I ran after them, pulling on his arm.

All I could hear were her words as she continued to bait him.

"Dex," I screamed out.

I felt arms around me. "I've got him," Dexter said as he appeared at my side.

I watched as they disappeared through a door to the side of the bar, D-J stood in front to stop a guy going to Honey's rescue. I caught his eye and he slowly closed them as he shook his head. I walked over.

"Let me pass, D-J," I said.

"You don't..."

"Let me fucking pass, now," I shouted.

"Let her in, we need this," Dexter said as he came to my side.

D-J stood to one side and I pushed through the door and into a storeroom. I followed her voice to another door.

I barrelled through it just to see Jackson push her roughly towards the bed. She fell forwards and immediately pushed her arms above her head and gripped the sheets; she parted her legs shoving her ass in the air towards him. Her short skirt rose and she wore no panties.

"Punish me, baby. I've got you so mad."

"Jackson!" I shouted.

She laughed as she looked at me.

"It's just role-play, sweetie. Join us? You'll have fun. Jack loves this; he needs this. Look at him; he can't even hear you. Watch us, sweetie, watch him fuck my ass. He likes to come all over my face, don't you, baby?" she said.

My stomach heaved. "Shut the fuck up," I growled.

"Honey," Dexter's tone of voice was low, making it clear it was a warning.

"She needs to know, Dex. Can he choke you and you enjoy it, love it even? Can you take a slap to your ass?" She looked at me as she spoke, and I watched Jackson as he reached forwards and wrapped her hair in his hand. He twisted it before yanking her head back. I heard her hiss in pleasure.

"Jackson, don't, please," I said.

She was right; it was as if he was in a trance, totally lost to me.

Dexter walked towards him; he stood between Jackson and her. He spoke quietly. For a minute or so there was nothing other than the sound of Dexter talking Jack down. I'd held my breath, feeling my heart beat furiously against my chest.

It was only then that I allowed the tears to fall. When he turned to look at me, I saw such anguish on his face but I was gone. I turned and ran.

I heard my name being called as I pulled a rack of boxes over after me. Bottles of beer smashed on the floor, halting whoever was chasing me. I ran through the door and back into the bar. It had emptied. I spotted Jackson's car keys on the side and grabbed them as I ran past.

I was in the car and trying to calm the shake to my hand, so I could get the key in the ignition, when Jackson ran through the bar door and into the car park. I slammed my hand on the door lock as he tried to wrench it open.

He was shouting out my name as I fired up the car and ground it into drive. He ran after it as I drove from the car park. I watched in the rear-view mirror as he fell to his knees. He cradled his head in his hands.

My heart was telling me to stop, turn the car around, and go back to him. My head was telling me to get the fuck out of there. I wasn't sure what I'd witnessed, it had all happened so fast. One minute we were dancing, the next, it looked like he was about to fuck her from behind without any regard for me. And what the fuck was she saying? Her words swam through my mind as I drove. Was that what he liked to do? Choke, slap, fuck arse. No matter how hard I tried, I couldn't get the words to leave my mind. Those were things I'd never entertain. Yet I'd helped him hurt. Confusion washed over me.

I tried my hardest to remember the route. I had no idea what I was going to do when I arrived home, though. I could hardly lock him out from his own house.

I struggled to see, my tears blurred my vision, and my hands shook on the steering wheel. I saw the house come into view and screeched to a halt. It then occurred to me that I didn't have a door key. I fumbled with the keys attached to the car key, in the hope one would open the front door, none did. I ran around the side of the house and through the beach car park. All the doors leading off the balcony were locked. I slid down my bedroom one, and cried.

CHAPTER FIFTEEN

Jackson

"Just fucking drive, D-J," I shouted.

I didn't want to talk, I wanted to get to the house as quickly as possible, and I prayed that was where Summer had headed. He cornered so fast I held onto the door to keep myself upright. I breathed a sigh of relief when I saw my car parked haphazardly outside. She wouldn't have a key though, and I scanned the front entrance to see if I could find her. Before D-J had even come to a complete stop, I was out of the car and running around the house. I slowed as I saw her slumped against her bedroom door and sobbing.

"Summer," I said as I climbed the steps.

She didn't look up.

"Stay away from me, Jack," she said.

I stopped at the top, unsure what to do. I wanted to go to her, I wanted to pick her up and hold her in my arms.

"I..."

"Don't fucking speak, okay?" she screamed at me.

I slid down the balcony's glass wall opposite her and hugged my knees to my chest. Neither of us spoke for a long time. The fear that ran through my body was escalating with every minute of her silence. The urge to cut, to punch the wall, to hurt, was beginning to overwhelm. I struggled to breathe evenly. I had fucked up, big time. There was no doubt in my mind that I had lost her. And I wouldn't try to stop her leaving. From the corner of my eye, I saw D-J.

"D-J can take you to the airport if you want to leave," I whispered, hoping that her answer was, 'no.'

"I need time to think. Open the fucking door," she said as she climbed to her feet.

It killed me to see her flinch when I reached over her shoulder with the key. Without a word, she slid her bedroom door open and the sound of the lock being engaged when she closed it echoed through my heart. Somewhere in my brain it registered that she hadn't said she wanted to leave, I tried to focus on that.

"Jack, go in the kitchen, dude," D-J said.

I nodded; I didn't want to torture myself anymore by hearing her pack, if that's what she was doing. I walked into the kitchen and sat on a stool. I crossed my arms on the counter and rested my head on them. I concentrated on getting my heart rate down and on squashing the urges.

"Let me go and talk to her," D-J said and I nodded.

He was gone way too long, although in reality it was probably no more than a few minutes. I heard his footsteps across the decking and rose to greet him at the kitchen door.

"Well?" I said.

"She asked me to leave her tonight, she'll make some calls tomorrow about rearranging her flight."

"Okay, so I have one night."

"For what?"

"To change her mind, of course."

"Jack, I think you should leave her alone, at least for tonight. She isn't strong enough for the likes of us."

"You don't fucking know her," I said as I pushed past him.

He tried to grab my arm; I yanked it from his grasp and walked to her door. Like mine, fine muslin draped the inside but I could see through. She had slid down the door with her back resting on the glass. She hugged her knees. I did the same.

"Summer?"

"I can't, Jack."

"Then just listen, please?"

There was no answer. I sat for a moment wondering what the fuck to say, where to start. D-J walked from the kitchen. I looked over to him and he gave me a sad smile. I nodded my head at him before he left and watched the sun begin to rise.

"I'm sorry doesn't cut it, I know. You know I said I had outlets? Cutting is one, Honey was the other, but that was before I told you how much I fucking love you, have always loved you. She's damaged, she pushes my trigger so I react and give her what she needs. I guess, for a while we fed off each other, it was symbiotic for a long time. I don't want or need that anymore."

The door slid open so fast I fell backwards into her room.

"Don't you fucking dare!" she shouted at me, at the same time she landed a kick straight in my side.

I imagined that kick hurt her way more than it hurt me by the grimace and hopping about she did. She leaned down to slap my shoulders as I sat up.

"She's damaged and you're helping her? Really! What are you, some sort of therapist now? How fucked up is that?"

The situation was serious, I knew that, but her feeble slaps to my shoulder, her kicks to my side had me stifling a chuckle. I sprang to my feet while she continued her assault. Right or wrong, the clenching of her jaw, the squinting of her eyes as her anger took over, had my cock as hard as wood.

"Would you have fucked her? I was there, Jack, would you have fucked her while I watched? Would you have...done all that *stuff* to her? Would you have *hurt* her?"

I grabbed her wrists and walked her backwards. We fell onto the bed and I pinned her underneath me. She writhed trying to break free.

"No. I would not have fucked her, and no, I wouldn't have done that *stuff* to her. And that's a first—believe me. Somewhere in my mind I knew you were there."

"But you would have, had I not been here, wouldn't you?"

I didn't answer. "Wouldn't you?" she screamed at me.

"Yes," I answered, quietly.

"You sick fuck," she said.

That comment sliced me deeper than any wound I could have inflicted on myself.

I stilled, pushing myself slightly away from her. My breath caught in my chest, as if captured by her words, words that had momentarily paralysed me.

Her knee to my groin was about the most painful thing I'd ever experienced. It felt as if my balls were forced halfway up my body. I groaned, I let her go and slid off the bed, curling into a ball. I was in total fucking agony.

"Oh my God, shit." I heard her say.

"I'm fine," I winced out.

"What do I do?"

"Kiss them better?"

I narrowly missed a second kick to the balls, her foot connected with my thigh instead. She stomped from the room and I groaned some more. When she returned she threw a bag of ice at me.

"Have that kiss it better."

I rolled onto all fours, trying to quell the nausea, and then eventually managed to stand. Summer had sat on the bed with her arms folded across her chest. There was a look of concern on her face, a look she was desperately trying to hide.

"I need to lay down."

"Go to your own room, Jack. You're not sleeping here."

"I can't fucking walk, Summer."

She stood from the bed and as she passed me, she bashed into my shoulder. I shuffled forwards and onto her bed. I took in some deep breaths and, after a minute or so; the pain subsided, leaving a dull ache.

"Sweet Jesus," I whispered, wincing as I turned on my side.

I woke with a start and gingerly straightened my legs. I exhaled the breath I had been holding when I realised I was no longer in pain, although I was sure if I'd checked I would be bruised. I climbed from the bed and swallowed down the fear that she would be gone. As I walked to the decking, she was curled on the daybed sleeping. I stared at her for a long time. Her cheeks were chapped from her tears; her hair was a tangled mess around her face. I'd done that to her. I'd caused her tears and sadness washed over me.

It was as she cried out my name in her sleep I knew exactly what I had to do. I was on the brink of losing her before we'd got started.

I walked to my bedroom and opened the drawer to my bedside cabinet. I took out the small cardboard box and unwrapped the tissue. My hand shook with desire as I held the blade. My stomach knotted with need and my head thumped. I walked to the balcony, down the steps, and onto the beach. I continued, stepping through people sunbathing and laughing, having a great time. I continued until I was chest deep in water and raised my arm. I hesitated. My fingers curled over the blade and I felt the sting as the metal sliced through skin.

Just one more time, I thought.

I threw it as far as I could. I lost sight of it as it sailed through the air; the sun had blinded me.

I waded back, ignoring the questioning stares of people I passed. Dripping in salt water, I placed the box on the barbecue and switched on the gas. I lit it and watched the box burn. I wrapped a tissue around my fingers to soak up the blood.

"Jack?" Summer had woken.

Maybe it was the sound of her voice, maybe it was the loss of my blade, or the fact she finally saw me the same way I saw myself, a *sick fuck*, but something knotted inside me. My heart felt wrenched, my chest constricted. The need, the urge to hurt rolled over me like a wave. I swallowed hard, trying to lubricate my dry throat as panic welled inside me.

Immediately, I felt like the times I'd seen D-J going through withdrawal. I knew it wasn't real, but my hands shook and beads of sweat formed on my forehead. There were a hundred things I could use as a replacement but I'd had that blade for years. I knew it was coming. I headed to my bedroom and closed the door. I lay on the bed, as his voice grew louder in my head.

'You see this, Jackson. This ends it all,' he said, as he handed me a packet with a razor blade.

'Jackson, all you need to do is cut, just across here,' he said, showing me his forearm.

"No," I cried out. My father's voice was all I could hear.

'You cry out for your mother, Jackson. Here, take this, be with her,' he said.

'If your mother had the C-section she might have lived, Jackson. They would have cut her stomach and pulled you out, but she didn't, and you killed her,' he cried when he'd said that.

'Your mother is all I cared about, she was my life and you took that from me,' he said, many times over the years.

'Oh, Jackson. Now you've surprised me. You cut, well done. Now do it properly,' he said, when he'd caught me sitting on the bathroom floor with the blood from my arm dripping on the tiles. I was eleven years old.

I thrashed about on the bed as sweat rolled from my body. I gripped the headboard; it was a subconscious way to keep me from climbing from the bed and doing exactly what he had drummed into my head, for years.

The words, 'cut her stomach' had morphed into 'cut my stomach.' I arched my body off the bed and my skin itched. It felt like a thousand ants had run across my cuts.

"Jackson?" There was a panicked edge to her voice.

"Dexter," was all I managed before I cried out again in frustration.

She ran from the room and it felt like hours passed before I heard footsteps returning.

"Son, relax. I'm here," I heard and opened my eyes.

Dexter stood beside the bed. "Tie my hands, Dex," I pleaded.

Summer had stood by the door watching.

He stood and looked around the room. "The drawer," I said through gritted teeth. If he didn't hurry up, I was going to tear my stomach apart.

I closed my eyes and listened as he opened the drawer to retrieved two pieces of rope. Pieces of rope I'd used on Honey many times but never myself. As the twine tightened against the skin on my wrist, pain shot through me where it rubbed against the raw tattoo. I welcomed in the pain.

"Let me give you something," he whispered.

I cried out in frustration as yet another wave of the imaginary ants marched across my body.

"No," I said.

"Think of her, Jackson. Think of her auburn hair; see her brown eyes, and the smile she gives you. Think of her tattoo, son. Remember dancing with her, do you remember the words you sang to her? Think, Jack, just think of Summer."

The ants crawled, my father's voice battled with Dexter's to be heard and brown eyes smiled at me.

I lost track of time. I think I slept, I wasn't sure. It was dark when I opened my eyes fully and realised I wasn't tied to the bed anymore. I was lying on my side and curled in a ball. A sweater, one I didn't recognise, lay across the pillow and under my head. It smelled of her perfume. Every time I breathed in, an image of her came to mind and it settled me.

My cheeks felt chapped and sore. I climbed from the bed and headed to the shower. The tattoo on my wrist itched like fuck and my stomach hurt. I stepped under the shower, adjusting the temperature to cool. I stood for a while, just letting the water run over me and thought hard about my future.

Dex was sitting on my bed when I returned. "How are you doing, son?"

"Hollow right now but calm. Great idea with the sweater, by the way."

"It was Summer's idea."

"Where is she?"

"I had D-J collect her, she's at my place with Alfie. He'll mother her, just for a day or so."

I didn't answer, just nodded my head. Although she had only been with me for a short while, the house already felt empty. I pulled on a t-shirt and shorts and Dex followed me outside. I sat and watched the people on the beach, the families, and couples walking, holding hands. I'd never have that, at least until I got my shit together.

"What do I need to do? I can't live like this anymore. I don't want Honey, or anyone else. I don't want to cut anymore."

"Then we're halfway there. What is your goal?"

"I want Summer. I want a normal relationship with her. I want to still work at the bar, do my art, but getting her back is more important, and I don't know whether I can stay here and do that. And, when I'm fit, I'll go home and confront him. I think I need to do that."

"Okay, then that's what we will work towards. I got you some new sketchpads. Every time you feel the urge, draw something. Design me another wall."

"Go home, Dex, and thank you, I needed you today."

He gave me a smile, a pat to the shoulder and then left. I sat the rest of the day, just thinking, watching the world go by and healing.

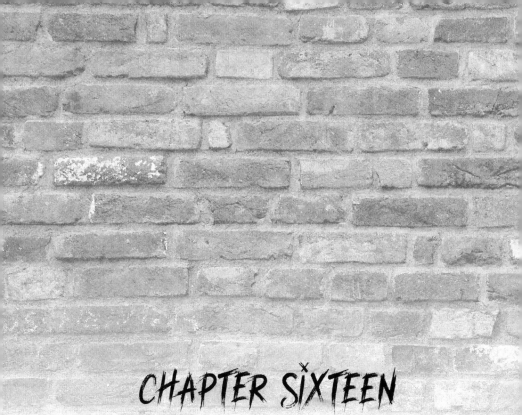

CHAPTER SIXTEEN

Summer

"Will you eat something?"

"I don't think I can, Alfie. But thank you. Have you heard from him?"

I paced their living room. Dexter and Alfie had a beautiful beachfront house, not far from the shack. I was surprised when Dex decided I was to stay with him for a day or so. I hadn't expected Alfie to open the front door when D-J had dropped me off. And judging by the photographs of them both that adorned every available shelf, it was clear they were a couple.

"A drink then? I don't think we have tea but I can make some lemonade. And no, not yet. Dex will call soon, I'm sure."

"A cold drink would be great."

"Come sit outside," he said.

I followed him through the small kitchen and onto the deck. Like Jackson's, it opened up onto the beach, although way down the coastline.

"You have a beautiful home," I said as I sat on a wicker sofa.

"Thank you, even though it's much smaller than our previous one, it suits us."

"Was that in New Orleans?"

"Yes, we lost our home, like many others in the last hurricane. It was just too much to start over, so Dex decided he wanted to run a bar and we came here. Ironic that an alcoholic wants to run a bar," he said and chuckled.

"I wasn't aware of that."

"Oh, he won't mind me telling you. He's been sober for a long time now, might have the odd beer, but that's all. So Jackson's on a downer is he?"

"Seems that way, however, before I came here, I didn't know anything about it."

"I'm not the therapist here, but I'd say keep the man you know and love in your mind, not the one you've seen lately."

"That's the problem, Alfie, I don't know him. I thought I did, but the Jackson I knew in the UK isn't the real one. Or is it? I just have no idea anymore."

"Did you love Jackson when you knew him in the UK?"

"Not like I do now. He was a great friend."

"Then my guess is; the Jackson you know is the one you love now, flaws and all. I don't know his issues, Summer, Dex doesn't betray their confidence but it's not hard to see he's a wonderful man with some serious problems. I've seen him on a low before, and I know what he does to himself. If Dex has such belief in him, and I've never known Dex to be wrong about someone, then he's all good in my mind."

I smiled up at him. He had a point. The Jackson I knew back home was a million miles away from the man just along the beach, and I ached to be with him. I was still upset, I was still angry, but there was something in me that needed him—and he needed me.

"I've got some chores to do, will you be okay for a while?" he asked.

I nodded my head and curled my legs under me on the sofa. I looked out to sea, the coastline was slightly different and not so popular with the tourists I imagined, and the beach was empty. I placed my earbuds in and left my music on shuffle. The album Jackson had download started to play. Tears welled in my eyes as memories connected with the songs, flooded my mind; the time we'd danced in the kitchen; the time he'd sung to me. My head was telling me to scroll on past, my heart wouldn't let me. I closed my eyes and absorbed every word.

A hand on my shoulder jolted me awake. I hadn't realised I'd fallen asleep until then. I pulled the earbuds out.

"Hey, how are you doing? Is Alfie looking after you?" Dexter said.

"He is, he popped out to do some chores. I think he's a wonderful and caring man," I said.

"I think so, too. He has to be to put up with me." Dexter chuckled at his comment.

For a moment we sat and looked at each other. "So, how is he?" I asked.

Dexter sighed before he answered. "He threw away his blade. That caused his anxiety attack. He's had that blade since he was eleven years old and having it beside his bed has been, strangely, a source of comfort. We need to replace that. I've told him to draw."

"I saw the pictures he did of me."

"He has given me permission to speak openly to you, not that he doesn't want to tell you himself. However, I think it's safer for him if I give you some background."

"I want to know everything, Dex. I want to know the answers to all the 'whys' I have floating around my mind. I can't help him if I don't know. I'm walking on eggshells because I don't know what his triggers are."

"And therein lies the problem. The obvious trigger is any reference to his family, but there are times when it could be a smell; it could be a situation that he can relate back to childhood, like being in a confined space, that sets him off. He spent some time in therapy in the UK, and for a while he seemed to be coping, but something happened for him to relapse."

"And you know what that is?"

"His father is dying and wants a reconciliation. Jackson doesn't. So right now, he has the anger and hatred for all his wasted childhood and the guilt that he doesn't feel anything about his father's news."

Alfie returned and our conversation was halted for a while. He had brought me tea, fresh, loose leaf tea. I had to show him how to make a pot and then Dexter and I settled back on the deck.

"So where do we start?" I asked.

"He thinks he's lost you and I'd like to keep that going. You have a week left of your holiday, so I don't know how hard that's going to be. You're going to have to act well. And then I think you need to go home."

"Go home?"

"Yes, you can't stay, obviously, but separation will be the test. As much as I'm asking you to be a good actress, he's an even better actor. Like any addict, and that's what he is, he will lie and manipulate all the time you're here. When you go, when he has to face time alone, that's when we will know for sure if he's on the right path. He will fall, Summer, you need to be prepared for that."

"If the cutting outlet has gone, Honey is the next and I can't deal with that," I said.

"Honey isn't going to be his outlet, I'll make sure of that. She is bad news, always has been. I've tried to help her many times but she's beyond my capabilities."

"Tell me what you can, start at the beginning." I settled back into the sofa, expecting us to have a long night.

"His mother died in childbirth, she had an illness. She refused the C-section to birth him early. From the age he was able to understand, his father blamed him for that."

"That's madness. Why?"

"There will be a lot of 'whys' I can't answer. He doesn't know why himself. His father loved his wife obsessively, from what I can gather. He never recovered from her death."

"A C-section? He has a pregnant woman tattooed on his stomach, right where he cuts. I knew that was significant somehow."

"It's a very emblematic tattoo for him. If he can bleed, she bleeds. He has it in his mind he's saving her. Whether that be he's 'aborting' or 'performing the C-Section' on her, is something I can't determine. He switches the why—depending on his mood. There are times, when he's at his lowest, he's terminating himself symbolically instead of really terminating himself."

I blinked a few times, letting those words sink in. "Jesus!"

I'd gathered Jackson was in a bad way but not to that point.

"Would he? You know…"

"I don't know. He asks how long it will be 'until he hangs;' he knows he's heading for rock bottom."

"What does he mean by that?"

Something in Dexter's face told me that was a question I shouldn't have asked. Pain flashed through his eyes. I reached forwards and placed my hand on his.

"I don't need to know the answer. Was his sister abused?" I asked to change the subject.

"No, his father dotes on her. I don't know how aware she was, or is, of Jackson's situation. He speaks to her frequently and she owns the house, of course. She works for the father; she's a lawyer in the bank. Jackson told me she did that to protect his trust, so I'm guessing she knows something."

"What else did his father do?"

"He gave him that blade, taught him how to cut and praised him when he did. The cutting not only releases the pain for Jackson, it became the only way to gain his father's approval and attention."

"Sick bastard!"

"Indeed. To the outside world, Brett Walker is a wonderful man. He brought up two children, owns a very successful private bank."

"Jackson said something about his wall. I can't remember the exact words, something like hell masquerading as heaven."

"The father would wheel out the kids for public appearances when necessary, he was the doting dad at those times. The confusion Jackson must have felt would have been immense."

We fell silent for a while. Alfie quietly made his way towards us with a fresh pot of tea for me and a jug of homemade lemonade.

"I wished I'd know some of this a long time ago," I said, as I sipped my tea.

"What would you have done?"

"I don't know. I don't know what to do now. I've never faced anything like this before."

"Jackson is a complicated man, there are many layers of guilt to shed. The rational part of him knows he could have done nothing to prevent his mother's death. But that rational part is often so overwhelmed by the irrational. I think we've talked enough for now. You've a lot to think about."

"Can I ask one question? The Honey thing, the rough...You know what I mean?"

"I do. It's a way of releasing anger for Jackson. It was a mutually beneficial arrangement in the beginning. She has a need to be dominated, to be controlled, and forced anal sex. She can't do vaginal. I'm not breaking a confidence, she'd tell you herself if she were here. He has a need to dominate, to control. For him, and I have no idea if you'll understand this, the anal sex is a punishment. It's a primitive act without feeling or emotion for him. He isn't making love to that woman, he isn't, and I hate the term, fucking even. There is no sexual emotion involved, for either of them. It's debasement, it satisfies his need to degrade in the ultimate way, in his mind of course."

"Does he...I don't know if I can say this. Does he imagine that

Honey is his father, when he's doing that?" I swallowed the bile that rose to my throat and took a sip of tea to cleanse the taste from my mouth.

"That's an interesting question. He doesn't visualise his father at all. He has no sexual urges towards him. He's not bi, he's not homosexual, but somewhere in his fucked up mind, he's robbing his father of his power. The Romans did it frequently. It was perfectly acceptable then for men to have sex with male slaves. Jackson doesn't see Honey as an equal, he sees her as below him, the way his father degraded him."

"She knows about him, doesn't she?"

"No, not as far as I'm aware. You, me, and D-J know nearly everything, no one else."

"She said, 'daddy' and it was that word that kicked him off."

"She stumbled across a couple of trigger words, words that are also significant for her, she built on that. She wants to punish her daddy."

A wave of nausea washed over me, I held my hand to my mouth as I dry-heaved. Tears welled in my eyes and such a depth of sadness washed over me, for Jack, for Honey even.

"Do you think Honey would talk to me?"

"I'm not sure that's a good thing right now, but maybe later, she doesn't have any friends, as you can imagine."

"Can you work with her again?"

"She needs more than I can offer. I'm not licenced in the U.S. to practice. What I do would probably put me in jail." He chuckled slightly but I saw the sadness in his eyes.

"I think that should be all for now. You've a lot to digest," he added.

"I'm exhausted, the time difference, late nights, and his mood swings are killing me," I said, trying to inject some light into the dark conversation.

"Why don't I show you to your room, take a nap, and I'm sure Alfie will let you know when dinner is ready."

"One last thing," I said. "I called Jack a *sick fuck*, that probably hasn't helped has it?"

Dexter exhaled a slow breath. "No, he now believes you see him in the same way as he sees himself."

I let the tear that had built up roll down my cheek. Dexter gave me a small smile and squeezed my shoulder.

I followed him to a bedroom off the hallway. It was a nice, light, and airy room, but I missed the sliding doors to the deck and the beach that I had at Jackson's. I missed Jackson. I set down a small holdall I'd brought and placed my toiletries in the en suite shower room. I placed my phone on the bedside table and felt a pang of sadness that I couldn't speak to him. Dexter had said that Jack needed to believe he'd lost me. The reality was, in a little over a week, I was returning to the UK. Neither of us could afford a long distance relationship, flying back and forth. One of us had to give up our life and move, and I suspected that would have to be me. I had parents, loving parents, back home. I needed to find a job; I'd given up work when Dane had died. I simply wasn't able to function for a while. And I needed to push through the sale of the apartment.

I pulled off my sundress, threw on a cotton shirt, and lay on the bed. I closed my eyes. I saw his smile; I heard his laugh and the song he had sung to me. I felt his arms as he held me to his chest when we'd sat on the daybed. My lips tingled at the memory of his kiss. Absentmindedly, I placed my hand over my tattoo. Although the skin was dry and flaking, I let my finger run over his name. A tear rolled down my cheek. Despite what I knew, what I'd seen, I hated to be away from him. D-J had offered me a ride to the airport, and I'd said I would make some calls to rearrange my flight. I wasn't sure I wanted to do that anymore.

———

I'd slept through dinner and breakfast. It had taken me by surprise to learn I'd woken at lunchtime and with a very grumbling tummy. I was hungry. I took a quick shower and dressed before making my way through the house to the kitchen.

"Good morning, is it still morning?" Alfie asked as he looked at his watch. "Goodness, no it isn't. How about I make you some tea and something to eat?"

"I'd love that and I can't believe I've slept for so long. I feel very refreshed today, though."

"I'm glad to hear that. Now go take a seat and I'll bring it to you."

"Where's Dex?"

"Gone to the bar, he'll be back shortly."

I made my way to the wicker sofa and sat in the same spot I'd occupied for hours the previous day.

"What will you do when you get home?" Alfie asked, as he placed his tea on a small table beside me. "I understand you're on the hunt for work."

"I need to be. My husband had an affair, I discovered he has a child, and the mother of the child wants his share of my apartment." I tried to conceal the bitterness that crept into my voice.

"I'm sorry to hear that. I imagine that was very hard for you to learn."

"It was, but Jack helped me come to terms with it. For now, I have no idea what I want to do. I had a thought about going back to university but I'm not sure for what."

"What interests you?"

"I'll tell you what does, not that I know anything about it, but psychotherapy, what Dexter does. I think I'd like to learn more about that, if only to be able to help Jack."

"UC runs courses, in what area of psychotherapy I'm not sure."

"UC?"

"University of California, up the road as you would say. Only need a student visa." Alfie gave me a wink, pushed himself from the sofa and headed back into the kitchen.

It didn't sink in immediately but then a grin spread across my face. Perhaps some investigation was in order. I picked up my tea and sipped. Although Alfie hadn't added milk, he had added a slice of lemon and the taste was growing on me.

I'd need a laptop for proper research. I scrolled through the Internet on my phone but the university's site was too complicated for me to navigate. 'Up the road,' he'd said. I wondered how far up the road it was.

Perhaps there was a chance for me to move to California, assuming Jack and I could make a relationship work, of course. And that was a big assumption. I'd decided to talk it through with Dexter.

I spent the day alternating between worrying, sleeping, and eating. Alfie was a wonderful chef and insisted on trying new recipes on me. I had told him if he wanted to go to the 'shack' he could, I'd be okay on my own, but he insisted on staying put.

CHAPTER SEVENTEEN

Jackson

It had been two days of pure hell. I missed Summer so much it hurt. I was a bundle of nerves and had typed, then deleted, so many messages. Dexter had said that she needed some time to think, alone. I needed to respect that. I was also pissed off that he had removed all the knives from the kitchen. As if that would stop me from cutting. I hadn't, but there were plenty of tools I could use had the desire taken over me.

The nights were the worst. I lay hour after hour thinking of her, of myself, and the fucked up life I was leading. When it got too much—I ran. I ran along the beach in the dark and again during the day. Dexter came over every day, D-J sometimes accompanied him and we sat. I itched to get to the bar; I hated being away, of having the feeling of being excluded, even though I knew it was for my own good. I didn't drink to excess, normally, but there was the risk I'd freak out and the bar wasn't the place for that.

It was late in the evening when a car pulled onto the drive. I had heard the crunch of tyres on the gravel while I'd sat outside watching the sun dip below the horizon. I heard voices and my heart missed a beat. Dexter and Summer walked around the side of the house and up the steps to the balcony.

I stood, unsure at first what to do. She gave me a smile but looked as hesitant as I was.

"I'll let you guys talk. If you need me, either of you, call," Dex said before making his way back down the steps.

"Hey," I said.

"How are you?" she asked. Then chuckled a little. "Dumb question, huh?"

"I've missed you."

She took a step towards me; I did the same. I sighed as she wrapped her arms around my waist and laid her head on my chest. I placed my arms around her and held her tight. I kissed the top of her head when I heard a gentle sob.

"Please don't cry," I whispered.

"I promised myself I wouldn't but…"

"I know. Come on, sit with me."

She left her holdall on the decking and I led her to the daybed. She curled up against me and placed her hand on my chest.

"I missed listening to your heart beating," she said.

"I don't want us to talk tonight, I just want to be with you."

"Same. No talking, just hold me close."

We stayed that way, in silence, for a while. She shifted slightly so her face was in the crook of my neck. I felt her lips brush against my skin and I closed my eyes.

"I can't..."

"I know, just let me do this," she said.

I wanted so desperately to fuck her, no, I wanted to make love to her, but I didn't know how. I knew only one way and I couldn't go there right then. I was pent-up with frustration and sadness; I didn't want to ruin anything by hurting her. It took all my restraint not to roll her to her back and at least kiss those lips that were tormenting me. She sighed as she pulled her head away.

"You understand, don't you?" I asked.

"I do. I just want to be close to you right now."

I slid from the bed and held out my hand for her. She took it and stood. I walked her to my bedroom and closed the door behind me.

"Sleep with me?" I asked.

She nodded her head and smiled. "Clothed?"

"Partially might be better," I replied. "I guess I better find some shorts."

She laughed as she stripped down to her panties, leaving her vest top on but undoing her bra and threading it through the straps. I pulled off my t-shirt and undid my jeans. Before I let them fall, I grabbed a pair of shorts and made my way to the bathroom to change. She was lying under the sheet when I returned.

It felt good to lie beside her, to hold her in my arms and feel her body against mine. I inwardly cursed the vest top but smiled to myself when I felt her hard nipples graze my side as she shifted to get comfortable.

With her in my arms, her hand on my chest, and her head in the crook of my neck, it was the best night's sleep I'd had in days.

—————

I woke before her. We had shifted positions in the night. She was facing away from me and I had my arms wrapped around her. I shifted my body slightly away; I didn't want her to feel my hard-on against her backside. The scent of her hair comforted me. I breathed in deep before sighing. I had no idea what the future held for us. She had to leave soon and I knew I'd have to follow. I couldn't live in the U.S. and have her back in the UK. Whether I could follow in a few days' time was something I was unsure of. The day I set foot back on UK soil was the day I would have conquered my urges. In one way I was glad she was leaving, it gave me a goal to work towards.

She stirred and turned in my arms. Her eyelids fluttered open and I watched as she smiled.

"Good morning," I said.

"Morning to you, too. Do we have to get up?"

"We do. I have to run."

"Have to?"

"Yep. I need to get the blood pumping around my cock right now to pump someplace else."

Her eyes widened before she laughed.

"We could…"

"No, Summer. The next time I have you naked underneath me will be because I want to make love to you, not fuck you. And I need to work on that urge, like right now."

I rolled from the bed and strode to the bathroom. Pissing was hard with a cock that wanted nothing more than to be embedded deep inside her. I changed my shorts, pulled on my trainers and smiled at her as I headed for the beach. I ran, dodging early walkers and dogs. I ran until the sweat rolled from my body and adrenalin pumped around my system. I ran until the blood that had kept my cock rock hard, was diverted to my needy heart.

When I arrived back at the house, Summer was in the kitchen. Music was playing and she was making herself tea. I jogged up the steps to the balcony and she smiled at me through the door.

"Coffee?" she asked.

"Sure. I need a shower first though."

I headed to my bedroom and stripped off my shorts. I stood under the jets of water, and despite my run, it took no more than a thought to have my cock hard again. I stroked, I pleasured myself until I came. It wasn't entirely satisfactory, but would do.

Summer had a coffee ready for my return and I took a sip.

"Want to come to the bar tonight?" I asked.

"Sure, is it open every night?"

"No, just Thursday, Friday, and Saturdays for now. I don't think Dex could cope with more."

"Will Honey be there?" She hesitated over her words.

"I imagine so. If she thinks I'll be there, then she'll turn up. I need to talk to her, Summer. I'm not sure what Dex has told you so far, but I need to tell her that there'll be no more."

She didn't speak for a little while. She did however pick up her tea and my hand and led me outside to sit. She snuggled with me on the daybed.

"It's okay. I agree that you need to talk to her. I don't think just walking away from her is helpful, to either of you. I know what you

168

do, with her, and I can't think that much about it. I understand; I don't like it, obviously. I'd never put choices in front of you, but I can't share you with her," Summer said.

She hadn't looked at me all the time she had spoken and I appreciated her honesty.

"You know it was never a relationship, don't you?"

"I do, I understand, sort of. I feel sorry for her, Jack. I wish she would get help."

"Dexter tried for a long time with her but she's too destructive. She needs me and for a while I needed her. I don't want to feel that need anymore."

"That scares me a little. You've thrown away that blade and you're cutting yourself off from her. How do you release your anger, your frustration now?"

"That's what I have to work on. Another outlet, a safer one."

We fell silent for a little while. "Your art is one, isn't it?" she said.

"Yes, but it's not enough. It's not physical, I can't punch it, hurt it, make it bleed."

"Is that what you did to her?"

I turned sharply to her.

"No, not in the way you imagine. I've never hit a woman, I never intend to."

"But you've hurt her, choked her, and slapped her ass?"

I took a deep breath; it wasn't a conversation I wanted to have with her at all. "After being begged to. It's not in anger, Summer, it gets her off."

"I don't want you to tell me the details, I'm just trying to get my head around it all. That's okay, isn't it?"

"Of course, I can't answer everything, Summer, it's not a part of me that I like. I want to get away from it."

"I'm scared to talk to you about any of it, in case it sets you off," she said, her voice had grown to a whisper.

"I guess we have to find some way of talking about it that suits us both. I've been like this all my life; it's going to be a hard habit to break. It's going to take me time—I just hope you'll wait for me."

She didn't answer; I didn't expect her to. I was asking a lot of her but she did give my hand a squeeze, it was enough. Summer and I sat in silence, a comfortable silence for a while. I'd always been alone. I guessed one of the reasons I could connect with her so much was that often we didn't need to be deep in conversation. She gave me breathing space and thinking time while being by my side.

"Can I see your drawings? I noticed they were of me," she said.

"Okay, but...fuck it. What harm can it do now?" I stood and she followed me to my bedroom.

We sat on the edge of the bed and I placed a pad on her lap. I watched as she slowly opened the cover. I heard her take a sharp breath in. She was looking at a picture of herself. She was lying on my bed, the sheets a tangled mess around her. Her back was arched from the mattress and her hand was splayed between her thighs. Her mouth was open and her eyes closed. She flipped the page after a minute or so. Each picture was of her in a sexual position but on her own. One had her on all fours with her head thrown back, as if my imaginary hand was pulling on her hair. Another had her arms raised above her head, holding the headboard and her legs spread wide.

When she came to the end of that pad I gave her another. With each turn of the page, the scenes became more erotic. I had started to draw myself with her. My head was between her thighs and my hands held her hips to the bed. In another, she was bent over the bed; my hand was between her shoulder blades while I fucked her from behind. As she closed that pad, I noticed her hand shake gently as she placed it on the bedside table.

She didn't look at me but stood. "I...err...I need..."

"Shit! Now you're mad at me, aren't you?" I said.

She turned to face me, her neck and cheeks were flushed, her pupils dilated.

"No, I'm..."

"Aroused?" I cut in.

"Very."

I stood and faced her.

"Do something about it. Show me what you do."

"I don't know if I can. Fuck, Jackson." She sighed and bit down on her lower lip.

I took a step closer. I didn't place my hands on her body, as much as I wanted to, but leaned down to whisper in her ear.

"Show me. Know I'm watching you. Know the sight of what you're doing is going to fucking turn me on, big time. I won't touch you, I'll smell you though, and I'll lick your juices from your fingers."

She moaned and her hands gripped the front of my t-shirt. I took a slight step back and grabbed her vest top by the hem. I raised it over her head. I unclipped her bra and slowly slid the straps from her shoulders. My knuckles brushed her skin as I unbuttoned her shorts and I heard her moan again. I lowered myself to my knees as I dragged her shorts and panties to her ankles. She stepped out of them. I breathed in the scent of her arousal.

When I stood, I unbuttoned my shorts and let them fall, kicked off my trainers, and stood naked in front of her. I wrapped my hand around my cock and watched as her eyes widened while she watched.

"Get on the bed, Summer," I said.

Without a word, she did as I asked. She lay down and I knelt at her feet. Her hand slowly moved to her pussy, and when her fingers connected with her clitoris, she moaned. It was fucking torturous, arousing beyond belief, sensual, sexual, every damn word and emotion flooded through my brain. I pumped hard on my cock as I watched her fingers, as I watched her face. I was desperate to bury myself in her, to fuck her so hard she'd beg me to stop. But I wouldn't. Not until I could control myself.

Her free hand gripped the bedding beside her. Her stomach tensed and her fingers worked harder.

"Look at me, baby," I whispered. She opened her eyes.

She watched my hand slide up and down my cock, and her fingers worked faster over her clitoris. They were slick and the sight spurred me on, as did her smell. A musky scent washed over me. Lying in front of me, in all her beauty, pleasuring herself without embarrassment was about one of the hottest things I'd seen. I fell in love with her more, if that was possible, at that moment.

I clenched my jaw shut but hissed out as she bucked off the bed. She moaned out my name and I watched her give in to her orgasm. Sweat had beaded on her forehead, and I wanted that on my body, I wanted her juices around my cock, around my fingers. I grabbed her wrist, forcing her to sit. I placed them in my mouth and sucked and licked them clean.

Her hand covered mine as I brought myself to my release. My

cum spurted over her hand, and what she did next nearly tipped me over the edge. She raised her hand and licked it from her thumb.

"Fuck. Don't do that, Summer. Fuck," I said.

My heart was still racing as she knelt in front of me. "Just kiss me, Jack."

It was all the invitation I needed. I grabbed her face in my hands and my mouth crashed down on hers. She bit my lip and it was painfully delicious. My stomach knotted at the sting. Electrical synapses fired off in my brain, as I tasted my blood and my heart pumped faster. I wrapped my hands in her hair and tightened my fingers, she moaned into my mouth. She wrapped her arms around my shoulders and ran her fingernails down my back. My cock hardened at the scratch. She had me dangerously close to losing control.

Just as I was about to throw her back on the bed, she broke the kiss and started to whisper to me.

"I love you, Jack, this is me, Summer. You love me, you don't want to hurt me."

While she spoke, she straddled my lap. One hand held my cock and guided it inside her. I was sitting back on my heels as she rode me.

"Tell me you love me, Jack," she continued to whisper.

"I love you, I can't..." I said with a grunt.

"You can, you look at me. Look straight into my eyes, Jack. This is me, it's Summer."

She said her name over and over, slowly. She whispered that she loved me; she didn't stop talking until I had come for a second time. I let my head fall on her shoulders and she held me while I cried.

"See, you can do it," she said after a few minutes. "You just need to focus on me, on us."

She slid from my lap and I let my body fall face first onto the bed. She lay beside me and her hand gently stroked the back of my head, my neck, and down my back as if she was comforting me.

"I can give you an outlet. I can make you bleed but in a more pleasurable way, Jack," she said, as she placed her finger to my swollen lip.

"That's not what it's about. That's not always going to be enough. I don't want to bleed, you'll never understand the reasons," I said quietly.

"I know it's not enough, I know I'll never understand, but it was something for now, wasn't it?" she said.

I reached out and pulled her close to me. It had worked, I guessed. However, what she didn't realise was I didn't have the urge, there was no anger flowing through my body, at that point. If she did that when I had, there was no telling what I was capable of.

"You can't do that again, okay? Let me get my urges under control. If you are my willing outlet, it doesn't get better, Summer. It gets worse with every abusive fuck I give you. The more you give me, the more I will take."

"But that wasn't an abusive fuck as you called it."

"No, because you took me by surprise and because I wasn't in a bad frame of mind. One day I might be and you'll push just that one wrong button..." I left the sentence hanging.

She sighed. "I wanted you, I needed you. Those drawings, Jack, they turned me on, you turn me on, and I can't help that."

"I'm pleased to hear that," I said with a chuckle.

"I'm serious."

"I know, and so am I. I don't trust myself and you are nowhere strong enough to stop me. I will do all I can to give you warning, and you need to promise me you will back off when I ask. Please, Summer, do that for me at least."

"Are we ever going to have a normal relationship?" she whispered.

Her words caused my heart to constrict.

"I don't know, is the honest answer. You need to work with me. I guarantee if I can do this, it'll be worth it."

I saw her smirk a little. "Worth it, huh? You better be, Jackson Walker, you better be."

———

The bar was clean and mostly prepped when we arrived, a little later than I would normally have liked.

"Dude, wasn't expecting you tonight," D-J said from behind the bar.

"Can't keep me away for long, my friend."

"Good, because we were fucking heaving last night. I barely coped."

I led Summer to the chair beside the bar end, where she had sat before. I handed her a cold beer and set about to line up the glasses D-J was polishing. That night we had a DJ, and while he set up on the stage, D-J decided to sing, loudly and off-key. As he belted out some country song, I aimed the soda syphon at him. The party was getting started way earlier than normal. Summer's laugh lifted me. I had worried about our earlier conversation. She must have been fucking exhausted with all my highs and lows. I knew I was.

An hour later, it was three deep at the bar. The noise level was at fever pitch, and I had to lean over the bar many times to hear the order. D-J and I spun a couple of bottles between us, made a few cocktails, and messed around, as usual. Dexter had the night off and we were getting behind with stacking the dishwasher. The bar was always busy but that night, one man down, we were struggling. I caught Summer's eye and indicated with my head for her to join me, she wouldn't have heard had I shouted. She slid from her stool and forced her way through the throng to the open end of the bar and joined us.

"Want to help? I need fresh glasses," I had to shout.

"Sure, just show me where."

I pointed to the dishwasher and D-J threw her a polishing cloth. She emptied, stacked it again, and set it to wash. She polished the glasses and shelved them, mopped down the bar and then served a couple of beers to a guy shouting for her attention. She smiled and laughed; she flirted with them, all the time with her hand on my arse under the bar. I gave her a wink and quickly showed her how the till worked. She was a godsend.

As the night wore on, she barely had time to speak. The DJ cranked up the music and when The Weeknd's *Wicked Games* started to play, D-J jumped on the bar and sang his signature tune. The crowd cheered and sang along, not one of them had a clue how significant that song was to him. Like me, D-J had songs that resonated with him. He sprayed the crowd, fuck knows how much soda we got through in a month, but they loved it. Especially the women with the see-through tops.

I watched as Summer leaned over the bar to hear an order. A guy I hadn't seen before reached forwards to grab her tit. It took no more than a second for me to be by her side. I grabbed his wrist, twisted his arm, and slammed it down on the bar.

"No touching," I growled. He raised his uninjured hand in defence and backed off.

"My knight in shining armour, again," she said.

"Told you, I am a jealous kind of guy," I said, before grabbing her face for a kiss.

"That was a little territorial," she said when we parted.

"Just wanted them to know not to touch." I gave her a wink and turned to serve the customer.

All serving stopped when *Jungle* by X-Ambassadors screamed out. The crowd sang along with D-J and me as we belted out the words and jumped onto the bar. All that could be seen were people bouncing on their feet in time with the music. I watched Summer kick off her shoes and climb up to join us. She raised her hands above her head, wiggled her arse over to me, and ground it firmly into my groin. I wrapped an arm around her waist and danced with her. She was sexy as fuck, her t-shirt was wet and nearly see-through, her wet hair whipped around her face as she dirty danced against my hardening cock. We were giving the crowd quite a show as I practically fucked her through her clothes.

She laughed and turned in my arms when the song came to an end. She placed her arms around my neck and kissed me hard.

"That was a little territorial," I said when we broke.

"Just letting them know not to touch," she replied with a laugh. "I get very jealous too, Jack. And it doesn't look like it's just the women that want to tear the clothes from your body."

I followed her gaze. A guy was standing against the wall and he raised a glass to me. I stared at him and was thankful to see him lower his eyes.

"Someone you know?" she asked.

"No. Now you've given these guys enough of a warning that you own me, shall we?" I held out my hand.

She laughed and I helped her from the bar. From the corner of my eye, I caught sight of Honey and she wasn't looking pleased. She was drunk, she often was, and swaying from one foot to the other, but certainly not in time with the music. I made a point of not looking directly at her. I didn't want to give her reason to approach me.

The night turned into the early hours of the morning and the bar started to wind down. When we had a handful of people left, it was time to kick them out and lock up. We wiped down the bar and cleaned all the glasses. The floor could be mopped in the morning.

"Breakfast?" I said as I took Summer by the hand.

"Absolutely, I'm starving."

"D-J?"

"Sure, usual?" he said.

I nodded and we made our way to our respective cars.

"I'm fucked," I said with a laugh as we drove.

"Where are we going?"

"A twenty-four hour diner. Half the customers will be in there. They party all night, eat, then go to bed for the day."

We pulled up outside something that looked like it hadn't changed since the 1950s. Neon lights buzzed and flickered outside. Inside the smell of fried food had my stomach grumbling. As predicted, the diner was nearly full, most of them greeted D-J and me as we made our way to the one spare table. Summer slid across the red leather seat and picked up a menu. D-J sat opposite and I took the seat alongside her.

"What do you fancy?" I asked.

"I have no idea," she replied with a laugh. "Got to be pancakes or waffles since I'm in the U.S., I guess."

We placed our menus back on the table as a waitress approached.

"What can I get you?" she asked.

I placed an order for pancakes, waffles, bacon, and eggs. I had to remember to ask for the bacon and eggs not to be on the same plate as the waffles. The Americans had strange tastes where mixing their sweet and savoury was concerned. She poured three cups of coffee from the jug she held and then left.

"Tonight, or last night, I guess, was amazing," Summer said.

"Sure was, couldn't do it every night though," D-J replied, followed by a yawn.

"What do you do the rest of the week?" Summer asked.

"Surf, sleep, surf some more," he replied.

I watched as he tried to very subtly unwrap something he'd pulled from his pocket. I stared at him as he popped that something in his mouth and then took a gulp of coffee. Summer was chatting about wanting to surf, but I kept my gaze on him. I sighed and shook my head gently. He cast his eyes down.

I guessed he'd taken amphetamine or some upper. It wasn't long before all signs of tiredness left him. We ate, we drank enough coffee to have us buzzing without the high he'd taken, and then as we stood to leave, Honey arrived.

I had hold of Summer's hand and we were making our way through the diner's doors, having said goodbye to D-J. Initially, Honey had been leaning against my car; she pushed herself off when she saw us. She looked a mess. Lines of black ran down her cheeks where her mascara had streaked, probably from earlier tears. Her hair was messed up and she was missing one shoe.

I came to a halt in front of her. "What happened?" I asked.

I felt Summer's hand tighten in mine.

"I...I don't have you anymore, do I?" Honey said.

"No."

She nodded and gave Summer a very sad smile. "Can you fix him?" she said, nodding her head towards me.

"I'm going to try," Summer answered gently.

She nodded her head. Something was very wrong though. This wasn't the Honey I knew.

"What have you taken, Honey?" I asked.

She smiled at me, "I need the pain to stop, Jackson."

I took a step towards her; she took a step back. She swayed a little, stumbling in her one shoe. I grabbed her bag from her hands and opened it. I pulled out an empty pill bottle.

"Go and get D-J," I said to Summer. At first she stood still and looked at me.

"Now!"

I watched her rush off. Honey fell against my car, she slid to the ground and I knelt beside her.

"You love her and you couldn't love me. I only ever wanted you to love me," she whispered. Her words were slurred.

"Talk to me, Honey," I said, fishing around in my pocket for my phone. I dialled 911.

When D-J arrived at my side, I handed him the bottle. "Fuck!" he said.

"What is it?" Summer asked.

"Some serious shit. Did you call 911?"

"I did, what do I do?" I asked.

"Fuck knows, keep her talking?" he replied.

Summer knelt down beside her.

"Honey, can you hear me? Give Dex a call," she said to D-J.

Honey opened her eyes slightly and looked at Summer. "I love him," she said.

"I know you do. When did you take those pills?"

Honey didn't answer; she slid a little further down the car. As she did, her short skirt rose. We all saw her blood stained thighs.

"Daddy's back," she said.

Those were her final words before she stopped breathing. I watched in stunned silence as Summer pulled her legs until she was lying flat. I watched in horror as she pummelled on her chest and vomit mixed with foam spewed from Honey's mouth. It all seemed in slow motion. The blue and red flashing lights lit up the car park, people were running and talking, and I didn't hear a word of it. All I heard was, 'Daddy's back.'

Coldness swept over me, I'd taken a step back—only seeing a blur in front of me.

'Daddy's back, Jackson. Are you ready? Are you ready to show me what a man you are now?'

'Cut, Jackson, show me how brave you are. Let me see you bleed like your mother did.'

'Did you know she bled all over the floor when they pulled you from her?'

'You did that to her, you made her bleed, Jackson.'

"Jack?"

"Dude, can you hear me?"

'Daddy's back, Jackson. That's another one you've killed.'

'Daddy's back, daddy's back, daddy's back, daddy's back.'

"Daddy's back!" I screamed out, bashing the side of my head with the heel of my hand.

I wasn't aware of who was around me, I felt hands on my arms, I heard words. I smelled her. Was that my mother? Could I smell my mum?

"Mum?" I said.

I fucking hated my mum, I hated her for dying, I hated her for leaving me with him, I hated her for not terminating me. I hated her for refusing the C-section. I hated my father for his years of abuse, for his torment and vicious words. I loved my daddy for giving me his blade; he must have loved me to do that, mustn't he?

"Jackson." It was a man's voice.

I grabbed his hair and dragged him to the side of the diner. I forced him face down on the hood of a car and stood behind him, readying myself. I heard a scream, a woman scream.

"It's okay, he knows what to do," I said to no one in particular, as I unzipped my jeans and pulled out my cock.

He was ready for me; he was always ready. Honey wasn't my only outlet.

I felt a punch to the side of my jaw; it knocked me from my feet. I landed heavily on my back. The wind was knocked from my lungs and I struggled to get my breath. My sight was blurry and there was a ringing in my head, but in the distance I could hear sobs.

"Summer?" I called out. I could hear her.

It took a moment for my vision to come into focus. She was being held by D-J, she was sobbing into his chest. Her ponytail, usually so neat, was a mess. I scrambled to my feet.

"What the fuck happened?" I shouted.

"You happened, dude. Stay there, Dex is on his way. And put your fucking cock away."

"What do you mean, I happened?" I fumbled to do up my jeans, not fully understanding why they were undone.

"Stay there, Jackson," he repeated. He held his hand out to keep me at arm's length.

I watched her bury her face in D-J's chest; she curled her arms under her chest as if she was trying to crawl inside him. He tightened his grip on her; he turned slightly so she was shielded from me.

"Summer? What happened?" I was shouting again. A crowd had formed outside the diner.

"Someone called the police, Jack, we need to get out of here," I heard.

I saw Dexter's hand on my arm. When the fuck had he arrived?

I was bundled into his car, all the while looking over my shoulder and calling out to her. I was confused. Where was Honey? We had just had breakfast, hadn't we? Why was Summer crying?

We drove the short distance to the bar. "Safe room, now," Dex said. I duly followed his order, without any understanding of why.

I sat on the bed and waited for him. I struggled to think, to slow down the rush of images in my brain. I couldn't focus. I stood and paced; I sat again. Dread and fear began to settle in my stomach. My skin itched and I scratched at my cuts. I eyed the drawer, my drawer. I strode over and tugged at the handles, I kicked it in frustration when it wouldn't open. My blood pumped faster around my body, my heart raced as adrenalin flooded through me. I began to mumble to myself. I looked around the room and smiled at a framed picture on the wall.

"Silly, fucking silly, Dexter," I said quietly.

I dragged it from the wall and slammed it to the floor. The glass frame shattered, it was the most satisfying sound I'd heard. I knelt, sifting through the pieces until I found the perfect one. I held it in my hand, closing my palm around it so tightly, and watched the blood seep through my fingers and drip to the floor.

I stood and raised my t-shirt. I sunk the piece of glass into my flesh and dragged it down my stomach. The relief that washed over me was like I imagined a first hit of heroin to be. The noise in my head quietened, the tension in my body lessened. I floated as warm liquid rolled over my skin, over my fingers.

Before I could make the second cut, something akin to a bulldozer drove me from my feet. I smacked my head on the floor and that was the last thing I remembered.

CHAPTER EIGHTEEN

Summer

"I have to go, D-J. Please, take me to him," I said.

My body shook and I struggled to breathe as panic welled up in me.

"No, Summer. Dexter said to take you home."

"I have to know what he was doing, damn it!"

"You know what he was doing, you saw him."

I spun in my seat and glared at him. "I know what I saw; I need him to fucking explain himself." My voice rose to screeching point.

I felt sick. Sick to my stomach at the sight I'd witnessed. I'd watched the man I love about to fuck another, but it wasn't him—it couldn't be. There was no emotion on his face as he held the man

I'd seen in the bar, down on the hood of a car. There was no struggle from the man, he was a willing partner, in fact, I'd seen him smile. The sick fuck had smiled at me. Jackson had lied to me; I'd asked him if he knew the guy and he'd lied.

I watched D-J sigh and his shoulders sag. He slowed the car from the breakneck speed to just fast. I also saw a tear roll down his cheek.

"I don't know what to do. I've never seen him like that," he whispered.

"Take me back to him, please," I said, gently.

He didn't answer immediately, and I was thankful for the seat belt as he pulled a U-turn worthy of a stunt driver.

"I just need to know he's all right, then you can take me back, okay? I need to leave, I need to go home, my home."

He nodded and didn't speak to me until we pulled up outside the bar.

"I don't know if Dexter will even let you in. Be prepared for that."

"I will, now open the door," I said, urgency laced my voice.

He fumbled with the key until eventually I took it from his shaking hands. Whatever he had taken, and it was obvious he was on something; it was making him very clumsy. His pupils were dilated, he constantly licked his lips as if his mouth was very dry, and he was trying to conjure up saliva. He was edgy, nervous, and it was as we came face-to-face with Dexter I understood why.

"Get the fuck in there," he said to him, pointing behind the bar.

I watched him walk away. "How is he?" I asked as I made to follow D-J.

"Not good, I don't want you in there, right now."

"I need to see him, I need to ask him one fucking question, and then I'll leave."

"He has no idea what he's done right now. What he does know is Honey died a half hour ago. I got a call from an old friend at the hospital. He believes he caused that. Right now, I'm allowing him an outlet, then I'll sedate him."

"What? Whoa, no. Hold on...You're allowing him to do what? Cut or fuck a man?" My breathing was erratic. "How could you have not told me, Dex? That's his other outlet, isn't it?" I spat the words at him.

"He cut. It was that or beat him unconscious, which I did earlier as well."

"He needs to be in hospital, Dexter."

"He can't afford to be in the hospital, Summer," he over pronounced my name.

"He must have insurance, doesn't he?"

Dexter shook his head. "There must be a free service here?" I asked.

Again, Dexter shook his head. "I have money, how much are we talking about here?"

"Thousands and thousands of dollars. I can manage this, Summer. You trusted me once, do it again."

I was hesitant. I looked at the man who stood before me; he looked broken himself. His boys were in trouble, they needed him, and right at that moment, Dexter needed me.

"Okay, what do I do?"

"Let the sedation start to take effect, let me calm him. He's distraught, he doesn't know what he did, but he suspects it was something bad. I worry that in the state he's in, if he sees you, those memories may surface. He heard you scream, he knows you were there, but he hasn't spoken at all about Ted. I fear that will be too much for him to handle right now."

"Ted?"

"The guy..."

I nodded my head. "I'll wait here. Am I completely losing it by wanting to see him? I need one answer, Dex, and then I have to leave. I can't do this. You have no idea how conflicted I am. I love him, but Honey, Ted, self-harm...I just don't understand. I thought I did, I thought I could cope, but..."

"You're the best thing that has happened to him," he said sadly. "But I understand, he'll understand."

"I talked him down earlier today. I had sex with him, Dexter. I took the lead, he didn't want to at first. I talked to him, reminding him it was me. I said my name over and over and he was okay. Why was he okay then and not now?" I was rambling a little, but I wanted Dexter to understand that there had been a shift in Jackson's behaviour.

"Was he as bad as now?"

"Well, no, but it still worked."

"I'd rather we wait until the sedative kicks in. It's fairly mild; he's taken it before with no ill effect. Grab a coffee and wait until I call you."

Dexter walked away and left me alone. I headed for the coffee machine, unsure at first how to operate it. Once I'd realised it needed to be turned on at the socket, I set about to make coffee. I'd watch enough baristas in the past, and a half hour later, I finally had a cup of coffee in my hands. I sat for a little while, just sipping it. But I needed to do something. I cleaned the bar and unloaded the dishwasher. I found a mop and bucket and filled it with soapy water. I started to mop the floor. I was halfway through when Dexter walked back into the room. I just needed something to wipe the image of Jackson and Ted from my mind.

"He's calm now, half asleep of course, so don't expect too much from him," he said.

I leaned the mop against the bar and followed him. We walked through the storeroom and into the room I'd only visited once before. Jackson was lying on his back on the double bed; he had one hand bandaged. D-J had his head in his hands; he was sitting in one of the small leather armchairs. He looked up at me and smiled sadly as I approached.

Jackson had his eyes closed as I sat on the edge of the bed. I wasn't sure what to do at first and looked over to Dex. He nodded at me. I reached forwards and ran my fingers down Jackson's cheek. He slowly opened his eyes. He didn't speak but a tear leaked from one eye and rolled down the side of his face. His brow furrowed as if he was trying to remember something.

"It's me, Summer," I repeated the words I'd used earlier.

His face relaxed. He nodded his head gently and closed his eyes again. He opened his mouth to speak but made no noise. I watched as he licked his upper lip.

"Are you thirsty?" I asked. He shook his head and opened his mouth as if to speak again.

"Do you want to tell me something?" He nodded that time.

Dexter stepped closer to me. He placed his hand on my arm to stop me from leaning down to him. I looked up at him.

"Not too close," he whispered.

I wasn't sure why but I did as I was asked.

"What do you want you want to say, Jackson?"

He closed his eyes and, for a moment, I thought he'd fallen asleep. And then I heard words that ripped me apart.

"I killed Dane," he said.

There was no sound in the room at all. I don't know how long it took for the words to register in my brain. I leapt to my feet, I stumbled backwards so fast I fell over the vacant chair. I scrambled to my feet in time to see Dexter's chin fall to his chest as he closed his eyes, in what? Shock? Resignation?

I wasn't able to speak; I willed my legs to move me backwards towards the door. I watched Dex walk towards me. I was in the bar before he spoke again.

"He didn't kill Dane, it was an accident."

"You knew? You fucking knew?"

"They fought over you. Dane tried to punch Jackson but he was drunk, they fought and he lost his balance. He fell back onto the wall. Jack tried to grab him before he toppled over. It was an accident. An accident Jack holds himself entirely responsible for. He believes if they hadn't argued, if Jackson hadn't confessed he was in love with you, the fight wouldn't have started."

"You fucking knew!" I screamed from the top of my lungs. "Accident or not, Jackson knew exactly what happened that night. I questioned and questioned, I drove myself fucking mad with wanting to know, Dex. All the time he knew."

I was shocked to the core. My body started to tremble again. Dexter took a step towards me, and I welcomed his arms around me as I gave into the sobs that overwhelmed me. I was glad for his strength; my legs were about to give out. I'd seen and learned way too much for me to take in, and I hurt. I physically hurt.

"I'm calling Alfie to take you home."

"I...I can't do this..."

"I know. I know. Go home, Summer. Let me fix him."

———

"Ma'am, can I help you?"

I stood in the middle of the airport with tears streaming down my face and no idea of where to go.

"I need to get home," I whispered.

"Let me help you. Home is where?"

"I'm not sure."

I turned, finally, to look at a woman in a uniform. I guessed she was some sort of walking information service for the airport. She had a kind face and a gentle smile for me.

"Why don't we sit for a moment?"

She led me to a row of plastic chairs.

"Now, where do you need to get to?" she asked.

"England. I need to get to Heathrow or Gatwick. My heart is here though."

"A boy?"

"A man, a damaged man. I'm sorry, I just need pointing into the direction of the ticket sales desks."

"Do you have a preference of airline?"

"No, the first one leaving I guess."

We stood and walked through the vast airport to the ticket desks. She went from one to the other speaking on my behalf until she waved me over.

"Cheapest, and soonest," she said.

I purchased a ticket, praying I had enough limit on my credit card and collected the document. She then placed her hand on my back and walked me through to check-in. She waited for me before showing me through passport control.

"I'm sorry about your man," she said as I smiled my thanks.

"So am I. Thank you."

I wandered aimlessly until I found a seat near my gate and waited. I had purposely turned off my phone but my hand itched to see if Dexter had called. No matter what I did, the tears would not stop rolling down my cheeks. People looked at me but everyone smiled, offering some comfort without words.

Eventually my flight was called. As I walked to the desk, I hesitated. At that moment I could have easily turned around and gone back, but I didn't. I boarded the plane, took my seat, and I buckled myself in.

I watched California fall beneath me as the plane climbed. I mentally said goodbye to the most intense couple of weeks of my life. I placed my palm on the window and whispered to him.

"I love you, Jack."

I was thankful that the seat beside me remained unoccupied. I raised the arm and curled up with my back against the window. I dozed on and off, I ate, and I listened to music. I played James Bay, *Incomplete* on repeat. It was the song Jack and I had danced to in the kitchen and every single word resonated with me. It could have been written about us.

It was the following day that I arrived home to a cold, soulless apartment in rainy London. I left my case in my bedroom, stripped off my creased clothing, and took a shower. I climbed in bed and buried my face in my pillow. I hadn't slept properly for over twenty-four hours and my body was totally fucked.

It was two days later that I had a need to leave the apartment. I had no food and headed to the supermarket. My head was full of Jackson as I placed random items in my basket. I chuckled bitterly at the checkout—my basket was full of the usual break-up crap. I had two tubs of ice cream, a bottle of wine, and chocolate. I had thought to buy milk at least.

When I arrived home, I unpacked. I'd checked my phone repeatedly and each time felt a pang of disappointment that there was no call or text. I thought long and hard about what Dexter had told me. Dane and Jack had fought; the words swam around my head.

Jackson had confessed he loved me. He tried to help Dane.

Had he though? How hard had he tried to save Dane? I pushed the thought from my mind. All the questions I had a year previous flooded my brain. Dane and Jack had been on a rare boys' night out. They hadn't done that for months. I'd been pleased because I loved them both and to see their friendship so strained had saddened me. I knew Dane was drunk at the time of the accident; I'd had the unhappy experience of sitting through the coroner's verdict. There had been no witnesses; it was dark. The train driver wasn't even sure what he'd hit at first. I closed my eyes and my stomach heaved at a memory. I'd overheard an official from the train company that day at the inquest.

'Thankfully, the train was slowing for the station, otherwise there wouldn't have been much to identify the poor kid by.'

My stomach lurched; I sprang to my feet and, with my hand over my mouth, ran for the bathroom. I only just made it before I threw up.

I seemed to be on autopilot. I went to bed and slept, I got up and ate, and I went to bed again. I'd been at home nearly a week before I got any communication from Dexter. He had sent me a text while I'd slept.

He's doing better, knows he's lost you, but he's determined to turn his life around to win you back. He hasn't cut at all.

It was good news, I thought, but not enough. Despite what I knew where Dane's accident was concerned, despite what I saw, I still loved Jackson. I couldn't switch that off, but the conflict inside held me back from replying immediately. Jackson knew what happened that night and he'd lied to me. His version, and the version given to the police was that Dane was drunk and decided to walk along the wall. He slipped; Jack was too far away to get to him before he fell.

I'd spent the previous few days trying to figure out why Jackson had lied. He wasn't to blame, if what he had said was true, they'd fought, but Dane had toppled over the wall. So why lie? What else wasn't I being told?

I scrolled through my phone. I had several missed calls from my mum but I didn't want to call, she'd be able to tell immediately something was wrong, just from the tone of my voice. I wasn't sure what I would say, I wasn't sure of anything other than one thing. I needed someone to talk to, someone who knew Jack. My finger hovered over a number I'd never used. I'd met Perri several times, and somehow I'd ended up with her mobile number in my phone. I dialled.

"Hello?" I heard.

"Perri, this is Summer, Jack's..."

"Hi, Summer, how nice to hear from you. How are you?" She cut off my sentence obviously remembering me.

"Erm, I'm..."

"Summer?"

"I just left Jack, he's not good."

"Are you in the UK?"

"Yes, I'm at home," I said.

"Give me your address, can I visit you this evening?"

"Of course, I need to talk to someone."

I gave her my address and she promised she'd visit. We said goodbye and I laid the phone down on the sofa beside me. I wasn't sure I had done the right thing; maybe she didn't know what he did. Maybe she did, and I was about to get an earful for leaving him. I thought back to the last time I'd met her. We had been at mutual friend's barbecue and it had been wonderful to see her with Jack. She was the big sister: teasing, hugging, and chatting to him and all his friends. She was polite, pleasant company and I'd spent some time chatting with her. She was a lawyer but it was never mentioned that she worked for her father. I often wondered how Jack felt about that. Did he think she supported what her father did?

For the rest of the day I paced, tidied up, paced some more, slept a little and as the hours wore on, I became anxious. By the time I heard the intercom buzz, I was a bundle of nerves. I released the main door and stood by the apartment one, waiting for Perri. She had opted for the stairs and smiled at me as she walked along the corridor.

"Summer, how are you?" she said, as she pulled me into an embrace.

"I'm okay, sort of." I led her into the kitchen. "Can I pour you a wine?"

"I think I'm going to need it, aren't I?"

I slowly nodded as I poured. We took our glasses into the living room and sat.

"Tell me," she asked.

"I don't know where to start, what you know, even." I twirled the glass in my fingertips.

Perri shuffled up the sofa until she was beside me, she took one of my hands in hers.

"He's loved you for years. Did you know that he saw you in the bar? He pointed you out to Dane and wanted to approach you first."

"Why didn't he?"

"I guess Dane decided that wasn't going to happen." There was a slight bitter edge to her voice. "I've known Dane since they were at school together, he was never the nicest of friends Jackson could have had."

"I wish Jackson had been the first one to talk to me," I said quietly.

"So what happened in Cali? I guess that's why you need to talk to me."

"He...I saw him..." Tears welled in my eyes and I choked on my words.

"He self-harms, that's what you saw, isn't it?"

I nodded. She sighed and leaned back into the sofa, taking a sip of her wine.

"I thought we'd gotten that under control. I hate that he is there, Summer. I hate that I'm not. I've tried for years to keep him in therapy. Do you know why he does it?"

"I know your father had him believe he killed his mum, and I think the cutting to his stomach is symbolic of the fact she didn't have the C-section."

Perri nodded. "I hate my father, Summer, so much. And I guess you want to know why I work alongside him?"

"It crossed my mind."

"I can keep control of Jack's trust fund. It's substantial, very substantial. It's enough to set him up for life, but he won't touch it and I won't allow my father to, either. I'm biding my time, like Jack. Soon that bastard will be dead and I can breathe, Jack can breathe."

Hardness settled over her face. "He adores me, Summer, only because I resemble my mother. For years I dyed my hair, changed my eye colour with contact lenses. Now I make a point of looking like her, it torments him further."

"Wow, I wasn't sure how you felt about him," I said.

"I called the police once. I found Jack slumped on the bathroom floor, surrounded by his own blood. It was one of many suicide attempts; he'd slit his wrists, as he'd been taught to do, but not deep enough. A mistake on his part, I think. My father is a very influential man, unfortunately. Nothing came of it but more torment for Jack. I had to make a decision, I had to keep quiet and help Jack without it being made public. I was fourteen years old, Summer, just a kid myself."

"I don't know what to say," I stammered.

"I'm okay, I toughened up, and I had the advantage. I could behave like my mother and my father fell at my feet. He would do anything I asked, except one thing; he wouldn't leave Jack alone. I got Jack out of the house as soon as he was old enough to fend for himself. I used my trust to pay for accommodations, bills, not that Jack knows. He thought the apartment he rented was super cheap," she chuckled a little at the thought.

"I'll do whatever is necessary for him. It's why I bought that house. I don't want an investment property in America; I wanted Jack out of the country with somewhere wonderful to live, to heal. I thought if he was abroad he'd be able to move on, I guess I was wrong."

"I think he was doing well, until I arrived," I said.

"Don't blame yourself. Who knows what set him off this time. He went long periods of time without hurting himself. All he wants is to be loved."

"I love him, I told him I loved him more than I ever loved Dane, and that's the truth, as painful as that is to admit."

She squeezed the hand she still held. "I heard about the child, I'm so sorry for you."

"It was a shock, for sure. I'm in the process of selling the apartment so the mother gets the child's share."

"Have you taken legal advice on that?"

"The solicitor that held the will said it was legally binding."

"Mmm, that may be the case, but there are other ways of dealing with that, you don't need to rush to sell your apartment. Even if you did, that child won't be entitled to the cash until he is of legal age. Is there a trust to be set up?"

"I don't know, I was just going to sell it and then ask the solicitor to hand it over, I guess."

"You'll do no such thing. I'll deal with it, Summer."

"The thing is, I don't want to live here anymore, it feels tarnished," I said.

She nodded and we paused our conversation while we both took sips from our glasses.

"I don't know what to do, Perri. I love Jack, I want to be with him, but there are other things I can't talk about right now. Dexter said to stay away for now. Jack is using the fact that he's lost me as his goal to sort himself out. Maybe he thinks he can win me back when he's well."

"Dexter is the bar owner? And what other things, Summer?"

"Yes, the local fixer-upper as they call him. He was a therapist in Australia before he moved to the U.S. I don't think what he does is legal but it seems to help. And...Jack has a need to dominate, to..."

"Sexually?"

"Yes, but not with me, with...others." I was finding it hard to speak the words, to tell her what I'd seen.

"Okay, I can understand that and when you're ready, tell me everything. I have to know it all; I can't help if I don't. And as for Dexter, legal or illegal, if it helps then we need to support that."

"What did your dad actually do?" I asked, not sure I really wanted to know.

Perri sighed. "I don't know all of it, he was a clever man, most of his torment was behind closed doors, and while I was out of the house. He would lock Jack in a cupboard, I know that much. He'd stand outside the door, sometimes inside, and just talk to him, scare the shit out of him. He'd tell him the monsters were coming. I heard him a couple of times but I was too young then to help. I know he told him he killed our mother, which simply isn't true."

"What happened to her?"

"She had pre-eclampsia, it's quite common, but with her diabetes, she developed complications. It's normal to have a C-section, and usually once the child is born, the mother recovers. My mother wanted a natural birth, my father begged her to terminate, which wasn't an option, obviously, she was too far into her pregnancy. She was mortified that he'd want that; I don't know this for fact, it's just what I was told by my grandmother before she died. Anyway, Mum didn't recover; she had a series of fits and died. It's possible that Dad wanted her to abort because he didn't want a son, an heir. Or he didn't want to share Mum with any more children."

"I'm so sorry," I said.

Perri smiled at me, "It was all a long time ago. So what to do about Jack?"

"I don't know right now. There's a lot I have to think about but I got a text, let me show you."

I reached for my phone and showed her the text message I'd received.

"Do you think I should fly out? Would that help?" Perri asked.

"I don't know, I can ask. I want to push through the sale of this apartment and then, who knows? There's a huge part of me that wants to return, Perri. I can't switch off my feelings for him, despite what I know, what I've seen. I thought I might like to go back to university and Alfie, Dexter's partner, said that UC has courses in psychotherapy. I'd like to explore that. I can go on a student visa, he said."

"I have contacts still at my old uni, Summer, why don't I see if I can find out. But are you sure? Your parents are still alive, how would they feel about you packing up and leaving?"

"I haven't mentioned it to them, I imagine they will be thrilled for me to be honest. They've always encouraged me to do whatever I want. But there's something else. Jack told me he killed Dane."

Perri leaned forwards and placed her empty wine glass on the coffee table. I watched as she took a deep breath. Her brow furrowed and she screwed her eyes shut.

"It was an accident, Perri. He didn't kill my husband, he blames himself for his death though." I then told her what I knew.

"I don't know what to say. I'm so sorry for you and I'm so sorry for my brother. His downward spiral has been since then, and now I know why."

"There isn't anything to say. I'm angry, of course, and hurt that Jack kept that information from me. I'm confused. I should hate him, but I don't. I should be disgusted with what he does, what I saw, but I'm not, and I don't know how to deal with that. I saw your brother..."

"What did you see, Summer?" There was urgency to Perri's voice.

"I saw him with another man. Dexter told me that he likes to do things but it isn't sexual, there's no feeling. It's a way of stripping power, or something. He likened it to the fucking Romans," I said. I started to laugh.

"What's funny?" Perri asked.

"Fucking Romans? That's ironic, don't you think?"

It took her a moment to understand. Her eyes widened and she covered her mouth with her hand.

"I'm sorry, I have no idea why I'm laughing. It's not remotely funny."

I started to cry then. Perri pulled me into her arms and I sobbed on her shoulder. Tiredness, jet lag, lost love, and loneliness washed over me.

"Is he gay?" she asked.

"No, that I doubt."

"Bi then?"

"I don't know. Dexter doesn't believe it has anything to do with sex. I don't understand and I didn't get an opportunity to talk to Jack about it."

"I need to speak to Dexter, I need to find out exactly what's been happening. Can I get his number from you?"

She took her phone from her handbag and added Dexter's number to her contacts.

"I'll give Dexter a call, see if I can get an update. They may be holding back for fear of upsetting you. Although, I'd like to think he'd be honest with you."

She stood and smoothed down the grey pencil skirt she'd worn. I imagined she had come straight from work.

"Can I ask one more thing?" I said as I stood. "What's wrong with your dad? Dexter thinks this episode is because your dad wants a reconciliation and Jack doesn't."

Her eyes widened. "Dad has cancer, it's terminal. But how did Jack know that? I never told him, I know not to mention him."

"I don't know. Could your dad have rung him?"

"Possibly, unlikely, I don't know. If he has Jack's mobile, we need to get that changed. Dad doesn't come into the office anymore; he has nursing care at home. I'm in the process of dealing with his affairs, his shares and all that. I'll speak to the nurse and see if he has spoken about Jack at all. Let's make a plan to meet again in a few days. I'll call you, if that's okay?"

"Of course, and thank you. I can't deal with this on my own," I said.

"You don't have to. I'm so glad you called. I can't do it on my own either but together, I think we'll make a formidable team."

She gave me a hug and left. I watched her give a little wave as she walked through the stairwell door. She had remained unemotional the whole time we'd spoken. I assumed that was Perri the businesswoman at work, possibly her way of dealing with the news. I didn't imagine her to be one to openly shed tears, and who knows, maybe that was a learned behaviour. Jackson was the emotional one, he'd openly cried. Perri seemed more controlled.

———————

Another few days passed. I visited my parents and told them about a tentative plan to study in America. As suspected, they were thrilled for me. My mum gushed about holidays on the beach; my dad beamed and was happy he'd be able to tell his friends his daughter was a doctor. I corrected him on that, of course, but he waved my correction away.

Perri and I talked on the telephone, she had texted Dexter, who told her to stay put with me. It took some convincing from me to allow Dex to work with Jackson, she had wanted for Dex to find a facility to take Jack in. To confine him would be his worst nightmare, I'd told her. I'd seen Dexter at work, I believed in him.

I received an envelope one morning, delivered by courier. I sat at my kitchen table and opened it. I pulled out a first class ticket with American Airlines, an open ticket and instructions that all I had to do was book a seat, it was paid for. Although there was no sender's name, I guessed it was from Perri. I texted my thanks.

You never know, you might be jumping on a plane tomorrow, so it's handy to have available, came her reply.

I dealt with the apartment sale and slowly started to pack up my belongings. I wasn't expecting to have to move for another few months, but it was an opportunity to 'clear out' my old life. I'd found some old memory cards from a camera and decided to take a look. I'd avoided anything with Dane for a long time after his death, it had been too painful, but I was ready to revisit my life with him and let it all go. I'd harboured such pain for so long, and it was only meeting up with Jack and that kiss the first night that I was able to set myself free.

I sat on the sofa with the laptop and downloaded picture after picture. It was with a little sadness that I realised the majority were of Jackson and me. If Dane was in the photograph, he was usually scowling. I began to remember times we had all been together and how fraught it had been. How jealous Dane was of Jack. But in all the photographs, I was laughing or smiling. I was having fun. I looked up at the mantel and the framed pictures of Dane and me. I had a smile on my face but I wasn't laughing. That smile never reached my eyes.

Had I ever been truly happy with Dane? We'd met and married quite quickly and I must have been in the beginning. It was in our last year of marriage that things started to change. He'd be out late a lot, stressed, bills were left unpaid, and it was only after his death that I realised why. He gambled, a lot. He owed money that I wasn't legally responsible for but felt obliged to clear.

———

My dad came to help move some boxes to their garage for storage. Other than a possible plan to return to California, I had no idea what I was going to do. And that plan wasn't concrete. I hadn't told Jackson and there was a small amount of doubt in the back of my mind. When he healed, when he recovered, would he still want me? Would I end up being a trigger that reminded him of the UK, of all the bad things? And more importantly, could I get over what I'd seen? If Jackson was bisexual, how would I feel about that?

It was killing me not being able to speak to him, not being able to see him or have him in my arms. It had been a week without any contact and each day I longed for him a little more. I was sure Dexter was right, this would help Jack but it was fucking hard for me. I played his favourite album, James Bay's, *Chaos and the Calm*, over and over. It was painful to hear the songs he'd sung, the song we'd danced to, but it did make me feel just a little closer to him.

CHAPTER NINETEEN

Jackson

Dexter was sitting on the deck with me, we'd had a long session that day and I was fucked. I didn't want to talk to him anymore, I didn't want to eat, I just wanted Summer, and to sleep.

"She saw you with Ted, do you remember that?" Dexter said.

"No, I remember every fucking thing but that."

For a few days, I'd been totally out of it, sedated I'd found out and, boy, was I pissed off with that. I was distraught to learn Summer had left, but I didn't blame her one bit. I'd confessed the one thing I didn't want to. Well, I wanted to, eventually, but not the way I did. To blurt that shit out while I was fucked up, bleeding, drugged—it was no surprise she had run and didn't want to speak to me. And as for what she saw? I had blocked that from my mind, I had no idea what I'd done, other than what I was told. It sickened me.

"Have you spoken to her? Does she ring to ask how I am?" I asked. I was desperate for news of Summer.

"Occasionally, but right now, I guess she needs time. Perri calls though."

"Why won't she ring me and ask?"

"Do you want her to?"

I stood from the daybed and paced. "Of course, I fucking want her to!"

"Then why don't you call her?" he asked.

I stopped my pacing and turned to look at him. "Because I'm scared, Dex. I can't hear the words that I know she'll say."

"What is it that you think she'll say?"

"That she wants nothing more to do with me, that she regrets coming here, that she's disgusted with me." My voice had trailed off into a whisper and I turned back to face the sea.

"Just keep your goal in mind, Jack. You want her back, you need to keep fighting the urges and work on yourself."

I sighed. That was easier said than done. I felt him pat me on the shoulder as he rose and left. I headed for the kitchen and pressed play on the music centre. I couldn't stand the silence. I grabbed a beer and took it back to the deck. At first, I wasn't concentrating on the lyrics of the song playing, but one line caught my attention. I listened to Paulo Nutini sing *Better Man*. Summer had told me once I had the same voice, gravelly. I recalled the day. We had been in a bar in London. I couldn't remember the song but I knew it was one I liked and knew the words to. I'd sung it as we danced. In fact, the more I thought, the more I realised, we'd danced a lot. We'd done a lot together full stop.

It was that fact that had caused the argument between Dane and me that night. He was pissed off that I hadn't wanted to visit a strip club with him after the bar trawl. I remember telling him that he had something wonderful at home, why the fuck would he want a stripper? The argument escalated from that point. He accused me of being in love with his wife, I spent too much time with her, and she only laughed when she was with me. All of that was true, I'd told him. I think I also told him that if she were mine I wouldn't be fucking every slut in town, and I wouldn't be squandering money in gambling dens. I'd be fucking her every night. He took a swing at me, I raised my arm to defend myself but he missed. I fought back, pushed him away. His body did a full rotation and he stumbled back against the low stone wall of the bridge we were on. I reached out to grab him, of course I did, but I wasn't quick enough.

I'd watched him fall; I heard the thump as the train hit him. It was a sickening sound. Then I heard the screech of the train's brakes as it came to a halt. I looked over the bridge; I couldn't see him. I could hear screams though. I was frozen to the spot with fear. A car pulled to a halt, a man approached me and all I could do was point. He called the paramedics, I think. The rest of the night was a blur.

I shook my head to clear the memory. No matter how much time had passed, it still made me sick to my stomach to think about that night. I was even sicker that I never told anyone what had really happened. I'd lied. To tell the truth would mean to tell Summer what we'd fought about, and at that point, I didn't want to tarnish her memory of him. Even after she'd found out about the child, I still kept quiet. I wanted her to think it was one indiscretion. The truth was, Dane was fucking her bridesmaid at their wedding and he'd continued to fuck anything that walked from that day on.

———

I drew a lot, all were pictures of her but not sexual ones. I drew her sitting on the beach, on the daybed. I drew her laughing and smiling. It was as I studied one picture of her face that I had an idea. I grabbed my phone and keys, locked up the house, and headed for the bar.

I had something to do. Dexter had said to give him some more art and I knew exactly what I wanted to do.

The front of the bar was just a brick wall, a miserable looking red brick wall with an iron door. There was nothing on the outside to indicate it was even a bar and Dex liked it that way. The people that visited were not the ones who were strolling the streets, looking for a drinking hole. They were people that knew Dex, knew D-J and me, and sought us and the bar out.

I wanted passion on that wall but not in the way Dex thought when I met him inside and explained my thoughts. He gave me free rein on the understanding that whatever it was I drew, if he hated it, it would be covered up. I agreed and grabbed my paints.

It took the best part of a week to complete, and every day Dex would stand beside me and smile at the progress. When it was done, I took a step back. It was just a painting of Summer's face, done in purple. She held a rose to her lips. Her eyes were why I then sprayed the word, 'Passion.' They were full of it. It was the eyes I saw when she looked at me, the eyes that I'd caused to shed tears, the eyes that sparkled when I held her; the eyes that had clouded with desire when I'd fucked her.

I took a photo using my phone. I wanted that piece of artwork framed. I wanted to be able to fall asleep each night looking at her and having those eyes bore straight to my soul.

"Fuck me," I heard.

D-J had climbed from his car and stood beside me.

"Most of your stuff is like, dark, fucked up mind shit. That is beautiful," he said with a laugh.

Between us we'd had a fucking rough week. His cheeks were as hollow as mine, his eyes dull and his normally tanned complexion gave way to a yellowish tint to his skin. Withdrawal was hard for him. But like me, he was determined to kick his habits.

"It can stay," Dex said. "Now, the bar needs cleaning up after last night. What the fuck goes on when I'm not here is beyond me. I might have to get behind that bar next week."

The previous night had been a raucous one. Not that anyone could tell, but D-J and my 'performances' were false. We didn't feel the party animals we portrayed ourselves to be. However, I liked being at the bar. It was less thinking time than if I had been alone. I didn't do alone anymore.

I finished the wall with my signature and packed up. I was covered in paint, the fumes had dried my throat, so I followed Dex in and grabbed a beer.

"You really should wear a face mask when you paint," Dex said as I gulped down a couple of mouthfuls.

I shook my head. "I could say something really deep like, I smell the paint, I feel the paint, I become the paint. But really I just don't like the thought of breathing in my own poison."

He raised his eyebrows at me. "Interesting."

I laughed, "I don't need analysing today."

"You need analysing every day. But it's nice to see you laugh."

"I'll get her back, one day." I placed my now empty bottle on the counter and with a wave over my shoulder, left for my car.

I drove along the coastline and pulled over before reaching the house. I sat for a while, just watching the beach, the surfers, the people, and the families. A few months ago just the sound of children laughing had my skin itching, it was a sound I didn't recall from my childhood. That day, however, I felt nothing but hope. I wanted to be a father, I wanted to father children with a wonderful auburn-haired, brown-eyed woman. I pictured our kids. Whose eye colour would be the dominant? Her brown ones or my blue?

When I arrived home, I sat on the daybed with my sketchpad and drew. I drew a family, the adults each holding the hand of a small child that they swung between them as they walked along the beach. I drew her standing naked, and as my eyes blurred with my tears, my pencil rounded her stomach and drew her hands held over it protectively. I never finished that drawing.

It had been a few weeks with no word from her. I'd typed many text messages but then deleted them. I hadn't returned any calls from Perri, not wanting her to pick up any sadness in my voice. Other than Dex and D-J, I didn't want anyone's help. I didn't want to drag anyone further into my pit. It was my problem to solve.

I thought of Honey a lot. No matter how many times D-J, even her sister, had told me she was on self-destruct and no one was ever going to help her, I felt guilty at the way I'd treated her. I didn't hold myself responsible for her death; I was rational enough for that. For a while we had helped each other, but that 'help' would have never healed us.

Dexter had told me her father had been arrested, finally. It was only then that her sister could speak of the horror the two girls had been subjected to. In my mind though, it was another mother who had failed her children. I wouldn't attend her service, I couldn't sit there and listen to the mother sob and wail at the injustice of life. The only injustice was that woman should have helped her daughter when her life spiralled out of control, even if she was totally oblivious to what her husband was doing.

I didn't want to think anymore, I wanted to 'do.' Maybe I was brushing aside my issues. Maybe I was unfair in my thoughts towards Honey's mum but dwelling, analysing, and apportioning blame, wasn't going to get me moving forward.

I didn't sleep well that night, and for the first time in a long while, it wasn't because I was in pain. A bubble of excitement had been building in my stomach at a plan that ran through my mind. I made notes, I scrolled through the Internet on my phone, and I made decisions.

———

"Well?" I said, after I'd explained my plan to Dexter.

We sat at the bar. D-J had his elbows resting on it and his chin in his hands. "I think it's a fucking awesome idea. I want in."

"We need to do a lot of research, Jack, on the legalities, the paperwork, the licences," Dex said.

"That's where Perri comes in. She's a lawyer, okay, a contracts lawyer but it can't be that hard for her to find out for us," I said.

"I like the idea. In fact, I think it's a fucking awesome, as cliché here says, idea." Dexter laughed.

"Less of the cliché. Can't help it, dude, if I'm the epitome of California," D-J said.

"Now we just have to figure out where to start," Dex said.

"Money. We need money first and I know where to get it, just not how," I said.

"You sure you want to do that? Won't that mean seeing you know who?" D-J asked.

"No, Perri has been managing it. It's mine by right, I just told him to shove it because it gave him control over me. And you know, say the word. My father, dad, daddy. It's not kicking off up here." I pointed to my head.

The word had been a trigger for a long time, and although only a short while ago it had, something had changed just by making the decisions I had. I was going to channel all that anger, all that frustration into something worthwhile. I was going to set up a facility to help damaged kids through art, through surfing if D-J had his way, and through therapy. Fuck knows how, but I was determined.

"I guess first port of call is, you need to get your licence to practice," I said to Dexter.

He had a demon to conquer. He had to overcome his fear that he'd misdiagnose again, and he had to legalise what he did at Passion.

"You weren't struck off, were you?" D-J asked.

"No, I quit. I wasn't fit to practice."

"But you are now," I said.

Dexter sighed. "I don't seem to be having much effect though, do I?"

"Dude, I'd be dead if it wasn't for you," D-J said.

"There's no way you'll be involved if you aren't clean, you know that, don't you?" I said to D-J.

"Yes, and until now I've never wanted to, if I'm honest. Maybe this project gives us all the incentive to sort our shit out," D-J replied.

We made plans, we got excited, but more importantly, we had a future mapped out, something we hadn't had before.

Dexter followed me to my car. "How are you, son?" he asked.

"Okay, I miss her. I need to talk to her at least. Can you ask her if she'll talk to me? I know you speak to her."

He nodded his head. I wasn't entirely sure he did, in fact, speak to her but I didn't believe she would leave without keeping any form of contact. Maybe that was conceited of me, but she'd want to know how I was doing, I was sure of that. It was my driving force. If I fell, she'd know about it and I'd blow any chance of getting her back. I cranked the music up in the car as I headed for the shack. Alfie wanted a little more art on his 'restaurant.'

"Hey, my man, Jackson. How the devil are you?" Alfie faked a British accent.

"I don't know anyone who uses that as a greeting, Alfie."

He chuckled as he handed over a bowl of rice and something unidentifiable.

"Taste, tell me what you think," he said.

"What is it?"

"Taste and tell me."

I took a small spoonful. "Fuck, Alfie. How much chilli do you have in this?"

"Too strong?"

"I'd say so. Jesus, give me drink, will you?"

He handed over a bottle of water, which did nothing to cool the burn in my mouth. Once my lips had stopped burning, I told him of my plan for the therapy centre. His smile grew broad as I detailed that I'd like to help children express their anxiety through art, D-J wanted to teach them to surf, not that we thought that was actually possible, but he'd be involved somehow. We needed therapists and I'd said that we wanted Dex to apply for his licence to practice in the U.S. I wanted a 'drop-in' centre not so much a therapy centre. I wanted kids to be able to walk into a safe environment when life got tough. If they wanted to spray paint a wall to let out their frustration, they could. If they wanted to sit and pencil draw quietly in a corner, they could. If they wanted to scream and shout, to blast out loud music to drown out the noise in their own heads, they could.

"I think it's an amazing idea," Alfie said.

I got to work to complete a side of art to his shack. It wasn't a shack as such, although it was wooden, it was a large beach hut of sorts. People drove for miles to eat his food or just sit with a beer on the sand. If there was ever a party, it was always at that part of the beach. He was a respected man, as was Dex. I remembered when I'd finished the first wall, the local officials had freaked and initially insisted it be repainted, it wasn't in keeping with the 'look' they wanted. The locals had started a petition to keep it. It was exactly what that part of town needed. It was urban, buzzing with a mix of nationalities, not so much a tourist area.

CHAPTER TWENTY

Summer

"Do you think you're ready?" Dexter said.

"I think so. It's been a few weeks now, is he ready? Is he ready to answer my questions without freaking out?"

Dexter had called me to ask if I wanted to speak with Jackson. He'd been doing well and it had excited me to hear that he was making plans for his future.

"I don't trust that he is in full recovery, just yet. He's gone a month without cutting before. As for answering your questions, is there ever a good time for that?"

"I talked to Perri, she wants to fly out. He didn't return her call recently."

"He didn't say she'd called. He has it in his mind that he needs to sort himself out before he speaks to her, though."

We finished our call and I sat for a while. I'd normally Skype Jackson but I was worried about actually seeing him. I was worried that I'd see his sadness, that he'd see mine. An idea came to me.

I settled on my bed and opened my laptop and the Skype app. My fingers shook a little as I dialled up his number. I watched a blue screen until it connected.

"Hey," he said after a slight pause.

I looked at his image on my screen. He'd lost weight, his cheeks were hollow, and his skin tone was pale.

"Hey," I replied.

"Turn your camera on, I can't see you," he said.

"I don't want to. I just want to talk."

He didn't answer immediately.

"I'm sorry. I miss you," he said. His voice caught and he coughed to disguise it.

"I'm sorry, too. How are you?"

It seemed a dumb thing to ask, really. I watched him sigh and bite down on his lower lip.

"I haven't done anything since you left. I'm determined, Summer. I don't want to live this way anymore. I know I've lost you, I hope it's only for now."

I let my fingers run over the screen, over his face and across his lips as tears rolled down my cheeks. I hadn't expected speaking to him, seeing him, to affect me the way it was. My heart was breaking at not being with him and in his arms.

"I'm glad to hear that, Jack."

"Is there any chance...?"

"I don't know yet. There are things I have to do, want to do, before I can think of us."

He looked dejected. "I understand. I mean, who the fuck would want to be with me right now?"

"Don't talk that way. I love you, Jack, that hasn't changed. I've seen and heard a lot that I need to get my head around before I can make any decisions."

My heart broke a little further at my words, words that were partly true.

"Ask me, Summer. Ask me about that night."

There was a pause as I replayed the things I saw in my mind.

"Are you gay?" I asked.

I saw him chuckle a little. "No, definitely not."

"Bisexual, then?"

He shook his head. "No."

"I don't understand then. How can you..." I struggled to finish my sentence.

Jackson took a deep breath, he let his head fall back, and he stared up at the ceiling. He didn't speak at first.

"I'm not sure how to explain it in a way that's easy to understand. In a way that doesn't make me look like an even bigger fuck-up. It's got nothing to do with sex; it could be anyone underneath me. It could be male or female, I..."

He was struggling. I watched him swallow hard. He ran his tongue over his lower lip before biting down on it. He looked around the room and I saw his brow furrow with, I imagined, frustration in finding the right words.

"Dexter said it was a power thing, maybe you're stripping your dad of control in your mind when you did...do that?"

"Yeah, I don't visualise my dad, you understand that, don't do?"

He seemed desperate for me to at least get that.

"I do. I just...well. What you did to me, the feelings you produced in my body, in my mind was like nothing I've experienced before. I'm confused that you can do that to me then..."

It seemed neither of us were able to actually say the words. I heard him sigh.

"I don't do that anymore, Summer. You have no reason to trust or believe a fucking word I say right now. I know it's going to take me a long time to gain your trust again, but know this; I love you. I've loved you from the moment I set eyes on you, and what we did bears no resemblance to what I've done to others."

"It's only been a month, Jack. What happens if you crash again?"

"I know, but I can promise you, if I do, that stuff won't happen again. Do you know how much it sickens me? Do you understand how much I hate myself? If I could erase all that, I would. I need you to forgive me, I need you to understand, that's not going to happen again."

"I just need a little more time, Jack."

"Will you come back? I want to tell you about that night, the night with Dane."

"I want to get this apartment sold and then decide what I'm going to do with my life. Nothing can change the past and knowing something different to what I've been led to believe isn't going to make any of it better, is it?" I tried to hide the bitterness from my voice.

"I should have been honest, but I didn't know if you'd believe me, I was protecting you. It's always been about you, Summer. Every choice and decision I made where Dane was concerned was always about you."

There was a short silence as I let his words digest.

"I keep listening to the songs you downloaded on my phone, they make me smile," I said.

"It's funny how a song, words, can do that."

I watched as he placed his palm to his screen, I did the same. I rested my hand on his.

"I dream of you, I draw you, all the time," he whispered.

"I..." I choked on my words. Emotion threatened to overwhelm me.

"Don't cry, baby. Please, don't cry. I've made you cry way more than I ever hoped I would, and it breaks my heart."

"I miss you."

"I can fly over. I'd pack up here tonight, Summer, if you just say the words."

"No, I don't want you to do that. You need to be there, you need Dexter and D-J."

"I need you more."

"I don't want you to need me, Jack. I need you to want me. When that happens, we'll find a way."

We fell silent as I let my words sink in. I saw him take a deep breath then release it slowly. He nodded slowly.

"Will you wait for me?" he asked.

How long for, though? How long would I wait before too much time had passed? Two weeks, two months, two years?

"Just concentrate on you, Jack. Get on top of your issues. No one is asking you to be 'cured' immediately."

I didn't want to add the words that were on the tip of my tongue. I didn't want to ask him to stay away from the women, from Ted, but I hoped that he did. I prayed that he'd choose to do that and find another way to cope.

"Can I call you tomorrow?" he said.

"Maybe, I don't want to be the reason you work on yourself. You have to do it for you. You have to want to stop the cutting, the...you know what I mean. When you've done that because you want to and not because I'm the goal, I'll never be your trigger, either. I can't walk on eggshells around you, not knowing if I'll say or do something that reminds you of your past. I don't want you flawless, Jack. But I want someone who I'll feel safe with."

"I scared you, didn't I?"

"Yes, and no. I wished to God I hadn't seen what I did, of course. It was the look on your face. A look of hatred for Ted. I want to know who he is but not now. We've said enough for now."

"I will do this for you, Summer. You're my goal because if I don't have that, I don't have a reason. You'll be the reason I will kick this, and when that happens you can decide if you feel safe enough, is that a deal? Give me that, at least."

"Okay," I said with a sigh. "I have to go now, it's way past my bedtime. Be safe, Jack."

"I love you, baby."

"I know you do." I whispered that I loved him too as I disconnected the call.

I closed my eyes and shut the laptop lid before placing it on my bedside cabinet. I climbed under the duvet and curled into a ball. That had been hard, but I was glad to have seen him, to hear his voice. I picked up my phone and scrolled through the music I had been playing. I selected a song, copied and pasted it to a text message. I smiled as I sent it to him. I then pressed play and listened to Mumford & Son's sing, *I Will Wait*.

———————

Two days passed before I met with Perri again, she had sent me a text wanting to meet at a coffee shop. I arrived early and ordered a latte. I took a seat near the window so I could watch out for her, and while I waited I opened my laptop to continue my research in courses at UC.

"I'm sorry I'm late," I heard as she took the seat beside me.

"Can I get you a coffee?" I asked.

"Got one waiting. They'll shout out my name when it's ready. I'm often tempted to give them a funny name to see what they do." As she finished her sentence her name was called.

"I found out how Jack got to know about my dad," she said, as she settled back after collecting her coffee.

"How?"

"The nurse. He asked her to send him a message. I'm still trying to work out where he got the number but I suspect that was from me, unfortunately. I'm the only one, other than you of course, that has his number. I wonder if he'd scrolled through my contacts one day."

"Did Jack ever reply?"

"No. Dad doesn't know where Jack is, I suspect. The nurse asked me some probing questions when I visited for some signatures. Have you spoken to him?"

I told her of the conversation we'd had, and that I thought he needed a little more time before we made a decision to head out to

California. She leaned over the table and took my hand in hers.

"He has to have you as a goal. You're the only thing that's important to him, Summer."

"I know, but it tears me apart each time I think of him and I'm worried. I'm not sure I can go back, yet I still love him. I have to get this, man thing, in my head straight. He's not gay, he's not bi, it's not a sexual thing, I understand all of that, but it still shocks me to the core when I think of what I saw."

She shook her head. "I told you before, he's loved you for a long time, that won't just fade away. No one ever measured up to you, you were all he spoke about."

"That's something that worries me, too. What if I don't measure up, Perri? What if I'm not the person he has built me up to be in his head?"

She smiled. "You're all he's built up and more."

"I've been searching for courses at UC, I have no idea how hard it's going to be to get in. I'm not sure I have the grades."

"That's something else I've been working on. An old uni friend of mine knows someone who knows someone. There seems to be a drive for overseas students."

"I've got the contracts through for the apartment, I'm going to mail those back to the solicitor this afternoon. I know you said to give them to you to check through, but I just want done with it all. I want to hand over that money, let the solicitor deal with it because that way, I've got no reason to be involved or reminded anymore."

"Fair enough. And having a little money in the bank will help with your student visa, too. I have some information on that, although UC will help, should you be offered a place."

She handed me a stack of paperwork that I folded and placed

in my bag to read later.

"I'm having the house signed over to Jack, as part of his trust. He has to buy it from me for a nominal fee, but that way he at least will always have somewhere to live. And I'm in the process of unlocking the trust and moving it to another bank. I think that will be the best way to safeguard it."

"Why now?"

If Perri could move his trust around, why wait until now?

"Because until now, Dad has always been in control. We have a board of directors, of course, but they never knew why Jack didn't access his account. I won't tell them, just let them know that he prefers another bank more accessible to him in the U.S."

"How is he able to stay in the U.S.? Surely he needs a visa himself," I asked. It was a question that had come to me in the early hours of the morning.

She smiled and raised her eyebrows. "He never told you?" I shook my head.

"He was born in America. Our mother was American."

"I never knew that. I wonder why he never said."

"He came to the UK when he was just a few months old, so he has no memory of being there."

"So you were, what, two years old?"

"Yes, consequently neither of us has an accent. My mother was from Boston; she met my father when he was on a business trip, I think. They got together and flew back and forth. I know we still have relatives there, although I imagine them to be distant. My mother was an only child and her parents died a long time ago."

"Does he have two passports? How does that work?"

"He travels on a U.S. one. If you're born in the U.S., you retain citizenship for life."

"I didn't know that. There's another thing I remembered last night. Dexter said he doesn't have medical insurance, is that something we need to sort out? Jack can't afford it, I guess. He earns from his art but I imagine not enough to keep paying a monthly fee."

"Yes, we do. I'll be honest, I just assumed it would be something he'd arranged."

We continued to chat, drink our coffee, and plan. We were both in touch with Dexter on a regular basis, as we didn't trust Jack to necessarily be honest with us.

———

"Is that the last one?" my dad said as he loaded a cardboard box into the back of a hired van.

I nodded my head, holding back the tears. "I'll take one look around and then I'll meet you at home," I said.

I watched him drive away, leaving me standing on the pavement outside my apartment block. I watched cars speed up and down the road, I watched people walk by, some smiling, some sad looking. I turned and headed back in. I took the lift to my floor and then walked into my empty apartment.

It hadn't taken long to pack all my belongings, I didn't own a great deal. I stood in the empty living room, recalling memories: Dane and I sitting on the sofa, watching a movie. We never snuggled, the more I thought about it, there was always distance even when we were at our closest.

I walked to the bedroom and checked empty cupboards. I stood where my bed had been, looking at the slightly different shade of carpet. It wasn't nights with Dane that came to mind, though. It was

Jackson. I relived the passion and desire he'd brought out in me. I'd loved Dane, but not the way I loved Jack. What Jack and I had was so much deeper. There was a connection that went way beyond anything Dane and I shared and that saddened me in a way. Had all my married life been a farce?

I walked back out of the apartment, locked the door, and took a slow walk down the stairs. I shut the main door and took the short walk to the estate agent, where I handed over the keys. That was it; the past three years were finished, packed up in small cardboard boxes and stored in a garage.

I made my way back to the car park and collected the car I barely drove. There had been no real need for a vehicle where we lived. I pulled out into the traffic, towards the motorway and my parents' house. It was going to be home until I could decide what my next move was to be.

I'd emailed UC for an application to start a course I'd selected. I'd completed the student visa forms, just in case. All I had left to do was wait. I'd wait for Jackson to be in a position to start his life with me.

CHAPTER TWENTY-ONE

Jackson

From the moment I'd made the decision that I wanted to do something for troubled kids, from the moment I decided that my life had to change, I had thrown myself into my plans. I wasn't someone who did things by half. Dexter and I decided that a vacant building next to the bar would be a perfect location for our drop-in centre. After borrowing a little money from Perri, we managed to secure a tenancy and set about cleaning the place up. It housed a large empty room that we'd fit with tables, chairs, workspaces, and sofas for relaxing. There was a kitchen and what looked like an old office. We decided the office space would become a therapy room.

I spent days creating a wall of art. It wasn't the usual dark, hell on earth stuff that I often painted. I wanted bright, fun, and cheerful. Even the usually lazy D-J did his bit. He cleaned and polished the wooden floor, and fixed windows with new locks that would open. He rigged up a music centre, arrived one day with a collection of two-seater sofas even. We didn't ask where he'd obtained them. D-J came from a wealthy family, and although he kept away from them, he had never worked yet seemed to have access to money.

The local authorities came regularly to inspect and demand, to set in place rules, yet refused to financially contribute. More importantly, Dexter enquired about how to obtain his licence to practice.

I called my sister a couple of times, she told me about my trust being moved and I'd soon have access. I'd been too afraid to actually ask how much it was worth. I'd learned to live so frugally over the past year or so. She also told me that I had bought her house.

"How? Did you fake my signature again?" I'd asked.

Her chuckle had me not wanting to know any more. She was a lawyer! When I'd arrived home that evening, I walked through the house inspecting it. I'd been there for nearly a year but never really taken the time to get to know each room. I hesitated outside the bedroom door that Summer had slept in. I hadn't been in that room since she'd left. I took a deep breath and turned the handle.

She had stripped the bed and piled the sheets on the end. I bundled them into my arms. She'd left some toiletries in the bathroom, and I smiled hoping that meant she planned on returning.

I took the sheets to the laundry room and loaded the washing machine. It was while I was in that room that I saw the sweater

Summer had placed under my head. I picked it up. There was a faint hint of her scent as I raised it to my face. I folded it and placed it on a shelf.

All the time I kept busy, I didn't think. I avoided looking into a mirror for fear of seeing my scars. The last few hadn't healed very well. Raised, angry lines ran across my stomach and occasionally I'd run my hands over them to remind myself.

The urge to cut was still there, the need to fuck simmered, but I fought both. The only person I wanted to fuck wasn't in the same country and I'd wait for her. It was as I thought of that, I remembered the song she'd sent me. I pulled my phone from my pocket and played it. I'd played it many times over and it gave me hope.

I focused and worked hard. I drew, I ran way more than I'd ever before, and I sat every day with Dexter in therapy, which often exhausted me. We spoke in depth about some of my issues, skirted around others. I confessed to missing Honey, I wanted to be honest. Although there was no relationship between us, in a conventional sense, I was saddened by her death.

Dexter had revisited his old office at his house, the office that held all his notes, records, and study papers from his days in Australia and then New Orleans. He slowly brought that office to the drop-in centre.

Dexter, D-J, and I sat down one evening to write a list of rules for those that used the centre. We knew we couldn't counsel; that was for Dexter and we'd need to find another volunteer for that. But D-J and I could be around to talk and listen.

"I'm so stoked for this," D-J said as he handed over three beers.

We were sat on my balcony watching the sun set.

"Same. Did I tell you I now own this house? Perri did some of her magic and worked it into my trust," I said.

"Fuck, that's awesome. So you're definitely staying then?"

"After what we've done the past few weeks, you thought I was leaving?"

"No, but I wondered, what with Summer being in the UK," he said.

My happy mood slipped just a little. "I'm hoping I can persuade her to come back, at least for a visit. I don't know what's going to happen there but somehow, one day, I'll have her back."

"So how much money do you have?" D-J asked, rather bluntly.

"I have no idea. I don't want to actually know. The bills get paid, that's all I'm interested in. I need a laptop, I want to pay Dex for the car, but other than that, it will stay a secret I guess."

"Did you sort out medical insurance?" Dex asked.

"I did, well, Perri did," I said with a laugh. Perri sorted everything, she always had.

The guys finished their beers and left. I sat and thought. If Summer didn't want to come back, I'd get on bended knees and beg if I had to. She was all I thought about, day and night. She was the reason for every thing I intended to do. I wasn't religious at all, but that night I sent up a prayer in the hope it would be answered. I asked that Summer would come to me.

I couldn't return to the UK all the time 'he' was alive, I didn't think I ever wanted to return permanently. I had a house on a beach, friends, and a lifestyle many would be envious of, yet I was lonely. All that was left was to hope that Summer would make my life complete. The nights were the worst. I longed to have her in my bed, in my arms. My fucking wrist ached with the constant masturbation

I needed to release the frustration I felt.

It was early hours of one morning, and I was still awake, when I thought of a way to tell Summer how I really felt. I grabbed a pad and pen and wrote. I tore page after page from the pad and screwed each into a ball. The floor around the bed was littered. As the sun rose, I thought I had the message I wanted to convey. I jumped from the bed and opened one wardrobe, sitting on the top shelf was an old guitar. Bridge had given it to me after it had been left unclaimed in the shop. I wasn't a great guitarist, I could strum a few chords, but I blew the dust from it.

I sat back on the bed and spread the pad alongside me. I familiarised myself with the strings and chords and then I sang the song I'd written. It wasn't going be a bestseller but it was from the heart. Another thought crossed my mind. I jumped from the bed and headed outside. It was early enough not to have any noise disrupt the sound of the waves as they broke on the shore. I held my phone slightly in the air and recorded the sound. I then scrolled through my app store to find something, at first, I thought impossible. I found an app to record my heartbeat.

When you can't sleep, baby, listen to this. This is my heart beating. This is the sound of the waves breaking on the shore. Both are waiting for you, Jack x

I attached the recordings and pressed send. As soon as I did, I regretted it. The sentiment was right but the wording a little stalkerish. I didn't want her to feel pressured; I just wanted to send her the two sounds she'd told me relaxed her.

I need that tonight, thank you. Summer x

I smiled at her reply. I decided to head for a run then try to get to some sleep. It concerned me that I was turning nocturnal and I'd need to get my sleep patterns back on track. I'd initially dismissed Dexter's thoughts that it might have something to do with being alone and in the dark. I'd slept alone for years with no issues, but now, I wasn't sure. When I thought about it, I never closed the curtains; there was always a sliver of light somewhere. Since receiving that text from my father, everything in my life had been turned upside down. I'd never replied, and I hadn't deleted it either.

I popped in some earbuds and ran. I listened to all my favourite songs while my feet pounded along the wet sand where the waves broke. I enjoyed the solitude, I enjoyed the way my heart pumped harder to keep the oxygen flowing through my bloodstream, and I enjoyed the sweat that rolled down my body.

When I returned to the house, I showered and lay on the bed. I thought about that text message and reached for my phone.

This is your father. I wanted to let you know that I'm dying. I have cancer and not a great deal of time left. You should visit.

There was nothing particularly friendly about his text, it was business-like but that was him all over. Dexter had asked me if I'd have any regrets by not replying, by not visiting. I'd have no regrets at all. There was nothing he could say to me that would make up for the years of abuse. There was nothing he could do that would turn back time and make me forgive him. Although my skin itched with urge, although his voice rang out in my head, both weren't as powerful as they once were. I deleted his message.

I slept on and off during the day, showered again and then headed to the bar. It was another raucous night but word had got around that we planned a drop-in centre and after offers of donations, D-J placed a wine bucket at the end of the bar.

After checking the time, I decided to Skype Summer. I tried not to text or Skype on a daily basis, I was sure that wasn't something she wanted, but it was hard not to either see or hear from her.

"Hey," she said when she connected and that time she had her camera on.

"Hi, you look tired. Are you sleeping okay?" I asked.

"Not really. I guess I miss my own place. Mum and Dad are great but it's not the same. I didn't really expect to move back home at my age."

She sounded sad and I wished I could have reached out to hug her.

"We should be opening the drop-in centre soon, just waiting on some paperwork," I said.

"Tell me about it, it sounds interesting."

I watched as she leaned back against the headboard of her bed. I told her all that we'd been up to, how excited I was about the project, and how much I thought the whole process had been a healing one.

"I'm so pleased for you, Jack. You look healthier. I like to hear your voice when you're excited about something, you sound so upbeat."

"What can I do, Summer? To make you smile?"

"Be happy, get well, just talk to me, Jack."

"Do you want to see the beach?"

"Yes, take me to beach."

I stood from my bed and took my phone to the balcony. I panned it around slowly, hoping she could see and hear the sounds I knew she loved.

"How was that?" I asked.

"It looks so beautiful, I miss it."

I noticed the 'it' and not 'me' as I walked back to my bedroom. "Come back, no pressure, you don't have to stay with me but come back for a while."

She didn't answer immediately. "Maybe, soon."

I wanted to ask when, I wanted to make plans but I knew I couldn't. I had to let her come to me when she was ready, when she wanted to and not because she thought I needed her, but it was hard not to ask.

"D-J's doing good. He's really up for the challenge. Did I tell you he turned up in a rusting old pickup with three sofas in the back?"

She did smile then. "No, where did he get them from?"

"No idea, didn't ask," I said with a laugh. "And Dexter is applying for his licence to practice. We need a therapist at the centre, possibly two."

I watched as she placed her fingertips on the screen. "Hold my hand, Jack," she said.

I covered them with mine and heard her sigh. "I want to wrap my arms around you right now, take away your sadness. I want to whisper into your ear until you fall asleep and then hold you all night," I whispered.

"I want that too."

We fell silent for a few moments. "Lay down, Summer."

I watched as she climbed under her duvet and placed her laptop beside her head.

"Close your eyes and just listen to me. I wrote a song for you, baby."

I propped my phone on a pillow and leaned down beside the

bed to pick up my guitar.

"You can play the guitar?" she asked.

"Not very well, I know a few chords that's all."

I strummed my fingers over the strings and sang the song I'd practiced and committed to memory.

When it's dark inside, I think of you, I dream of you.

I see the light that surrounds you, and peace washes over me.

Although you're so far away, I have you in my heart.

It hurts, and that's okay. One day I'll set that pain free.

I don't wanna look back, I don't wanna look down.

I want to take one step at a time, one step at a time.

Always moving forward with you by my side.

I'll learn how to heal; I'll learn how to breathe.

I'll love my scars as a reminder.

Of a time when it was dark inside. And I'll think of you, I'll dream of you.

I hadn't gotten to the second verse before I noticed her eyelids droop. I watched her fall asleep and when her breathing deepened, I logged off.

CHAPTER TWENTY-TWO

Summer

When I woke, I was surprised to see the sun high in the sky; its rays brightening the room. I checked my watch. I'd slept for nearly twelve hours straight. I smiled as I looked at my laptop, which had put itself to sleep. I closed the lid and chuckled. Jackson had written a song for me. He wasn't going to win any awards for it, but he'd done that for me. No one had ever done anything like that before.

I stretched and climbed from the bed. I could hear movement downstairs as I made my way to the bathroom. I showered and dressed before joining my mum in the kitchen.

"Morning, or is it afternoon?" she said with a laugh.

"I haven't slept that well in ages. I spoke to Jackson on Skype, he sang a song to me, I must have fallen asleep halfway through."

"He's such a nice guy. I hope you can work things through with him. Take a seat, I want to talk to you."

I had told my mum a little of what happened in California, she had placed her arm around my shoulders and told me how proud she was of the way I was handling it all.

"Do you love him?" she asked.

"I do, and I hate to say this but more than I loved Dane. Does that make me terrible?"

"No, it makes you lucky. After what you've been through, you deserve Jackson. For all his faults and troubles, he obviously loves you, he's loved you for a long time, by all accounts."

"I know. I thought I was doing the right thing, this staying away from him, so he has a goal, but I don't know how long I can do that and then..."

"And then what, darling? Are you hesitant because of us?"

"Yes. I don't want to be so far away."

Mum smiled and took my hand in hers.

"If you stay here, if you lose that chance of a second love with Jackson, that would break my heart far more than you being only a few hours away. You need to go, you need to start a new life, and all the time you are here, you'll be reminded of what an utter shit Dane was."

"Mum!" That was the first time I'd ever heard my mum curse, albeit a fairly mild curse word.

"He was, it was just a shame that we didn't see it before. I think that disappoints me the most, he fooled us all. You have the money from the sale of the apartment and Dad and I have money saved for you. We want you to go, we want you to study, get that degree and do some good with your life. Don't sit here and fester, there are no prospects here for you, you know that."

"Thanks and, thanks, I guess," I said with a laugh.

"You know what I mean, you'd need to move back to London to get a decent job. Most of your salary will be taken up with rental and for what? You'll be miserable because he isn't with you. Go, heal that man, and enjoy being in love. What I wouldn't give to live on a beach!"

"I can't go until I know what's happening with the course," I said.

"Yes, you can, you can wait it out there. You don't want to be here, I can see that. Every day since you arrived, you've looked a little sadder, more so after you've spoken to him. Book that flight, Summer. Do it for me and your dad, if nothing else."

I slid from the stool I had been sitting on and rounded the table. I wrapped my arms around my mum and held her tight. For the first time in days, I smiled.

"Oh my God, I'm going to do it. I won't tell him, I'm just going to arrive," I said, trying hard to control the excitement.

I picked up my phone and called Perri. I told her of my plans and had to pull the phone away from my ear to avoid a burst eardrum from her squeal. I then sent a text message to Dex. I wasn't sure what his response would be, but I'd stayed away from Jack long enough. I had no idea what would happen to us, I had no idea if I could put aside those memories of my last night there, but I had to try.

Mum spent the next two days washing, ironing, and packing my suitcase, not that I wasn't capable of doing it myself, of course. Dad handed me an envelope with instructions not to open it until I had arrived, I stuffed it in my flight bag. I emailed UC and explained that although I was waiting on a decision, I would be making the journey to California anyway. I hoped it might help speed up my application.

"Hey, how are you?" Dexter said when I'd taken his call.

"Good, excited. How is he? He doesn't know I'm coming but I can't wait any longer, Dex. I'm sorry. I need to be there."

He chuckled. "He's doing good. I'll pick you up at the airport if you text me over your flight time."

"That would be amazing. I think Perri is going to fly over in a week's time as well. She's desperate to see him, too. And I'm still waiting on a decision from UC, the new year starts in a couple of months, would they normally leave it this late?"

"I don't know, let me see what I can find out. If you miss the chance at UC it's no problem, I've found some other courses you might want to take first."

"What happened with your licence application?"

"It's in the process, we have the final papers for the drop-in centre, so as soon as I'm licenced, we're ready to go."

"What did you call it?"

"We haven't, I guess we should give it a name," he said with a laugh.

We said our goodbyes and I texted him the flight details. I couldn't eat that evening; I didn't sleep. Excitement bubbled inside me. The sun hadn't risen as I hugged my mum on the doorstep, both of us trying our hardest not to cry. Dad packed my luggage into the boot of the car and we made our way to the airport.

I tried to be cheerful; I tried not to cry when he dropped me off. I hugged him tight as he kissed the top of my head and waved me off. He'd told me he didn't want to come into the airport, he cited the growing traffic as an excuse to rush off, but I saw him wipe his eye as he climbed back into the car.

I had three hours before my flight would leave, three hours of sitting on a hard plastic chair or a crowded coffee shop. I tried to read, the noise of the airport distracted me. I shopped, well, browsed; I didn't want to waste money on duty-free goods. Eventually I saw that my flight was being called.

———

It had been the longest journey I'd ever experienced. I tried to sleep a little, read, and listened to music. I even watched a movie. When the plane touched down in California, I couldn't stop the broad smile. It took forever to get through the airport and I panicked a little at immigration. I watched as the brow furrowed of a rather intimidating officer. He would know that I'd been in the U.S. only a short while before and he questioned me thoroughly. My heart hammered in my chest as I explained that I was applying for a student visa, but in the meantime wanted to explore the university first hand. I had friends, I gave Jackson's address, I had money to support myself and eventually I was let through. I collected my suitcase and made my way out. Dexter was standing in the hall, waiting for me. He spread his arms wide and pulled me into a fierce hug.

"It's so good to have you back. Did you have any trouble?" he asked.

"No, the immigration man questioned me but I guess he was happy with my response. I mean, I am allowed here on a tourist visa for now."

He took my suitcase, pretending to damage his back as he dragged it behind him, and we made our way to his car.

"Is he at home?" I asked.

"He is, I called him earlier and asked what he was doing today. He said he was working on some new designs at home. I guess that means he's drawing."

"Be a nightmare if I get there and he's gone out."

"I'll hang about for a moment, let you greet him yourself."

"Thank you. I can't believe how nervous I am."

My palms sweated the closer to the house we got. Dex pulled up just short of the drive and I climbed from the car. I walked around the side of the house, down the little path and along the beach. I couldn't see him on the balcony but his bedroom door was open. I smiled as I kicked off my shoes and climbed the steps. I crept along the decking. I could hear his shower running as I stepped into his room. I stood quietly and waited. I heard the water shut off, I heard something fall into the sink, I imagined, and him curse. Then I heard the pad of his bare feet on the wooden floor as he left the room. He walked into the bedroom with just a towel around his waist, water dripped from his body. He came to an abrupt halt. For a moment neither of us spoke. We just stood in the centre of his bedroom, looking at each other.

He strode towards me, his hands grabbed the sides of my face and his mouth was immediately on mine. I wrapped my arms around his shoulders and my fingers gripped the hair at the base of his neck. His kiss was fierce, like the others, he took my breath away. His fingers dug into the side of my face and I felt his tears on my cheeks.

When we broke apart, he rested his forehead on mine.

"You came," he whispered.

"I did. I tried to stay away longer but I couldn't."

"I didn't think you'd come back."

"I guess I was always coming back, Jackson. I just had to give you time and space."

I heard the clunk of a suitcase being dragged up the stairs.

"How did you get here?" Jackson asked, before looking over my shoulder towards the noise.

"Dexter," I said.

"You can leave the case there, we'll see you tomorrow, maybe," he said.

Jackson returned his gaze to me, his eyes clouded, and my pulse rate increased. He ran his fingers down my cheek and his thumb grazed over my lips. Nothing was said as he ran his hands down my sides and to the hem of my t-shirt and pulled it over my head. He lowered his head to the side of my neck. I felt his sigh against my skin as he kissed. He reached behind me and unclipped my bra, as his mouth travelled over one shoulder, he slid the straps down and it fell to the floor.

He took me by surprise when he lifted me in his arms and walked me to his bed. He gently laid me down and whipped off his towel. He climbed on the bed and sat astride my thighs. Way too slowly, he undid my jeans and I lifted my hips as he slid them, and my panties, down. He rose to his knees so I could kick them off.

He placed his palms on my stomach, slowly circling my skin and leaving a tingle. He ran his hands upwards until each cupped a breast.

"I know this body so well," he whispered.

He lowered his head and took a nipple in his mouth; he held it between his teeth just flicking the hard nub with his tongue. I ran my hands through his wet hair and moaned. He rolled to my side and slid his hand down my stomach, his fingers brushed over my tattoo, and then further down, until they caused an electric shock to wash over me. He teased my clitoris until I raised my hips off the bed.

I heard him chuckle as he inserted two fingers inside me. At the same time, I pulled his head towards mine. I took his lower lip between my teeth and bit down, I heard him hiss at first, and as I applied more pressure, a growl rumbled from his chest. He pulled away.

"Be careful," he whispered before kissing me hard. I could taste the faint tang of blood on his lip.

His fingers stroked, faster and deeper. His mouth travelled down my throat, kissing and licking a path down my chest as he slid down the bed.

"Come for me," he said. His breath skimmed over my skin, skin burning with heat.

With his fingers stroking, he positioned himself between my thighs. He lowered his head and as I was about to come, his tongue swiped over my clitoris. He fucked me with his fingers, with his tongue, as the most intense waves of heat, of desire, and of static coursed through my body. I cried out his name as I let go and spiralled into an orgasm.

Before I'd caught my breath, I felt his cock at my entrance. He held himself above me and I opened my eyes to look at him. His lips glistened and I watched as he licked them.

"I love you, Summer," he said as he pushed inside.

At first he moved so slowly, so deliberately but I wanted more.

I wanted hard and deep. I wrapped my legs around his waist and my arms around his back. I dug my nails into his skin and his eyes darkened.

"Be. Careful," he hissed through gritted teeth.

"Fuck me hard," I whispered, as I dragged my nails down his back.

He did. He fucked me until my body jerked up the bed, until my legs ached from holding him tight, and until my heart hammered in my chest so hard, it hurt. Sweat rolled from his forehead, his arms shook as he held himself above me until he sank to his elbows. And until an orgasm rolled over me that had tears spring to my eyes.

He wasn't done with me though. Once I'd relaxed my legs back on the bed, he pulled out and rolled me over. He lifted my hips, as he had done once before, until I was on my knees.

"Hold the headboard," he said. I complied.

He pushed into me again and at the same time reached around to tease my clitoris. His other hand held my hip, his fingers dug into my skin as his release built. I buried my face into the pillow to stifle my moans. My hands gripped the headboard so tight they ached, but each time he thrust into me I pushed back against him. He let go of my hip and wrapped his hand in my hair; he pulled my head up. His fingers worked faster, he slammed into me hard and I screamed out his name. As my body shook, as tears rolled down my cheeks, he let go himself.

"Fuck," he said as he came.

He pulled out of me and I slumped onto the bed, he lowered himself until he lay beside me. I turned my head to face him.

"Wow," I said.

244

He chuckled. "Not bad, especially since it's been a long time."

He reached out to tuck a strand of hair behind me ear.

"One thing, Summer. Be careful when you test me. Right now, I have restraint, one day I might not."

"When I test you?"

"Yeah, when you mark my body, when you draw blood. When I taste that, something fires off in my brain. When I feel your nails on my skin, I want more."

I looked at him for a little while; there was something in his eyes. When he spoke that way his eyes darkened, his pupils dilated. The normal bright blue became sapphire in colour.

"When you need it, I can give it," I whispered.

"It's an addiction I'm trying to kick, remember? Although I think I might have just found something to replace it. Do you know how fantastic you taste?"

I gasped and widened my eyes. "I'm not sure fantastic is the word I'd use."

"If you weren't filled with my cum, I'd run my fingers over your pussy and have you suck it off."

My breath hitched in my throat at his words. I turned on my side to face him. "And talking of my cum, let's hope one of those little fuckers does his job right."

I laughed out loud. "On the pill, as you well know, and no, not yet."

I was surprised by his comment but didn't want to pursue it. I wanted children, in the future, but bearing in mind his issue over his mother, the comment wasn't something I expected from him.

Jackson pulled the sheet over us and although it was mid-morning, he wrapped his arms around me.

CHAPTER TWENTY-THREE

Jackson

It felt so good to have her in my arms, to inhale the scent of her. When I'd seen her standing in my bedroom, my mind froze initially. I'd hope she'd return; I had no idea it would be so soon.

"What made you come back?" I asked.

"I think, in the back of my mind, I was always coming back. I just needed to give us both time. We spoke about it."

"We?"

"Dexter and me. We've been speaking over the past month, I often rang to find out how you were."

"He never said. I'm not entirely sure I like decisions being made about me."

"It worked though, didn't it? You haven't done anything, have you?" She hesitated over her words.

"I haven't cut, and other than fucking my wrist up with the constant wanking, I've been waiting for you for anything else."

I watched her blink a few times at my words, and then a large grin spread over her face. She started to laugh until tears rolled down her cheeks.

"Are you laughing or crying?" I asked, concerned.

"Both, I think. Oh, Jack. I've missed you so fucking much."

I pulled her close to my chest and sighed. "You have no idea how much I want you here. I even thought about flying home. I'd do anything for you; you know that, right? I will kick this, it'll take time, but I don't want that life anymore. I want something else, I want you and a future."

"But can you stop, just like that?" she asked.

"I doubt it, but when you left all I focused on was you. I drew you, I pictured you in my mind, it drove out the shit and his voice."

"Will you tell me about that night, the night Dane...?" she whispered.

I didn't need to ask what she meant. "You asked me that once before, would it make a difference?"

"I don't know, but you know exactly what happened and I don't want any doubts about you keeping things from me. Good or bad, tell me the truth?"

"He was never faithful to you, Summer, and that killed me. It killed me that he didn't know what he had in you. It killed me that your face lit up when you saw him, and I knew what he'd been doing just a half hour before. I hated him; I hated what he did. I stuck around because of you. We'd been to a bar with a couple of the guys.

Dane wanted to go to a strip club, there was one he used a lot.

"We got drunk and I got pissed off watching him. I wanted to leave, he didn't, but I wasn't about to sit around anymore, knowing what he'd do. I left, and he followed. We walked across the bridge and he started shouting at me, he asked me outright if I loved you and if that was why I hung around. I told him that was true, so he took a swing at me. I pushed him away but he kept on swinging, rotating until he'd backed up to the wall and lost his balance. He fell. I didn't get to him quick enough."

She stayed silent for a while. "But you said you killed him."

"If I'd stayed in the club, if I'd kept my mouth shut, it wouldn't have happened. If I'd done the right thing and stayed away from you, it wouldn't have happened."

I shifted slightly on the bed so I could look at her. Tears rolled down her cheeks as she silently cried. I brushed my thumb under one eye catching them.

"I'm so sorry. I never told you because then I'd have to tell you why we argued. I'd have to tell you everything he did."

"You're not telling me anything. Did he fuck those women?"

"Yes."

She slowly nodded her head. "Why didn't I know? Why was I not good enough?" she asked.

"You were too good for him, Summer. Way too good."

"Am I good enough for you?"

"You're more than I could ever dream for, ever hope for. I'm the one not good enough. I want to be, though."

———

Other than to collect Summer's suitcase and to get some bottles of water, we didn't leave the bed that day. I fucked her repeatedly; I had her screaming out my name, over and over. I watched her ride me like she'd never experienced that before. Sweat glistened on her body and tears rolled down her cheeks as she came. As the sun began to lower, she fell asleep in my arms.

Her tear-stained cheeks were flushed long after her breathing had deepened. Her hair was a tangled mess, fanned around her face. Her lips were slightly swollen from our kisses. I didn't think she'd ever looked as beautiful as she did then. I grabbed my pad and sat up. I drew her. Her naked body lay on top of a tangled sheet; her lips were slightly parted as she drew in breaths. The only colour was her butterfly tattoo.

I stared at her for a long time, I had no need to commit her to memory, I'd done that years ago. I knew every inch of skin, from the subtle childhood scar on her shin to the small freckles smattered across her nose. I could smell our sex; it permeated the room. It made my mouth water at the thought and my cock twitch, again. I smiled as I placed the pad on the bedside cabinet and gently rose from the bed. I quietly walked to my wardrobe and pulled on a pair of shorts. I left her sleeping and headed for the kitchen. I hadn't eaten and after that workout, I was starving.

I raided the fridge for some cold meat and I buttered sliced bread. I loaded a plate with my sandwich, grabbed a beer, and headed for the balcony. I sat on the daybed and watched the moon reflect off the sea. Maybe my prayers had been answered after all.

I heard the shower run and waited for her. She appeared in a pair of panties and a vest top. She smiled as she walked towards me and wordlessly snuggled on the daybed next to me. She picked up my arm and placed it around her neck before she settled down.

"Hungry?" I asked.

"Mmm," she replied, before she reached over and took half of my sandwich.

I handed her my beer and watched her mouth close around the rim.

"What are you smirking at?" she asked after she'd taken a drink.

"Just imagining how your mouth would look around my cock."

I hadn't let her suck me off, she'd wanted to, but our day in bed had been all about her. It was all about pleasuring her in every way I could.

"You have a wonderful way with words, Jackson."

"I know. Now don't tell me that didn't have you squirming."

"Funny enough, no. Although, I do look forward to knowing what your cock bar feels like in my mouth. I have to admit, it feels pretty amazing everywhere else," she said then gave me an innocent smile.

"Keep talking dirty to me, baby, and you'll get your wish right here."

"I've missed your smart mouth," she said with a laugh.

"Judging by how often you took advantage of me in there, that's not all you missed."

She raised her eyebrows at me. I gave her a wink.

"I applied to UC while I was at home. I want to retrain to be a therapist," she said.

"That's fucking amazing. Did you get in?"

"I don't think so, the new year starts in a few weeks and I haven't heard a word."

"I'm sure there are other places you can train. Did you speak to

Dex?"

"He's going to investigate for me. It would have been handy to get a student visa, I was told that would be quicker and easier."

"I take it you intend on staying then?"

"For now," she said.

She took the bottle from my hands and placed it on the ground, I did the same with the plate. She shuffled her body until she was straddling my thighs, and with her lower lip between her teeth, she lowered my shorts. My cock sprang free and she clasped her hand around it.

I watched as she lowered her head and her tongue licked the length of my shaft, pausing slightly over my piercing. She opened her mouth and took me in. Her long hair fell to the side and hid her face. I wanted to watch her. I wrapped my hand in her hair and held it to the back of her head. I encouraged her lower; I wanted to feel the back of her throat.

I felt her grip tighten and saw her eyes water; I chuckled a little.

"We're going to need to train that gag reflex of yours," I said.

Her response was to run her teeth along the underside of my cock. I removed my hand from the back of her head and lay back, enjoying her pleasuring me. She sucked hard, she licked, her hands slid up and down my shaft before her nails gently scraped over my balls. I felt my stomach muscles tighten and my cock pulsed in her hand. She raised her head and continued to pump, my cum spurted over my stomach, catching in her hair.

"I don't think I'm very good at that," she said, as she slid her body up mine. She rested her head on my chest.

"Wouldn't have come if you weren't, but you're welcome to practice any time you like."

She looked up at me, her chin rested on her folded arms across my chest.

"When I fuck your mouth, for real, I want all of it," I said.

"I've only ever had sex with Dane, and you of course. I guess I have a lot to learn."

"And I'll enjoy teaching you." I brushed my fingers through her hair, cupping her face and pulling her towards me for a kiss.

"How many women have you made love to?" she asked.

"One. You're my first."

"I don't understand."

"I fuck, a lot, Summer. Correction, I fucked, past tense. I didn't know any different. I didn't know how to be tender, or whatever the fuck it is. In the past, it was all about my release but with you it's different. I want to please you. I want you writhing beneath me, screaming out my name. I want to watch you come around my fingers, in my mouth, on my cock. I want to fuck you every which way, anywhere, and everywhere. And then I want to make love to you."

I noticed her breathing change; the subtle moistening of her lip with her tongue and the way she gently ground her pelvis into mine.

"I've never known anyone to speak the way you do, with such passion," she said.

"I haven't started yet, baby," I replied with a smirk.

"You're getting me a little hot here."

"Good. But now, it's time for me to get some sleep."

I rose from the bed, lifting her in my arms at the same time.

"You pig," she said as she laughed.

"Can't have my body on demand, Summer. I'll be worn out before you know it."

She laughed as I walked us to the bedroom. I gently laid her down on the bed, untangled the sheets, and stripped off my shorts. I climbed in beside her. She nestled into my side and placed her hand on my stomach.

I felt her fingers gently brush over my scars.

"I love these, I love that they are part of you," she whispered. "But don't do it again, please, for me?"

"For you, I'd do anything."

We fell asleep, only waking when the sun was high and its rays blasted through the still open doors.

"Hi, just checking in," Dexter said when I'd answered the phone.

I was sitting on the deck, with a coffee in my hand, when my phone had rung.

"All good here, Summer's sleeping," I said.

"Will I be seeing you today?"

"Yeah, I'll be along later. I have some things to talk about."

"Okay, I'll be at the bar all day, we should get the paperwork for the drop-in centre soon."

"Sounds good, I'll see you later."

"Morning," I heard. Summer was walking towards me. I smiled over at her.

"Want a coffee?" I asked.

"No, tea would be good, though. I can get it."

"Take advantage of my domestic skills while you can. I'm sure I'll turn into Neanderthal man soon enough and expect to be waited on."

She laughed as she passed, slapping my shoulder. I rose from the bed and joined her in the kitchen. I poured a coffee while she filled the kettle. She placed her hand on my back as she reached up and over my shoulder for a mug. As she made her tea, I planted a kiss on her temple before taking my coffee back outside.

"I need to go the bar in a bit, I have a session with Dexter," I said when she joined me.

"Can I come?"

"Sure, not in the session though. You'll have to wait in the bar."

"What do you talk about? I guess I shouldn't ask really, should I?"

"Anything, everything, whatever's on my mind."

"Do you talk about us?"

"Yeah."

"Will you be open with me as well?"

"As much as I can be. Sometimes I have to talk it out with Dex first, so I get my feelings straight."

She smiled at me. "I love you, Jack."

———

I cranked up the music, Black Sabbath's *Paranoid* blasted through the car as we headed to the bar. From the corner of my eye, I watched her hair blow in the wind and she rested her feet on the dash. She nodded her head along, she looked happy and I laughed. I sang at the top of my voice as she pretended to play the guitar.

Dexter's smile was broad as we walked in. I had my arm slung around her shoulders.

"How are you both?" he asked.

"Good," we both said at the same time and then laughed.

255

"Let's not do that, no being 'in sync.' We'll be wearing matching clothes next," I said.

"Yeah, I can just see you in my panties."

"Sshh, he'll have me locked up," I said, nodding towards Dex.

"In the back, you. Summer, do you want to take a look next door? See what we've done so far?"

"That would be great, thank you."

He handed her the keys, and I gave her a wink before I headed to the safe room.

Dexter closed the door behind me. "That's a smile I haven't seen in a while," he said.

"Let's hope it lasts."

"So, talk."

I took a seat in the leather chair and he sat opposite me. He always sat in the same position, with one leg crossed over the knee of the other, his arms always on the armrests. He was 'opening' his body as an invitation to talk freely.

"She did something I'm sort of unsure about. She marked me, drew blood. I told her to be careful, she did it again as if she was testing me."

"How did that make you feel?"

"I liked it. But I don't trust myself. She's not that sexually experienced, and I need to remember that."

"Have you spoken to her about that?"

"Not yet. She said something like, 'when I need it, she can give it.' I like that idea, but it defeats what I'm trying to do here."

"Do you think you can ever stop harming yourself?"

"Yes, I believe I can. I haven't for over a month now, but when she dug her nails in my back and scraped them down my skin, that something fired off in my brain. It wasn't the same though; it wasn't a compulsion to feel pain. I can't quite explain it."

"When you're with her, how do you feel? How does that feeling compare to the others, say Honey?"

"It's different. I don't want to just take, does that make sense? Honey gave me something that Summer never will, and that's okay, because I don't want that anymore. It's hard to describe what I feel inside."

"Try."

"With Honey it was just fucking, just a release of frustration and aggression. How do I say this?"

"Say what, Jack. You can speak freely in here, you know that."

"With Summer, I feel something so deep inside me. I want to just please her and my release is secondary to that. With Honey, it was important that I came over her. I needed to see that, it was as if it degraded her in some way. That fucks me up a little. That I wanted to do that—degrade her. It's making me feel like a fucking shit and full of guilt, again."

"It was a mutual decision, Jack. Remember, I sat you both down one time. I counselled her, as best I could. She needed that at that point in her life as well. You didn't do anything she didn't want you to do, right or wrong."

"I wish I could turn back the clock. I wish I could talk to her, especially that night. I ignored her in the bar. I made a show of dancing with Summer, and deep down I knew what I was doing. I didn't want her anymore, and I went about showing her that in a fucking shit way. It's only after yesterday, spending the whole day in bed with Summer that I'd realise."

"Realise what?"

"It was a pretty cowardice way to do it, wasn't it?"

"Perhaps. But hindsight is a wonderful thing. Her father returned, Jack, you saw her. You know what happened. I don't think it would have mattered if Summer was there or not that night. She'd come to the end, for her. She suffered way more years before she found you. And yes, for a while, you two worked, in a sense. She knew it wasn't a relationship, you weren't the only one she was with."

"Yeah, well, that makes me feel a hell of a lot better," I said, hoping the sarcasm would be understood.

"Don't get shitty, as you Brits say. It's a fact. You can't absolve yourself in her eyes; she's not here to do that for you. You can in her name though. Focus on sorting yourself out, on building a life with Summer, and helping others. You can't feel guilty if you did the best you could."

I raised my eyebrows at him.

"Yeah, fuck off now. Giving advice and taking are two different things," he said with a chuckle.

"So what do I do?"

"I can't give you answers, Jack. I can only lead you to where you want to be. Talk to her, always be honest and open. She knows you well, son. Probably better than you know yourself. Even after what she saw with Honey, after what you did with Ted, she still loves you. She needed space and she was scared, but it was my idea for her to return home."

"She said, I'm not sure I like you making decisions for me, without me knowing. And that's another thing, we've only briefly spoken about Ted. I'm not sure I can explain what I did."

"I did what was best at the time and you were in no position to make a decision. You will, you'll find the words when they're settled in your own mind. You do know why you did what you did, you've explained it well enough to me."

"But it's different. I love her. I want her. I'm not sure I can be as open with her as I am with you."

"You're in a different place, mentally, now. Even after only five weeks or so. Let it go for now, move on. When the time's right to talk about him, then you'll be able to. I have spoken to him, he understands what's happened between you and Summer and that he's no longer required."

I sat for a while digesting his words.

"I told her about Dane, what happened that night."

"How did she take it?"

"She cried, obviously, but didn't say anything."

"If she gets a place at UC, one thing they'll do is offer therapy. It's important that anyone coming into this profession does so after coming to terms with anything in their own lives. Maybe that will be the time she deals with that."

"She doesn't think she has a place. I mean, they would have told her by now, wouldn't they?"

"I imagine so. I'll make some calls."

I stood from the chair; the session was over for me. I'd said what I wanted to and preferred a shorter expulsion of my shit than D-J. He could be in there for hours.

When we walked back to the bar, Summer was behind it. She was cleaning up and making a coffee. She smiled over to me.

"Coffee? I think I have finally mastered this machine from hell," she said.

"Sure, why not."

Dexter and I sat and watched her master, unsuccessfully, the machine from hell. She made a fucking mess with the coffee, but eventually we had three cups.

"Next door looks fantastic, I love the wall, Jack," she said.

"We just need to name it," Dex said.

"I had an idea for that," I said.

Both looked at me. "Honey Bees, without them, there would be no life."

She leaned forwards and placed her hand over mine. "I think that's a wonderful idea, and she'd have loved that, too."

"You're not upset?"

"She loved you, Jack, in her own way. It's okay to acknowledge that. I think it's a fitting tribute. You save just one child in that place, and you save a little bit of yourself, of her. She was a large part of your life, an important part. We don't need to forget that. I think you also need to paint her, put her on the wall, like you did me. She meant something to you, whether you care to admit that or not, honour her."

"I think I might be out of a job," Dexter said as he smiled at her.

I laughed, "Never."

———

Dexter received his licence, the drop-in centre was granted its paperwork, and we had an opening day. I'd painted Honey on the wall, she was smiling, the sun shone down on her, and she was without the worry and anxiety that normally graced her face. Her sister came; she stood in front of the wall and cried. I stood beside her.

"You were the one she loved, weren't you? She never said your name, just there was a man who helped her."

"Yes, although I wasn't aware she loved me. It wasn't that kind of a relationship."

"I know, but thank you. And thank you for this." She gestured towards the wall.

I placed an arm around her shoulder and she turned to cry into my chest. I rested my head on hers and looked over to Summer. She smiled at me and nodded.

CHAPTER TWENTY-FOUR

Summer

"Oh, shit! I got a reply from the uni, Jack," I shouted.

He was in the shower and I'd rushed into the bathroom. "Look, I got an email and I fucking missed it."

He stepped from the shower and grabbed a towel from the rack. He'd only been home an hour from a night at the bar.

"What does it say?" he asked.

"I didn't get an interview."

UC had emailed me, I had applied too late, but they mentioned that I should reapply when the new term started. I took that to mean, sometimes students dropped out and I might be able to get in then.

"Ah, baby. Don't be disappointed, Dex is looking at other options for you, as well."

"You know what? I'm not. It was probably a little too optimistic thinking I'd walk straight in anyway. But now I have to panic about a visa."

"If we can get you on other courses, that visa will still be valid, I think."

I watched as he rubbed his hand over his face. He had worked hard that night, Dexter had helped and D-J had been in attendance, of course, but the bar had been busier than he'd ever seen it before, he'd told me.

"Get some sleep, we can talk about it later," I said.

"I'm fine, come and lay with me. Let's have a look at some other options."

I lay beside him and propped the laptop on his chest. I Googled courses and smiled as I watched him struggle to keep his eyes open. I took the laptop from his chest, closed the lid, and placed it on the bedside table as he fell asleep.

I watched him for a while. His long eyelashes, eyelashes I was jealous of, rested on his cheeks. His hair was still wet from his shower and in need of a cut. If he wasn't careful, he'd be looking like D-J! I ran my fingers over the slight stubble on his chin and he murmured in his sleep. I loved to look at his tattoos, especially my name that ran down his side. A dragon twisted in and out of the Gothic style letters and I wondered if there was significance to that. Even with most of his skin covered in ink, Jackson was a very attractive man. Not that I believed he would cheat on me, but my stomach knotted every time a woman stared at him, or licked their lips suggestively, when he served them at the bar. He would flirt, take their money, then always give me a wink. That night had been the first I hadn't accompanied him. It was a fun place to go, but I didn't want to sit in a corner three nights a week while he worked.

I slid gently from the bed and made my way to the kitchen, collecting my laptop as I did. I sat at the breakfast bar and brought up UC again. I read through the course, what was anticipated of me, and was pleased to see they expected me to gain field experience. I wanted to work at the drop-in centre with Dexter. I made a mental note to thank Alfie, it had, after all, been his idea.

I emailed my mum to let her know and it was as I did that I remembered the envelope I'd stuffed in my flight bag. I hadn't opened it. I crept back into the bedroom and to the closet. My bag was stored on a shelf. I pulled it down and opened the zipped compartment. Once I'd pulled out the envelope, I crept back towards the door. Jackson was lying on his back, the towel had slipped from his waist, and even in sleep he sported a semi hard-on. He was insatiable; I couldn't recall a time Dane had made me come as many times. In fact, towards the end of our relationship, I didn't think he even managed once. Sex with Jackson was mind-blowing. I struggled to keep up with him, yet there was always the knowledge that he was holding back.

"You can stand there and watch, or you can come and fuck me," he said, with his eyes closed.

I watched as he reached down with one hand and started to stroke himself.

I giggled as I walked towards the bed and placed the envelope on the bedside table. He opened his eyes once I'd gotten close. I sat on the edge of the bed and watched him. Dane would have never done that, pleasured himself while I watched. I had to make an effort not to compare them; there was absolutely no comparison.

"Gonna help?"

"I like watching you," I replied.

His hand slid up and down his cock, his thumb ran across the top. I watched his knuckles change colour slightly as his grip tightened. Before I had time to react, he grabbed my arm and pulled me towards him. I landed heavily on his stomach and he grunted.

"Fuck," he said before laughing. "Panties off, Summer. Before I rip them from your body."

I wiggled them down my legs. "Now ride me," he said.

I straddled him, placing my hands on his stomach. He held my hips and tipped his head back as I slowly lowered.

"That feels so good," he said with a groan.

I rose and lowered slowly at first. He raised his hips to meet me halfway. With every thrust he made, I pushed harder down on him. It was only as he gripped my wrist and pulled one hand from his stomach that I realised I'd been digging my nails in his scars. It hadn't been intentional, but as my desire grew, as my orgasm built, I'd curled my fingers into his flesh.

He sat up suddenly, grabbing my legs to wrap around his waist. I placed my arms around his neck as he rolled us over. He was still inside me but he stilled, looking at me.

"Hold on tight, baby," he said.

I tightened my legs around his waist as he fucked me hard.

———

"You are so sure of yourself, aren't you?" I said afterwards.

We were lying side by side; he was propped up on one elbow with his fingers tracing my tattoo. My sundress had landed somewhere on the floor earlier.

"Yep."

"Arrogant, too."

"Yep."

"Good-looking, though."

"Yep."

"Crap in bed."

"Ye...What?"

I laughed. "Kidding."

"You fucking better be. You've soaked the sheets, baby, think that says something about my abilities. I'm the one that has to sleep on a wet patch all the time. In fact, I'm going in the other room."

"You are so..." He silenced me with a kiss.

Jackson wasn't arrogant, he was sure of himself though; he had a level of confidence that didn't fit with his insecurities. As I'd said before, he was a mass of contradiction.

He knew exactly what buttons to push to have me, 'soak the sheets,' as he so eloquently put it. I loved his humour; I loved the banter I had with him. In one way there was immaturity about him, humour I'd expect in someone younger, at other times, he was a man twice his age. I guessed that went back to childhood.

"I'm going to cook you dinner," he said, as he rolled to the edge of the bed.

He grabbed his towel, wiped himself down then pulled on some shorts.

"It's not dinner time," I said.

"It's always dinner time."

He laughed as he left the bedroom. I smiled at his retreating back. I shook my head to stop the comparison, but it was too late,

Dane had never cooked me dinner. I rolled to my side and picked up his sketchpad. I loved to look through his drawings, most of which were of me. I flicked through the last few pages and paused at one of a pregnant me. The pencil was slightly smudged by what looked like a droplet of water; it had stained the page.

That was one of the things I loved about Jackson the most. He had no fear of showing his tears, of showing his vulnerability. I ran my fingers over the drawing, over my extended stomach. One day, I'd love to give that man a child. But only when I believed he would be the best father he could be, only when I was confident he had conquered his demons.

———

The smell of steaks grilling on the barbecue wafted down the balcony as I walked towards it. When Jackson said he was cooking dinner, it was always something grilled and a salad. He was a very healthy eater. I'd never seen him eat sweets or chocolate. He drank beer, he drank shots of Jack Daniels, but mostly, he drank water.

"Look what my dad left for me," I said waving the enveloped I'd opened.

"What is it?"

"Five thousand dollars!"

"Wow, that's kind of him."

"It will keep us going for a little while," I said as I kissed his shoulder.

Jackson had plated the steaks and gestured for me to sit.

"I have money, Summer. I will keep us going. You use that for studies or whatever."

"I want to pay my way."

He shook his head as he ate. "Don't emasculate me." He smirked.

"I thought you said Neanderthal wasn't due just yet?"

"Yeah, well. He made an early return. I have money. Once we find you some courses, we'll sort out a car for you."

"I can drive yours."

"You cannot drive mine. That is a classic, and mine; all mine. And anyway, what do I do if I need to go out? Or I can pick you up each day. We'll look like something from a fifties movies."

"I'll be the oldest in the course, I imagine."

"I doubt it. Now, are you eating that?" He pointed over to my steak.

"Yes, go grill another if you're still hungry."

He huffed and winked as he stood. I watched Neanderthal wash up and dry the dishes, and I laughed. Jackson was about the most considerate, caring man I knew.

CHAPTER TWENTY-FIVE

Jackson

Most of my adult life I'd 'taken,' I guessed I was a selfish person in one way. I didn't necessarily consider others and was often wrapped up in my own misery. But with Summer I wanted to be different. I wanted to be the boyfriend she deserved. I wanted to look after her. I wanted her to feel secure and loved. I also found it hard work.

Until Summer, I did what I wanted, when I wanted. I didn't have to think. I had no emotional ties, other than her from a distance, to anyone. I loved my sister, of course, but our lives couldn't be further apart if we'd tried. We kept in contact, we met up, and I knew she suffered working with my father for one reason only; to protect what was mine.

I listened as Summer called her dad and thanked him for the money he'd left her. A pang of jealousy hit me in the stomach. I didn't have it in me to make amends with my father; I had no desire to do anything but watch the bastard suffer. I didn't care what he wanted to speak to me about; to be in the same room as him would have been torture.

From as early as I could remember, I'd wanted children and I'd love those children as if my life depended on it. And it did, I guessed. I had a need to prove that I could be the father I never had; I had a need for unconditional love. Somewhere in the back of my mind, a little niggle would chastise me for those thoughts, I shouldn't use a child to prove anything.

I watched Summer from the kitchen window; she was smiling and laughing as she spoke. She thought I had all the confidence in the world, but inside my stomach had churned at the thought of her going to uni. There was a little part of me that was thankful she hadn't got her place, and I mentally cursed myself for that.

I hated that I felt insecure. I hated that I didn't have the confidence everyone thought I did.

I headed to the bar and the drop-in centre. Dexter had told us the local social services had called a meeting and had some children they wanted to introduce to him. He had offered his services for free, and I guessed they wanted to take him up on that.

"Hey, so who do we have here?" I asked, when I walked in the centre.

A woman had her hand on the shoulder of a young boy, maybe

early teens, and he had a scowl that could out-scowl any I'd seen before.

"Hi, Jackson. This is Dylan."

Dylan was looking at the wall.

"Do you like it?" I asked.

He shrugged his shoulders. "Okay, I guess," he said.

"Think you can do better?" I said with a wink.

He shrugged his shoulders again.

"Dylan is a brilliant artist," the social worker informed me.

"Is that so? Want to show me some?"

He didn't respond but I heard the sigh that left his lips.

"How about you and I sit at that table and you can draw something, show me how great an artist you are?"

Without a word he walked away and sat. He placed his hands on the table but did nothing else. I wouldn't get to know his story, unless he told me himself, of course.

"I'm going to grab a coffee," his social worker said.

I sat opposite him and pushed a sketchpad and pencils towards him. He stared at them.

"I don't want to be here," he whispered.

I pulled the sketchpad back towards me and opened it. I drew. I drew Dylan but with a huge smile on his face.

"So what would this Dylan draw?" I asked as I pushed the pad back towards him.

He studied the page for a while before picking up a pencil. I watched the concentration on his face as he drew a woman. It was an amazing piece until he picked up a thicker, black pencil and drew vertical lines over her. He then pushed the pad to me and sat back in his chair. He didn't look at me as he folded his arms. Dylan was going to be one tough cookie to crack.

"She's beautiful, who is she?" I asked.

"My mom. She's in prison."

"Metaphorically?"

"If I knew what that meant, I'd answer."

I chuckled and saw a ghost of a smile on his lips. He was an intelligent boy, for sure.

"In art, we can take the bars away, Dylan. There doesn't have to be any barriers, we can express exactly how we feel. Come with me, let me show you something."

I stood and waited. After a little while, he pushed his chair back, scraping the legs against the wooden floor. I caught the social worker's eye as I walked to the door. Dylan followed and I took him into the bar.

He walked straight to the wall without any prompting and stood. I watched his head as he started at one side and scanned the whole piece. He then took a step closer to study it. I watched as he reached forward, placing his finger next to my father.

"He's out of place, so I guess that makes him significant," he said.

"You're only the second person to see him without him being pointed out. Tell me what you see?"

"A man in a suit, not that hard to see him, is it?" There was a slight challenge to his voice.

"The whole thing, what do you see?"

He walked the length of the wall, stopping to study small areas as he did.

"I know what this is, but I don't know the name. Something to do with God and all that shit. But it's all in hell, isn't it?"

"Yes. That's *The Last Judgement*. The souls rise, or fall, depending on Christ's decision. Do you know why they are all naked?"

He shook his head.

"It makes them all equal. It doesn't matter what clothes we wear, where we live, what car we drive, underneath we are all the same."

"Why have you put it in hell?"

"Because for a long time, and especially when I was your age, that's what my life was like. To the outside world it was heaven but it wasn't really. Now step back and look from a distance."

He shuffled back a few paces. "Now what do you see?" I asked.

"It's not so scary, I guess."

Dylan made his way back to the centre; I followed. Silently he took a seat at the table and picked up an eraser. As careful as possible, he rubbed out the vertical lines across his mother.

"She shouldn't be in prison. She was just trying to take care of me," he said.

I didn't speak or press for further information. Instead, I helped him draw. We corrected the contours of his mother's face to make her more proportional. After a half hour, he sat back with a small smile on his face.

"I'd like to learn to do that," he said as he pointed to the wall.

"If you can draw, you can do street art. Why don't you take a sketchpad and a couple of pencils home with you and design something. I might even let you paint next time."

He looked at me, and although his expression was one of suspicion, he at least smiled.

"Time to go," I heard.

His social worker and Dexter walked across the room. Without a goodbye, he headed off.

"He's a nice kid," I said.

"In temporary care, at the moment. Sad story really, but you seemed to have gotten on well with him. According to Sally, the social worker, he doesn't speak much. She hoped he might find it fun coming here."

"He said his mum was in prison, he drew her and then bars, I guess, over her face. What's she in prison for?"

"Murder."

"Murder? Fuck!"

"She killed her abusive husband, took a lot of shit then finally cracked."

"Jesus, what's going to happen to him?"

"They're looking for a permanent place for him, but it's not so easy at his age. He has a younger brother and that's where most of the problems are. He wants to care for him, which he can't of course, and they're separated."

"That's got to be so fucking hard on him."

"Yep."

Dexter left to grab a couple of coffees and I sat and looked at the drawing Dylan had done. I hoped that we'd see him again.

———

"Hey, baby. Good day?" I heard when I walked through the front door.

"Sort of, a young boy, well early teens, came into the centre. He's an amazing artist."

"That's good, did you draw with him?"

I told Summer of Dylan, she sat across the breakfast bar as I spoke.

"Poor kid, I'm not sure what to say, really," she said.

"Hopefully, he'll come back. I gave him a sketchpad and told him to design something for one of the walls, I thought it might give him a distraction."

"That's a good idea. Do you want a drink?" she asked.

"Yeah, I'll have a beer. Perri phoned earlier, she's coming out in a week. She'll be in touch when she's booked her flight."

"I'm looking forward to seeing her again."

"Again?"

"We met up, when I was at home. She paid for my flight back out here, Jack."

"I didn't know that. What did you talk about?"

I wasn't sure I was comfortable with Perri telling Summer things that should have come from me. It was enough to know I'd been kept out of the loop with conversations between Dex and Summer. I took the beer she had held out and made my way to the deck. It was my favourite place to sit. Summer nudged me with her elbow as she shuffled on the daybed beside me.

"You, we talked about you mostly. I needed to talk to someone, someone who'd understand."

"Did you tell her everything?" I asked.

There was a pause. "I did. I'm not going to apologise for that, Jack. I needed to talk. You have Dexter, I have no one."

I placed my arm around her shoulder and pulled her close into my side.

"I'm trying hard, Summer. I want to tell you everything, every dirty little secret, but it's going to take me time."

"I'm not asking you to rush, I'm just explaining that I also need to talk this through with someone other than you. You need to accept that."

"I do. I'm just not sure I wanted it to be my sister."

We fell silent. Was I being unreasonable? As she pointed out, I had Dexter to talk to. But my sister? She knew about the cutting, she'd help me clean up when I was young, but the other stuff was something I'd rather she hadn't known about.

CHAPTER TWENTY-SIX

Summer

I heard my phone buzz; indicating I'd received a text message. I climbed from the daybed and made my way to the kitchen. I'd left it charging on the counter. It was a text from Perri. I opened it and wished I hadn't.

Summer, my father died this morning. I'll need to stay here and sort his affairs. I'm not sure if you want to tell Jack or let me. Perri

I immediately replied.

I think it might be better coming from you, call him now, and I'll sit with him when he answers. I want to say I'm sorry, Perri, but I can't.

As I placed the phone back on the counter, I heard his ring. I made my way to sit beside him as he answered.

"Hey, how are you?" he asked as he answered.

I watched his face. He licked his lips just the once, he nodded, but didn't speak. He turned his face to me. I took hold of his hand.

"Okay. Give me an hour or so. I'll call you back," he said, then cut off the phone.

"My..." he said.

"I know, Perri texted me."

He stretched back out on the daybed, pulling me alongside him. We lay in silence for a while. I wasn't sure what to say, what to do.

"I need to call her back," he said.

I watched him while he dialled his sister back, looking for any telltale signs that he might be stressed. I wondered if I should send a text message to Dexter, just in case. Other than a clenching of his jaw as he waited for her to answer, he displayed no emotion at all.

"So, tell me," he said when his call was connected.

He listened for a while, interjecting just on the odd occasion with a question or two. It was hard to follow the one-sided conversation.

'I doubt it, Perri. Although, I'd like to see the fucker finally lowered into the ground."

He listened some more.

"Okay, I'll sort that out."

He finished his call and placed his phone on the floor beside the daybed.

"Are you okay?" I asked, wincing at such a dumb question.

"I think so, I'm not sure how I feel, to be honest. I've waited for this day my whole life."

"Do you need to fly home?"

"I don't *need* to, but there's a part of me that wants to. I guess there'll be paperwork and shit to deal with."

"What can I do?"

He took a deep breath, held it, and then exhaled slowly.

"I don't know, be with me, I guess."

"Do you want me to call Dex?"

He looked over at me. Slowly he shook his head. "No, although, I guess I need to tell him we're heading home for a few days."

I studied his face, trying to work out if I could see anything to indicate a meltdown on the horizon. There was nothing, other than sadness, which surprised me. I wasn't expecting that.

"How do you feel?" I asked.

"I don't know. I feel a little confused right now. I know what I should feel, I should be fucking over the moon, jumping for joy, but I'm not."

"When do you want to fly home?"

"I need a day or so to think about this. I feel like a shit leaving it all to Perri, but I'd be a hypocrite if I went to his funeral. And I don't want to sit here any longer talking about it."

He swung his legs from the daybed and stood. He held out his hand for me. "Let's take a walk," he said.

We walked, hand in hand, along the beach. He was silent for most of the way and I just let him be. The sun had started to set as we made our way back to the house. Dexter was standing on the balcony when we arrived.

"Hey, Perri called," he said.

"I wondered if she would," Jack replied.

"Need to talk?"

"No, I need to eat though. What has Alfie got on tonight?"

"Some mad concoction, I imagine, want to go find out?"

Jackson nodded his head before heading inside to collect his phone and car keys.

"How is he?" Dex asked.

"I'm not sure. He hasn't said too much, other than he doesn't feel overjoyed and he thinks he should."

"He needs to understand that it's okay to be sad. His father, good or bad, has been a powerful influence on his life, so I imagine he'll feel conflicted."

"He wants to fly home for a few days, although I don't know if he wants to go to his funeral or not."

"Might help him to find closure if he does."

Jackson joined us back on the balcony, and after locking up, we walked around the house to where the cars were parked.

"Meet you there," Jack said as Dexter walked to his car.

Jack opened the car door for me and I climbed in. He didn't have his usual bounce as he walked around the car to the driver's side. He wound down his window and started the engine.

"I don't know what to say, to make you feel any better," I said.

"What can you say? He's dead. I just need to figure out how I feel about it."

I took his hand as we drove along the coastal road. I was at a complete loss as to what to say or do. Perhaps an evening with his friends was needed, the distraction of being around *the misfits*, as he called them, might help to settle his mind.

The beach was heaving, a queue had formed around the shack, which Jack ignored as he strode straight to the counter. I expected to hear grumbles but the crowd parted to let him through. It was only then that I realised how highly regarded he was. He collected a couple of bowls of food and two bottles of beer, and we found a spot near a bonfire someone had lit.

D-J came and sat with us. He didn't speak, just clinked his bottle against Jack's in a silent toast. We sat and watched the night draw in and the party ramp up a little.

We didn't stay late, and I was glad. Jackson had knocked back a few too many beers, I thought, and I wanted him to have a clear head for the morning. He had arranged with Dexter that we'd travel to the airport and get the first flights out we could. I'd offered to go online and book but that wasn't Jack. Everything he did was spur of the moment. And I wondered if, by turning up at the airport, there was that chance there wouldn't be available flights. That gave him a get out if he needed one.

CHAPTER TWENTY-SEVEN

Jackson

It felt strange to be boarding a flight to London. I hadn't expected to be returning home so soon. Summer and I settled in our seats, and I rested my head back and closed my eyes. The previous night had been a nice distraction from the news I'd received, but my head was pounding, paying the price for the many bottles of beer I'd drunk.

"I called my mum, she said we can stay with her, if you want to," Summer said.

"That's kind of her. Perri expects me at her place to start with; there are things we need to discuss. I don't want you to feel obliged though, if you want to visit your mum, that's fine, I can drive you home."

"I'd rather stay with you."

I took hold of her hand and gave it a gentle squeeze. "I'd rather you stayed with me, too."

I slept on and off for the journey, but it was as we made our descent into London that my stomach started to knot.

Summer and I had to separate at immigration. I was travelling on an American passport, and although I had legal status in the UK, getting through was always a nightmare. I found her waiting by the luggage carousel and even though we only had a small case between us, it still took an age to finally walk through the airport. I had texted Perri when we landed and was pleased to see her, coffees in hand, when we finally made it out into the arrivals hall.

"Jack, look at you," she said, as I swept her up in my arms.

"I haven't been gone that long," I said.

"Nearly a year, that's too long. You need a haircut," she replied, and then chuckled.

I watched her embrace Summer before we made our way to the car park. The closer to London we got, the quieter we all became. Perri had an apartment in Canary Wharf, in the same block as my father, although he had his sprawling monstrosity of a house in Surrey, as well. I shivered as we climbed from the car and not with cold. I hadn't been to that apartment block in a long time. My father had the penthouse, Perri a couple of floors below, but as we stepped into the lift, I felt his presence.

"Would you rather go to a hotel?" Summer asked, I guessed she'd seen the involuntary shudder.

"No, I'm fine. I need to do this."

The lift door opened on Perri's floor and we stepped inside her apartment. My art was hung on her walls, giving the otherwise stark apartment some colour and warmth.

"Why don't you take a nap before dinner?" she said.

"I might do that, if you don't mind," Summer answered.

I gave her a kiss to her brow before Perri showed her to the guest bedroom.

"So, what do we have to do?" I asked as we settled on her sofa.

"He made all his funeral plans, I've spoken to his solicitor; the funeral is in a couple of days. He left a will, Jack, all his assets are to come to me, but I want to hand half of those over to you."

"I don't want them, Perri. I know fuck all about running a business and I'm not staying. My life is in Cali now."

"How does Summer feel about that?"

We had lowered our voices so as not to disturb her.

"I don't know. She didn't get into uni, so we need to work on a visa for her. There's nothing here for me, you understand that, don't you?"

"I do, although I don't know how easy it will be for her to stay with you, Jack."

"What do I have to do?"

"Marry her? Although, I don't know how easy that would be either."

I chuckled. "I'd marry her tomorrow if she'd have me, but even that doesn't get her an automatic visa."

"She loves you, even after everything you've done. I wish I'd known, Jack. I could have helped."

"No one could have helped me. Dexter does his best, but for a while; I was on self-destruct. I don't want that life anymore. I have something far better sleeping in that guest bedroom of yours. I can't fuck up again. I can't lose her. She's the only thing I need, other than you, of course."

"Yeah, well, thanks." She shoulder bumped me in mock annoyance.

"You know what I mean. I've loved her for years and when I'm with her, I feel good. I feel normal and I haven't felt that way in a long time."

"She's an amazing woman. It killed her to leave you, you know that, don't you?"

"She did the right thing."

"Can you talk about it?"

I shook my head. "Not now. I haven't explained everything to Summer yet. It's a conversation that, thankfully, keeps getting delayed. I don't have answers to why I did what I did that anyone would understand."

"He really damaged you, didn't he? I feel partly responsible, I should have done more," Perri said, her voice had lowered to a whisper.

"You were a child yourself. All I want now is to see him lowered into the fucking ground, and then I can truly move on."

"You might be disappointed then, he's being cremated."

"Even better, I'll watch the fucker burn then I'll go home."

———

Two days later wearing a pair of dark jeans and a shirt, I climbed into a black hearse to attend my father's funeral. I didn't believe I was being disrespectful in not wearing the obligatory black suit; I wasn't in mourning. Summer and Perri joined me as we followed his coffin to the crematorium. For a man who liked to display his wealth, he'd made a point of organising a very basic funeral.

I was greeted by men I hadn't seen in years, the board of directors, many of whom hated my father as much as I did. I was greeted by people I hadn't met before: colleagues of Perri's, old family friends, and neighbours. I shook hands, I accepted their condolences with a mock frown and I sat and listened to his service.

When it was done, I breathed a sigh of relief. It was over.

"I want to go somewhere," I whispered to Summer as we left the crematorium.

I took her hand and we wandered to a bench under a tree. We sat in silence for a moment.

"My mother's ashes are there," I said, indicating towards the tree. "I haven't been here in years."

"I thought she died in America?"

"She did, my father brought her ashes here. He couldn't be parted from her, even in death."

"Tell me about her?"

"I don't know her. I never met my mother. I've seen photographs, of course. She looked like Perri."

"You know you weren't responsible for her death, don't you?"

I shrugged my shoulders. "Why not have the operation, though? Why did she decide on a natural birth? Sometimes I hate her for making that decision. I don't want to hate her but I can't help myself."

"What about her parents? Did you ever get to spend time with them?"

"A little, not that I remember them either. From what I know, my grandmother raised me for the first couple of months and then we left. He isolated us all from them. My care was left to his mother and a nanny. I have a vague memory of a woman with blonde hair but I'm not sure who she is."

"Maybe Perri will know."

I placed my arm around her shoulders and pulled her close. "I don't need to know. I have my family right here with me. I don't need anyone else."

The temperature had dropped, and after I felt her shiver, we stood and left. Perri was waiting by the car, talking to a man I didn't recognise. She smiled at him as we approached.

"Mark, I'd like you to meet my brother, and Summer," she said.

"Jackson, it's good to meet you finally, Perri often talks about you," he said.

Mark, it transpired, was the family solicitor and judging by the way Perri continued to smile at him, a *friend* as well.

"We have some documents that need to be dealt with, when you're ready," he said.

"Summer and I will be heading back to California in a day or so," I said.

"If tomorrow is not too soon for you, perhaps we can meet then?"

We made arrangements before climbing back into the car.

"Is there a wake?" Summer asked.

"No, my father wouldn't have wanted people celebrating on his money," Perri answered with a chuckle.

Instead, we drove back to the apartment. The day had been a little surreal, Brett Walker, a powerful banker in the city, a very disliked man, had died, and there was no celebration of life, no outpouring of emotion or tears. I started to laugh.

"I hope he's looking down now. I hope he can see that most of those there today were like me, just wanting confirmation he was fucking dead and gone."

"What happens now?" Summer asked.

"The house will go up for sale, once all the legal stuff is taken care of. Neither of us wants it; it holds too many unpleasant memories. I'm also going to sell my shares, Jack. It's time for me to move on as well," Perri said.

"What will you do?" I asked, surprised.

"Tell me about this drop-in centre, maybe I can be of use there."

We chatted about the centre, Dexter and D-J, our plans for the future; the more we spoke, the more excited we became. If Perri could pass the bar in the U.S., we could really do some good for those that needed help yet couldn't afford it.

———

The following day, we sat in a plush office in the heart of Mayfair with Mark and two of his colleagues. A boardroom desk was covered in documents that needed our signatures. It took all morning to go through each one. Perri was the only beneficiary of my father's will, but my trust fund was now legally mine. Although she had transferred it to another bank, we were surprised to find out a secondary trust had been hidden. My mother had left her estate to be divided between us, which had never happened.

"So what is this all worth?" I asked, as I signed the last document.

"Once the sale of the property is complete, Perri wants that money divided equally, and your mother's estate is released, your net worth will be approximately fifty million pounds," Mark said.

I stood, in stunned silence. "Fifty million pounds?"

"Yes, and I advise that you speak with a colleague of mine in America as to where that money is best placed or invested."

"Fuck."

"Fuck, indeed," he said, as he took the last of the documents from me.

"Of course, Perri's net worth is considerably higher, bearing in mind your father left everything to her."

"Guess I can buy a decent car then," I said.

CHAPTER TWENTY-EIGHT

Summer

We decided to hire a car and spend a couple of days with my parents. Jackson was still reeling from the knowledge he was a very wealthy man. It scared me a little. He was totally grounded, he had plans to invest some of it in the drop-in centre, but I worried.

There was a little part of me nervous when Jackson met my parents; I had no need to be. My mum welcomed him with open arms, dabbing a tear away when she thought we weren't looking. My dad immediately embraced Jack into the family. Not before giving him the cringeworthy 'talk' about treating his daughter right.

"Richard, I promise you, I'll take good care of Summer," he'd said.

"Enough of the father chat. Jack, let's get some fresh air," I said.

"Nothing is going to change, you know that, right?" he said, as we took a walk with the dog.

"Of course it will, Jack. That's a fucking lot of money," I said.

"And we will do a lot of good with it. I don't want a penny of his, Perri can keep all that. That was my grandfather's, my mother's money that should have been given to me a long time ago. Think of all the things we can do with it."

He listed his plans. He wanted to buy the premises the drop-in centre was housed in, and buy into the bar as a way to lessen the stress for Dexter. He wanted to set up charities to help the children that had started to visit the centre.

It was all swimming around in my head. I had no concept of that kind of money, no idea how he would even manage all that.

"I have an idea. Someone will have to manage this charity, I've never worked, Summer. But you have. I don't want to be bogged down with paperwork and office shit, I just want to work with the kids. How hard could it be to run this?"

"I don't have a clue. I mean, I can learn, I guess."

The more we talked, the more real it all became. With help, and between us all, we could manage a charity; we could do some real good. By the time we had returned back to my parents, The Walker Foundation was born.

We spent another day with Mark, outlining plans for the Foundation. Perri was on board, Mark instructed a legal team in California, and Jackson called Dexter. For the first time in years, I watched him smile, laugh, plan, and become animated. His whole demeanour had changed. He had a purpose, something positive to concentrate on. There would be something worthwhile to come from all his pain and suffering.

The more I watched him, the more I realised; that was the real Jackson. I had eventually peeled back the layers, I was seeing the man I loved transform yet again. As much as he'd told me I was emerging from my cocoon, so was he.

There were no tears as we said our goodbyes to my parents, to Perri, at the airport. Plans had been made for visits and there was a level of excitement and desire to return and get started. Perri was going to investigate a new visa for me; technically I was about to be employed by an American company. So the hope was that a visa would be easily obtained. And if it wasn't, we'd cross that bridge when it came.

We flew home first class and chuckled with embarrassment as we took our seats in our jeans and t-shirts among the smartly dressed. It was to be the one luxury Jackson insisted on before we got back to real life.

Dexter met us at the airport, full of hugs and excitement as he caught us up to date with the drop-in centre. Dylan had returned, although disappointed that Jackson wasn't around, he got stuck into designing a piece of art that he wanted to show off. He'd also started to talk. Dexter had already had a couple of sessions with him, and although he had a long road ahead of him, progress was being made.

"It's good to be home," I said as I dumped our bag on the bed.

Jackson wrapped his arms around me. "That's the first time you've referred to here as home," he said.

"It feels like home now. It was lovely to see my parents, but look, how could this compare to a dreary day in London?" I'd stepped out onto the balcony to look out over the beach.

"Sleep with me?" he whispered as he nuzzled my neck.

"Just sleep?"

I turned to face him and wrapped my arms around his neck.

"Unless you want to take advantage of my jet-lagged body, of course. I wouldn't say no to that."

"I'd love to take advantage of your jet-lagged body, sure you're up for it?"

"Baby, don't tease," he said, as he scooped me up and walked me back to the bedroom.

He set me down on the bed, and I watched as he slowly stripped off his t-shirt and jeans. His muscles rippled with every movement. He'd lost a little weight over the past couple of months, which made his muscles more defined. While he ran his hand over his already erect cock, I wiggled my jeans down over my hips. I pulled my t-shirt over my head and deposited it on the floor. As he stalked towards me, I unclipped my bra and slid it from my shoulders.

Jackson climbed on the bottom of the bed; all the while his hand ran up and down his cock. He reached up and hooked his fingers inside my panties.

"Lift," he said, as he dragged them to my ankles.

For a moment, he sat back on his heels and looked at me. He then stopped pleasuring himself and lay beside me.

"Do you know how much I love you?" he whispered, as his fingers trailed a slow path down my stomach.

"Yes, but do you know how much I love you?" I asked.

He gave me a smile as he covered me with his body. His kiss

was gentle at first, but as his hunger for me grew, the kiss became deeper, more urgent.

He slid his body down mine, his lips trailing a path to the dragon through my navel. He took it in his teeth and tugged. I dug my fingers into his scalp as my stomach somersaulted. His teeth nipped as he moved lower until I could feel his breath at my very core. He swiped his tongue over my clitoris, sending shockwaves through my body. I arched my back slightly, wanting his tongue inside me. Instead of giving me what I needed, he pushed himself up on his hands and looked at me.

"Summer, when did you last have your period?" he asked.

"Huh? When did I what?" I stammered, terrified that I just had.

I reached down between my thighs, as if to check.

Jackson rolled to my side. "You haven't had your period since you've been here. Or while you were here before."

I stared at him. "And you just thought of that? Like, right now, you just thought of that while doing...that?"

"Yeah, I just thought of that," he said.

"Jesus Christ, Jackson. I don't know, maybe it's not due yet. That is about the most inappropriate timing you could have managed."

"It hasn't crossed your mind?"

"No, funnily enough. I'm on the pill, there's the time difference to get used to, we've flown across the fucking globe and back within a week, I guess my body is a little messed up."

"You're mad at me, aren't you?"

"I'm not mad, I was kind of enjoying that, you know?"

I rolled from the bed, pulled on my panties and then a vest top. With my hands on my hips, I stood and stared at him. He was naked; all cock sure on the bed with a grin on his face.

"Don't even go there, Jackson. I'd know, okay?"

He raised his eyebrows and continued to smirk.

"Would you? On a scale of one to ten, just how mad would you be?"

"I'm not even having this discussion with you. I am not pregnant, just late. Don't for one minute think your super-sperm has done its job."

"Super-sperm? I like that."

I heard myself growl at him, partly in frustration and partly in annoyance. "I'm getting a drink, do you want one?"

CHAPTER TWENTY-NINE

Jackson

Summer having missed her period had been on my mind, although I guessed I'd not thought of the timing when I brought the subject up. I imagined she was pissed off with me. I didn't claim to be an expert on women's menstrual cycles, but in the few months we'd been together, she hadn't bled. She'd had no cramps, no cravings for chocolate or any of that other shit women do. She hadn't tried to stab, strangle, or sexually molest me, although I wouldn't have minded the latter. No, no signs at all. Sure, she was on the pill, but she still should have bled at some point.

She returned with two bottles of water and climbed back into bed. We didn't speak for a few minutes. I leaned up on one elbow as

I sipped my drink and watched the emotions cross her face, she was thinking about it, for sure.

Eventually, she shook her head. "No, not possible."

She reached over to the bedside cabinet. "See, all up to date," she said, showing me her packet of pills.

"Maybe you're right, maybe it's just the time difference and all that," I said.

I snaked my arm under her neck and pulled her close. She settled into my side.

"So, where were we?" I said as I ran my hand up her thigh.

"*We* are about to get some sleep, you sort of killed my mood, Jack."

I laughed as I rolled onto my back. Sleep didn't come immediately for either of us, and as the night progressed, I began to regret speaking out. I'd love a child with Summer. I wasn't so sure she felt the same way.

The next couple of weeks flew by in a whirl of meetings with solicitors, setting up the trust, working at the bar, and spending days at the drop-in centre. There were times when both Summer and I just flopped straight into bed, exhausted, and other times we spent the night tangled in the sheets, fucking. She was as desperate for me and I was for her at times.

I didn't say another word about her missing her period, but I certainly researched. In just the two weeks since my observation I noticed subtle changes. She had winced when I'd taken one of her nipples into my mouth, something she had never done before. I'd asked her if they were tender, she shook her head. She was forever rushing to pee, but it was when she threw up for no reason, I knew.

"Don't say a word, okay?" she growled at me as I held back her hair.

We had been sitting on the balcony after a long day at the drop-in centre. We'd eaten a steak and salad. She'd drunk a couple of bottles of water, and after an hour or so, rushed from the daybed to the bathroom.

Once she had finished throwing her guts up, she rested back on her heels.

"Let me guess, dodgy lettuce?" I said.

I rose to get a washcloth and ran it under the cold water tap. I held it to her forehead, noticing that she was hotter than normal. Maybe she did have a bug after all.

We sat in silence for a moment, until I saw a tear leak from her eye and roll down her cheek. I scooped her up in my arms and carried her back outside.

"Okay, talk to me," I said as I laid her down on the daybed.

"I'm scared, Jack."

"About what?"

"You, me, us." She pointed to her stomach when she said that, and I had to conceal the grin that wanted to spread across my face.

"So am I. How about we make a doctor's appointment before we get any more terrified?"

"I don't know if we're ready for this," she whispered.

"I know I am. I've been ready for this for years, Summer. We have money, more money than we'll spend in our lifetime, we have a wonderful house on a beach, and I love you, so, I'm ready."

"That's just it, *you* have money, *you* own a house on a beach..."

I cut her off before she could finish her sentence. I knew this was hormones, I hoped it was hormones talking. She wasn't insecure about herself, or our relationship, but I'd do whatever I had to make her happy.

"So tomorrow we'll get married, then half of it is legally yours. I'll call the lawyers, have them draw up a will, I'll do whatever I need to, Summer."

"We are not getting married just because I'm..."

"Say the word, baby, go on."

"We're...oh fuck, Jack, we're pregnant!"

It was only then that she smiled, a fucking huge smile that lit up her face, making her eyes sparkle and glisten with more unshed tears.

"Well, technically you are, but I'll take some accolade for my part," I said.

I placed my hand over her stomach; she covered it with hers.

"You knew weeks ago, didn't you?" she said.

I nodded. "I don't know how, instinct, whatever. Or the fact your tits hurt, you've been moody, pissing all the time, and all you want to do is fuck the life out of me. I read about it, I like this stage of pregnancy. Can we stay at this point forever?"

She started to laugh and then cry. I pulled her to my chest and rocked her gently.

"Don't cry, baby, we've got this, trust me."

"I don't know why I'm crying. We need to do a test. I can't wait for a doctor's appointment. There must be an all-night chemist somewhere," she said.

I untangled myself from her and stood. "Leave it to me, I'll be back as soon as I can."

I rushed from the house, stumbling as I fiddled with my car

keys in the door lock. I drove to an all-night pharmacy and rushed through the door. The pharmacist looked up from reading a magazine.

"My girlfriend is pregnant, what do I need?" I asked as I approached his counter.

"Congratulations, how far along is she?"

"I don't know, we need to do a test and I need...things," I said.

"Okay, I can tell you're a little excited. Let's start with a test." He produced a slim box from behind him and placed it on the counter.

"Vitamins, and shit like that. I want her to be healthy, what do you recommend?"

He proceeded to place a couple of boxes of vitamins and *well women* tablets, as he described them.

"There must be other stuff we need," I said, as I looked at the small horde on the counter.

"It's a little early to be worrying, she needs to take the test first. You also need to make an appointment at her doctor's as soon as possible. They'll advise on the next steps."

I paid and as I grabbed the bag from the counter, he wished me luck. Did I look like I needed luck? I ran all the way back to the car.

My fingers itched to make calls, to tell Perri and Dexter. I wanted the world to know I was going to be a father. I didn't think I'd ever been excited about something as much as I was that night.

"Baby, get your arse in the toilet, did you drink more water?" I called out as I barrelled through the front door.

I heard her sigh. "I have vitamins and *well women* shit as well. We need to work out a healthy eating plan," I said. She sighed again.

"Oh, and no more of that." I snatched the bottle of water from her hand.

"Jack, for fuck's sake," she said.

"That plastic has chemicals, we'll get a proper water bottle or something."

"Yeah, a proper *plastic* one. Just give me the damn test kit."

I stood, hopping from foot to foot as she peed over the stick. We then waited, counting down the minutes. I checked my watch constantly.

"Is it working?" I asked, after a couple of minutes.

"It says to wait four and yes, I think it's safe to say it's working."

She held up the stick and already a faint blue line was visible in the small window. I held my breath as the line darkened and was joined by a second one. I had the instruction pamphlet open and I read out the results, results I already knew.

"Baby, you're pregnant!"

CHAPTER THIRTY

Summer

Jackson drove me nuts, for that first month after the 'great discovery,' as he called it. I was wrapped in cotton wool and not allowed to do a thing for myself. He was the font of all knowledge; even telling the doctor exactly what was going on with my body when we went to have the pregnancy confirmed. It took me threatening to go home until the baby was born for him to calm down, a little.

His excitement was a wonderful thing to see, I only wished I could muster up the level of energy required to join in. I couldn't believe how tired I was all the time.

I was scheduled for a full check-up. Jackson had insisted, and it was only after I had explained to the doctor how his irrational behaviour came about, they'd started to accommodate his fears.

"You do know what happened to your mum was rare, don't you?" I said as we drove to the clinic.

We were having a scan and after, we'd decided, we would let everyone know.

"No, it isn't rare, Summer. It's quite common, but if we can avoid it, we will."

"I can't go six months, Jack, with you worrying about everything, and I mean, *everything*. I get you're scared, I am too, but you're becoming irrational."

"My mum died, Summer, I was left to live a life of hell, there's nothing irrational about that," he said, and I winced at my error.

"I didn't mean it like that, I meant, you're suffocating me, Jack. I want as normal a pregnancy as possible; I don't want to be stuck with needles every five minutes because you're panicking. I want us to enjoy this."

I placed my hand on his thigh as we drove. As usual he had the windows wound down and his music playing, although not loud. He'd convinced himself that he didn't want to upset the baby's ears with loud rock music.

"I can't lose you, Summer, or the baby."

We continued our journey in silence.

———

"Hey, my favourite people are here," Dexter said as we walked into the drop-in centre.

I was pleased to see it busy. Two boys were arguing over a drawing one had done, a young girl was rubbing down a surfboard with D-J, and Dexter had his hand on the shoulder of Dylan, who gave Jackson a broad smile.

"We have news," Jack said, and then looked at me with a smile. I gave him a nod.

He held out the scan photograph for Dexter to see.

"You're kidding me? Is that what I think it is?" Dex asked.

I nodded. "It is. We're having a baby."

"Dude, did I just hear that right?" D-J said as he wandered over.

"We're having a baby, just had the scan," Jack said.

"Fuck me." I laughed as Dexter scowled at D-J.

"You didn't say," Dexter said.

"We wanted to make sure she had all her fingers and toes before we shared the news," Jack said.

"She? We don't know what we're having yet," I said.

"Oh, it's a girl, I just know it."

"This calls for a celebration. Kids, sodas all round, Jackson and Summer are having a baby," Dexter called out.

We left the drop-in centre and headed for the bar. I wondered how appropriate it was to take the kids into the bar but since the drop-in centre was right next door; the kids had often nipped in to pick up a drink or two.

Dexter and D-J fussed around, making sure I had a stool to sit on, getting me a bottle of water as they toasted with soda, forgoing a beer because of the kids. Jackson revelled in the congratulations and I was happy to let him. Although he had his sister, those guys were the only family he had and I needed to remember that. I also had no doubt he was going to make an amazing father.

I took a photograph of the scan and sent it by text to my mum;

I wanted her to see it as soon as she woke. We did the same for Perri.

I didn't need to wait until Mum woke, I smiled as I answered her call and heard her excited screams and cries. She was unable to talk and handed me immediately to my dad.

"Oh, baby, we're so pleased for you. What do we need to do? Is there anything we can send you?"

"No, Dad, but thank you. I'm just over three months so there's plenty of time to gather what we need. I'd love for you and Mum to come over for the birth, if you can?"

"You bet we'll be there. I'm going to put your mum back on and I'll make plans. I'll call you tomorrow. You get plenty of rest, you hear me?"

He sounded as much of a nag as Jackson was turning out to be. I had a lovely chat with my mum, who still couldn't contain her excitement. I handed the phone to Jackson so Mum and Dad could talk to him.

———

We stopped at the supermarket on the way home, a weekly shop took twice the length of time it should have. Jackson insisted on reading every ingredient to make sure there was nothing *harmful* to the baby or me. I laughed as he tutted and sighed, moaned about the level of chemicals in food, and as he grabbed a passing employee to help us decide which meats were free-range.

"We need tit pads," he said as we browsed the toiletries aisle.

"Tit what?"

"Tit pads, you're going to start leaking all over the place at some point."

"How the fuck do you know all this?"

"Told you, research. It can happen as early as fourteen weeks in," he said, with a level of authority that surprised me.

"What else should I know, Dr. Walker?"

"Your body is already changing shape, your tits have grown. They used to be a handful, now they're about one and a half."

He reached forwards with cupped hands. I slapped his arms away.

"Thanks, I'm not sure I want my *tits* measured in handfuls."

"I want to know everything, Summer. I want to see every change to your body, and we should discuss birthing options."

"I think we have plenty of time to worry about that, now let's get this shopping done before my tits leak all over the place, as you've informed me they might."

As much as Jackson wouldn't allow me to carry a bag, to lift anything heavy, or take part in anything strenuous, he didn't have the same concerns in the bedroom. And I was thankful for that. As the months wore on, it had come as yet another surprise to realise how horny pregnancy made me. I wanted sex all the time and more than once a night. Jackson was more than happy to oblige, and I thanked my lucky stars that he was more than capable of satisfying me as many times as I wanted.

***

"I don't want to hurt the baby," he'd said one night, I was coming up to eight months pregnant.

"You are not going to hurt the baby, didn't you ask the consultant whether it was safe?"

I thought back to our last appointment, where I'd cringed with embarrassment at the conversation.

"I know, but let's take it slow from now."

"My parents will be here tomorrow, so we can limit our *gymnastics* then." I was aware of how whiney I sounded.

"That's another thing, I need to ask your dad for your hand in marriage. We're going to do that as soon as she's born."

"We don't know the sex, and I'm not marrying you just because we have a child."

I sulked a little but he wasn't giving in. "We're getting married, Summer. No argument."

Jackson had spent the past half hour rubbing oil into my stomach. He did that every night after my shower. He massaged my aching feet, my shoulders and back. He spent ages talking to the bump, telling 'her' all the things they were going to do together.

I'd had a fairly easy pregnancy, I was fit and healthy, and there had been no complications. Although I felt the size of a horse, Jackson constantly told me how beautiful I looked. He drew pictures of me; he spent weeks decorating the nursery, although it wouldn't be used for a while. I'd watched with tears of laughter rolling down my cheeks as he struggled putting a cot together. Eventually calling on Dexter and D-J to help. They were shaping up to be the best uncles our child was ever going to have.

D-J had been clean for months, although he struggled at times. His need to help at the drop-in centre, and then his need to be involved with my child, was all the motivation he needed. The baby was a godsend for all.

CHAPTER THIRTY-ONE

Jackson

The nursery was finished, Summer's parents and Perri had arrived, all we were waiting on was the appearance of labour. That was when I started to panic. I tried my hardest to not let how anxious I was getting show. Every wince or furrow of her brow had me jumping from my seat and asking Summer if she was okay. I knew I was frustrating her no end, but I couldn't help it.

I'd spoken for hours about what happened to my mother. I'd consulted books and the doctors to be told Summer was fit and healthy, the chances of her developing pre-eclampsia were low. But I wouldn't rest easy until that baby was in my arms and Summer was home, safe and sound.

"Jack, wake up," I heard. Summer nudged me hard in the ribs.

"Huh? What's wrong?"

"I think I'm in labour."

"What do you mean, you *think* you're in labour?"

I jumped from the bed, tripping over the pile of clothes I'd been leaving handy for that moment.

"Fuck, right, calm down. Breathe, okay?"

She chuckled before sucking in a deep breath.

"Okay, let me think. The bag's packed, where are your clothes? I told you to leave a pile of clothes," I said, rushing around, trying to do up my jeans and find her clothes at the same time.

"Jack, *you* need to breathe and calm down. Go get my mum," she said, wincing through a contraction.

I rushed from the room and upstairs to where her parents were sleeping. I knocked on the door, and then shouted for Perri as well.

"Is it time?" Katie said as she answered the bedroom door. She was tying a robe around her waist.

"Yes, you need to get dressed, we need to go. I need to call the hospital, oh, fuck. What else do I need to do?"

"You need to calm down," she replied.

I rushed back down the stairs and to the bedroom. Summer had made it off the bed and was holding onto the frame. She smiled and panted a little when she saw me.

"Oh, baby, what do I do?" I asked.

"You've practiced this for a month now. Get my bags in the car, call the hospital...Aww!"

Her cries tore through me. I hated to see her in pain, knowing there was nothing I could do. I rubbed her lower back as her mum came into the bedroom, closely followed by Perri.

"Mum's here, take a deep breath, darling. You're doing fine," Katie said.

"Oh shit, Jack, what do we do?" Perri asked. Her face displayed the same level of panic that I imagined mine did.

Neither of us had been around babies or pregnant women before, we were clueless.

"Take my bag to the car, for fuck's sake!" Summer shouted.

Perri grabbed the bags and rushed from the room, colliding with Richard on the way.

"I'll start the car," I said, following her.

The journey took half the time but then I had practiced the route many times. Summer had thought it funny at first, but looking over at her doubled in pain, with tears on her cheeks, I was glad I knew every shortcut. Perri was following closely behind with the in-laws, and we screeched to a halt outside the hospital at the same time.

I ran through the revolving doors, leaving Summer in the car.

"My girlfriend, the baby, it's on its way," I said, as I grabbed the first nurse I saw.

"Okay, what's mum's name?" she asked.

"Huh?"

"Your girlfriend, what is her name?"

"Oh, Summer Kimms. She's in the car and the baby is coming," I said, my voice rose in panic.

My heart was beating at a frantic pace in my chest. Shit just got real. All the months of planning, of researching and asking questions, fell apart as I watched Summer being wheeled into the delivery suite.

I held onto her hand, whispering words of comfort, or so I thought. I swear I heard a bone crack as she squeezed my hand when another contraction hit her. It was all happening way faster than I thought it would. Sweat beaded on her brow, and she was turning a horrible shade of grey.

"She's ill, look, she's gone grey," I said as they hooked her up to machines.

"She's having a baby, Jackson, she's fine," I was informed.

I wanted to follow the nurse from the room as she left to call the obstetrician, but Summer wouldn't let go.

"Breathe, baby, breathe through it. Remember how well you did with your tattoo?"

"My tattoo? Fuck you, Jackson," she said through gritted teeth.

It took too long before the room filled with people. Summer was prodded and poked, scans were done before it was announced the baby was breech. I watched as her stomach was manipulated, they were trying to turn the baby; it didn't work.

"We need to do a C-section," the obstetrician said.

"Whoa, what?"

"A C-section."

"I know what one is, oh shit, can't you turn the baby or something?"

"We've been trying that. The baby is getting distressed, Jackson."

He proceeded to tell Summer what was needed. I saw her eyes widen as she looked over to me before nodding. I didn't get a chance to speak again before the sides of her bed were hooked up and she was being wheeled from the room. I ran alongside and was ushered into an anteroom to change into scrubs. My stomach started to knot, bile rose to my throat at the thought, and it took all my control to not pass out when I saw the largest fucking needle being pushed into her spine.

Everything was moving too fast, I didn't have time to process. I asked one nurse to tell her parents, not knowing where they were. I stood at the side of the bed, holding her hand and mopping her brow as they got to work.

It was a sickening sound as they cut into her. But it was the sight of the blood that nearly had me losing it. There was too much blood, and even I was able to see the barely concealed panic on the consultant's face. Words I didn't understand were shouted, people started running and someone grabbed my arms. I fought until I saw my baby being lifted from her stomach and handed to a nurse. I thought it was all over when I heard my baby scream. I turned to Summer.

"Summer, look. Summer? Summer!"

"We need you out, now, Mr. Walker," the nurse said.

"What's happened, why isn't she answering me?"

Summer wasn't moving, her eyes were open and she stared straight at me, but I knew she couldn't see me.

"What the fuck is happening?" I screamed out.

Someone dragged me to the door. I twisted and turned. "Summer! Baby, talk to me."

"Jack, what's happened?" I heard. Katie, Richard, and Perri were rushing along the corridor.

"Something's gone wrong, I don't know. There was so much blood, I..."

I started to sob, I leaned back against the wall, glad it was supporting me, and cried out her name over and over.

A nurse left the room and I ran over.

"Summer? What's happened? Please, you have to tell me."

"I don't know yet. I will find out though. Please, wait in here until I have more news," she said, as she reached behind me to a door I hadn't noticed.

"My baby?"

"Your daughter is fine."

"Why was there so much blood?"

She didn't answer as she left the room.

I heard Katie sobbing as she slumped onto the couch. Richard had his arm around her shoulder.

I paced for what seemed forever until the door opened again. It was the same nurse that had ushered me from the room.

"Would you like to see your daughter?" she asked.

I nodded my head. "I want to know what's happening to Summer, as well."

"The doctor will be with you shortly, but come and meet your daughter."

I followed her to a small room. There were four plastic cots and she led me to one. Lying wrapped up was the most beautiful thing I'd ever seen. She had dark brown hair and a screwed up face, as if angry at having been taken from her mother so brutally.

"You can pick her up," the nurse gently said.

I reached down for her. As I lifted her into my arms, she opened her eyes. Brown eyes stared back at me and her face softened. I watched my tears drip onto her forehead. I looked around for a chair and then sat. It was as I did that I fell apart. I hugged my baby to my chest and I cried like I'd never cried before.

"Please tell me, is Summer…" I couldn't finish the sentence; the words physically choked me.

The nurse knelt in front of me. "The blood loss was because an artery was nicked in the rush to deliver this little one. We had to act fast, Jackson, your daughter was in distress. There is always a risk when that happens. But it seems Summer developed a blood clot, that clot could have been there for a while and was dislodged. She suffered a pulmonary embolism."

I didn't understand what was being said. "The doctor is waiting for you, he's with her parents right now."

"What do I do?" I whispered, holding my daughter tighter against my chest.

"Let me take the baby."

I handed over my daughter, but not before kissing her forehead. With every step I took back towards the family room, dread set in. My footsteps were heavy and my heart broke the closer we got. I could hear crying. I hesitated before opening the door; my hand shook as it gripped the door handle. I closed my eyes and swung the door open, believing I was about to walk into my worst nightmare.

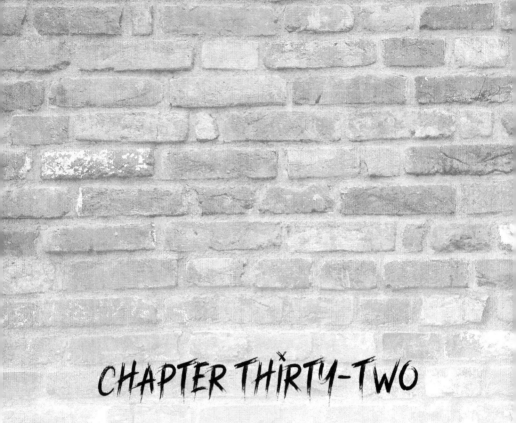

CHAPTER THIRTY-TWO

Jackson... One year later

"Baby, come on. We need to get you cleaned up," I said, as I picked my daughter, Bryony, up from the beach.

My phone rang in my pocket; Perri was calling. "Hey, we're just heading back to the house, we've been building sandcastles."

"That sounds wonderful. Now, did you pick up the cake?"

"Yes, I picked up the cake, and the balloons, and the plates, and everything else on the list. I'll see you later." I shook my head as I disconnected the call.

Bryony was about to have her first birthday party, not that she was completely aware of that fact, of course. I grabbed her with one arm and laughed as she squealed with delight.

"Dada," she said.

"Yep, Dada. Now, we need to get washed or we will both in trouble, young lady."

I stripped her of her sandy clothes and stood with her in the shower. Bryony loved nothing more than to stand and be showered down, she was most certainly my daughter in hating baths. I remembered when I'd brought her home from the hospital. Her cries as I tried to bathe her in the plastic tub we'd bought had me in tears. In the end, I stripped to my shorts, sat on the shower seat and held her as a gentle stream of water washed us. She'd loved it, despite the horror on Katie's face, who thought I was about to drown my child.

Once dried and dressed, I buckled her into her car seat and she clapped her hands. That was her cue for music; again, she was most definitely her father's daughter.

"So what does her ladyship want to listen to today? How about your mummy's favourite song?"

I doubted Bryony understood but she clapped her hands when James Bay started singing *Hold Back the River*. I was immediately transported back to days dancing around the kitchen.

"Shall we go see Mummy?" I said, catching sight of her wriggling in her car seat in the rear-view mirror.

The sun shined that day as we pulled into the car park of the crematorium. I unbuckled her and carried her on my hip.

Ahead of me I saw a group of children, they were about to let off Chinese lanterns and I held back. I didn't want to intrude in their ritual. They were kids from the drop-in centre and were learning about loss and letting go of loved ones that had died. It was something the Foundation had set up for them, just a small way of connecting with and supporting each other in times of grief.

When all the lanterns had been released, I continued to walk among the graves. I was just a short distance away when she stood. Her auburn hair caught the sun's rays and shone. She turned to me and smiled.

"Momma," Bryony gurgled and held out her hands.

"Hello, baby, have you had a good day?" Summer walked towards us and held out her arms to take Bryony from me.

"We have, we made sandcastles," I said, and I wrapped my arms around my wife and my daughter.

"And now we are ready for a party," Summer said.

"Perri has been nagging me all day, this better be the one and only party. I don't think I can cope with a sweet sixteen. How are the kids?" I asked, nodding towards the small group watching their lanterns float off.

"Good, this has been a great exercise for them, I think we ought to do it regularly. Tanya is taking them back to the centre."

Tanya was Summer's assistant at the Foundation, although Summer was in charge, she'd needed a second in command when she'd started to take some classes in counselling. It had been Summer's idea to take the kids out for a therapy session.

Things could have been so different. Just a year ago, I'd nearly lost Summer. A blood clot had reached her lungs. It was only the quick thinking of the doctor on the day that had saved her life. I thanked that man every morning when I woke and saw my gorgeous wife and my beautiful daughter.

Summer and I married in a quiet ceremony just a couple of months after Bryony had been born. I vowed Bryony would be the only child I'd ever have. I was not going to go through that again, no matter how many times Summer nagged for a brother or sister for her.

Arm in arm, we walked back to the car, my baby had her first birthday party to attend and we were already late. Dexter had texted, D-J had texted, and Katie was getting stressed. Bryony's guests had arrived and the belle of the ball was clapping in the car, listening to rock music.

As I laid my daughter down for a nap, still dressed in the purple princess dress she'd been changed into after opening that gift from Perri, I sat in a chair. I just stared at her. Summer walked into the bedroom and curled into my lap.

"She's perfect," I whispered, even with her tangled hair and cake smeared over her cheek.

"She is, and so are you," Summer said.

"Can you believe we're here? After all the shit, we're sitting here, married, and with our daughter."

"Sometimes I have to pinch myself. I look at you, Jackson, and I'm in awe of what you've overcome. I fall more in love with you each day, as you grow, as you change into the most wonderful man."

"You mean I wasn't wonderful before?" I teased.

"Conceited, for sure; wonderful, of course. What you are now bears no resemblance to the man you were," she said with a quiet chuckle.

I tightened my arms around her. "It's all because of you," I said, nuzzling her neck.

"Do you ever wonder what it was that your dad had to say to you?" she asked, somewhat randomly. I looked at her.

"No. I assumed he wanted a reconciliation but the fact he left everything to Perri showed he hadn't. Maybe he wanted to torment me one last time, his last little kick before he fucked off."

"Will you ever tell Bryony about your parents, she's sure to ask at some point?"

"I don't know, to be honest. I guess we just say they're dead and nothing more."

We fell silent for a while.

"Will we ever have that *conversation* again, the one you don't want?" Summer said, glancing at Bryony as she did.

I sighed. "Baby, I'm still traumatised by what happened. I look at you, and her, and the thought either of you might not be here right now, cuts me to the core. Give me a little more time?"

Bryony was only a year old but Summer was broody. I was still terrified.

She smiled at me, and placed her hand on the side of my face.

"You know what we could do? We could pretend that we're practicing to get pregnant," she said with a smirk.

"Pretend that we're practicing? Mmm, I think I could do that. That's like, three steps away from getting pregnant...I'm good with that."

I stood, carrying her in my arms to our bedroom. She laughed as I dropped her, unceremoniously, on the bed.

I watched as she pulled her t-shirt over her head, and before she had a chance to remove her jeans, I climbed on beside her. I kissed her stomach, letting my lips run over the faint silver lines that criss-crossed her skin. We were both scarred but for very different reasons, and we loved our scars.

After all, pain is good if something beautiful comes out of it.

The End

ABOUT THE AUTHOR

Tracie Podger currently lives in Kent, UK with her husband and a rather obnoxious cat called George. She's a Padi Scuba Diving Instructor with a passion for writing. Tracie has been fortunate to have dived some of the wonderful oceans of the world where she can indulge in another hobby, underwater photography. She likes getting up close and personal with sharks.

Tracie likes to write in different genres. Her Fallen Angel series and its accompanying books are mafia romance and full of suspense. A Virtual Affair is contemporary romance, and Gabriel and A Deadly Sin are thriller/suspense. The Facilitator is erotic romance.

Books by Tracie Podger

Fallen Angel, Part 1

Fallen Angel, Part 2

Fallen Angel, Part 3

Fallen Angel, Part 4

The Fallen Angel Box Set

Evelyn - A Novella – To accompany the Fallen Angel Series

Rocco – A Novella – To accompany the Fallen Angel Series

Robert – To accompany the Fallen Angel Series

Travis – To accompany the Fallen Angel Series

Taylor & Mack – To accompany the Fallen Angel Series

A Virtual Affair – A standalone

Gabriel – A standalone

The Facilitator – A standalone

A Deadly Sin – A standalone

Harlot – A standalone

Letters to Lincoln – A standalone

Jackson – A standalone within The Passion Series

Coming soon

The Beautiful Journey

The Fight of my Life

Stalker Links

https://www.facebook.com/TraciePodgerAuthor/

https://twitter.com/TRACIEPODGER

http://www.TraciePodger.com